Part One

Master Li

1.
The Village of Ku-fu

I shall clasp my hands together and bow to the corners of the world.

My surname is Lu and my personal name is Yu, but I am not to be confused with the eminent author of *The Classic of Tea*. My family is quite undistinguished, and since I am the tenth of my father's sons and rather strong I am usually referred to as Number Ten Ox. My father died when I was eight. A year later my mother followed him to the Yellow Springs Beneath the Earth, and since then I have lived with Uncle Nung and Auntie Hua in the village of Ku-fu in the valley of Cho. We take great pride in our landmarks. Until recently we also took great pride in two gentlemen who were such perfect specimens that people used to come from miles around just to stare at them, so perhaps I should begin a description of my village with a couple of classics.

When Pawnbroker Fang approached Ma the Grub with the idea of joining forces he opened negotiations by presenting Ma's wife with the picture of a small fish drawn upon a piece of cheap paper. Ma's wife accepted the magnificent gift, and in return she extended her right hand and made a circle with the thumb and forefinger. At that point the door crashed open and Ma the Grub charged inside and screamed: "Woman, would you ruin me? *Half* of a pie would have been enough!"

That may not be literally true, but the abbot of our monastery always said that fable has strong shoulders that carry far more truth than fact can.

Pawnbroker Fang's ability to guess the lowest possible amount that a person would accept for a pawned item was so unerring that I had concluded that it was supernatural, but then the abbot took me aside and explained that Fang wasn't guessing at all. There was always some smooth shiny object lying on top of his desk in the front room of Ma the Grub's warehouse, and it was used as a mirror that would reflect the eyes of the victim.

"Cheap, very cheap," Fang would sneer, turning the object in his hands. "No more than two hundred cash."

His eyes would drop to the shiny object, and if the pupils of the reflected eyes constricted too sharply he would try again.

"Well, the workmanship isn't too bad, in a crude peasant fashion. Make it two-fifty."

The reflected pupils would dilate, but perhaps not quite far enough.

"It is the anniversary of my poor wife's untimely demise, the thought of which always destroys my business judgment," Fang would whimper, in a voice clotted with tears. "Three hundred cash, but not one penny more!"

Actually no money would change hands because ours is a barter economy. The victim would take a credit slip through the door to the warehouse, and Ma the Grub would stare at it in disbelief and scream out to Fang: "Madman! Your lunatic generosity will drive us into bankruptcy! Who will feed your starving brats when we are reduced to tattered cloaks and begging bowls?" Then he would honor the credit slip with goods that had been marked up by 600 percent.

Pawnbroker Fang was a widower with two children, a pretty little daughter we called Fang's Fawn and a younger son that we called Fang's Flea. Ma the Grub was childless, and when his wife ran off with a rug peddler his household expenses were cut in half and his happiness was doubled. The happiest time of all for the team of Ma and Fang was our annual silk harvest, because silkworm eggs could only be purchased with money and they had all the money. Ma the Grub would buy the eggs and hand them out to each family in exchange for IOUs that were to be redeemed with silk, and since Pawnbroker Fang was the only qualified appraiser of silk for miles around they were able to take two-thirds of our crop to Peking and return with bulging bags of coins, which they buried in their gardens on moonless midnights.

The abbot used to say that the emotional health of a village depended upon having a man whom everyone loved to hate, and Heaven had blessed us with two of them.

Our landmarks are our lake and our wall, and both of them are the result of the superstition and mythology of ancient times. When our ancestors arrived in the valley of Cho they examined the terrain with the greatest of care, and we honestly believe that no village in the world has been better planned than the village of Ku-fu. Our ancestors laid it out so that it would be sheltered from the Black Tortoise, a beast of the very worst character, whose direction is north and whose element is water and whose season is winter. It is open to the Red Bird of the south, and the element of fire and the season of summer. And the eastern hills where the Blue Dragon lives, with the element of wood and the hopeful season of spring, are stronger than the hills to the west, which is the home of the White Tiger, metal, and the melancholy season of autumn.

Considerable thought was given to the shape of the village, on the grounds that a man who built a village like a fish while a neighboring village was built like a hook was begging for disaster. The finished shape was the outline of a unicorn, a gentle and law-abiding creature with no natural enemies whatsoever. But it appeared that something had gone wrong because one day there was a low snorting sort of a noise and the earth heaved, and several cottages collapsed and a great crack appeared in the soil. Our ancestors examined their village from every possible angle, and the flaw was discovered when one of them climbed to the top of the tallest tree on the eastern hills and gazed down. By a foolish oversight the last five rice paddies had been arranged so that they formed the wings and body of a huge hungry horsefly that had settled upon the tender flank of the unicorn, so of course the unicorn had kicked up its heels. The paddies were altered into the shape of a bandage, and Ku-fu was never again disturbed by upheavals.

They made sure that there would be no straight roads or rivers that might draw good influences away, and as a further precaution they dammed up the end of a narrow little valley and channeled rivulets down the sides of the hills, and thus produced a small lake that would capture and hold good influences that might otherwise trickle away to other villages. They had no aesthetic intent whatsoever. The beauty of our lake was an accident of superstition, but the result was such that when the great poet Ssu-ma Hsiang-ju passed through on a walking trip five hundred years ago he paused at the little lake and was inspired to write to a friend:

> The waters are loud with fish and turtles,
> A multitude of living things;
> Wild geese and swans, graylags, bustards,
> Cranes and mallards,
> Loons and spoonbills,
> Flock and settle on the waters,
> Drifting lightly over the surface,
> Buffeted by the wind,
> Bobbing and dipping with the waves,
> Sporting among the weedy banks,
> Gobbling the reeds and duckweed,
> Pecking at water chestnuts and lotuses.

It is like that today, and Ssu-ma Hsiang-ju was not there in the season to see the masses of wildflowers, or the tiny dappled deer that come to drink and then vanish like puffs of smoke.

Our wall landmark is far more famous. It is only fair to point out that there are many different stories concerning the origin of Dragon's Pillow, but we in Ku-fu like to think that our version is the only correct one.

Many centuries ago there was a general who was ordered to build one of the defensive walls that were to be linked into the Great Wall, and one night he dreamed that he had been summoned to Heaven to present his plan for the wall to the August Personage of Jade. At his subsequent trial for treason he gave a vivid account of the trip.

He had dreamed that he had been inside a giant lotus, and the leaves had slowly opened to form a doorway, and he had stepped out upon the emerald grass of Heaven. The sky was sapphire, and a path made from pearls lay near his feet. A willow tree lifted a branch and pointed it like a finger, and the general followed the path to the River of Flowers, which was cascading down the Cliff of the Great Awakening. The concubines of the Emperor of Heaven were bathing in the Pool of Blissful Fragrances, laughing and splashing in a rainbow of rose petals, and they were so beautiful that the general found it hard to tear himself away. But duty called, so he followed the path as it climbed seven terraces where the leaves on the trees were made from precious stones, which rang musically when the breeze touched them, and where birds of bright plumage sang with divine voices of the Five Virtues and Excellent Doctrines. The path continued around the lush orchards where the Queen Mother Wang grew the Peaches of Immortality, and when the general made the last turn around the orchards he found himself directly in front of the palace of the Emperor of Heaven.

Flunkies were waiting for him. They ushered him into the audience chamber, and after the three obeisances and nine kowtows he was allowed to rise and approach the throne. The August Personage of Jade was seated with his hands crossed upon the Imperial Book of Etiquette, which lay upon his lap. He wore a flat hat rather like a board, from which dangled thirteen pendants of colored pearls upon red strings, and his black silk robe rippled with red and yellow dragons. The general bowed and humbly presented his plan for the wall.

Behind the throne stood T'ien-kou, the Celestial Dog, whose teeth had chewed mountains in half, and beside the Celestial Dog stood Ehr-lang, who is unquestionably the greatest of all warriors because he had been able to battle the stupendous Stone Monkey to a standstill. (The Monkey symbolizes intellect.) The two bodyguards appeared to be glaring at the general. He hastily lowered his eyes, and he saw that the symbol of the emperor's predecessor, the Heavenly Master of the First Origin, was stamped upon the left arm of the throne, and on the right arm was the symbol of the emperor's eventual successor, the Heavenly Master of the Dawn of Jade of the Golden Door. The general was so overcome by a dizzying sense of timelessness in which there was no means of measurement and comparison that he felt quite sick to his stomach. He was afraid that he was going to disgrace himself by throwing up, but in the nick of time he saw that his plan, neatly rolled back into a scroll and retied, was extended before his lowered eyes. He took it and dropped to his knees and awaited divine censure or praise, but none was forthcoming. The August Personage of Jade silently signaled the end of the interview. The general crawled backward, banging his head against the floor, and at the doorway he was seized by the flunkies, who marched him outside and across a couple of miles of meadow. Then they picked him up and dumped him into the Great River of Stars.

Oddly enough, the general testified, he had not been frightened at all. It was the rainy season in Heaven, and billions of brilliant stars were bouncing over raging waves that roared like a trillion tigers, but the general sank quite peacefully into the water. He drifted down farther and farther, and then he fell right through the bottom, and the glittering light of the Great River receded rapidly in the distance as he plunged head over heels toward earth. He landed smack in the middle of his bed, just as his servant entered to wake him for breakfast.

It was some time before he could gather enough courage to open his plan, and when he did he discovered that the Emperor of Heaven—or somebody—had moved the wall 122 miles to the south, which placed it in the middle of the valley of Cho, where it could serve no useful purpose whatsoever.

What was he to do? He could not possibly defy the mandate of Heaven, so he ordered his men to build a wall that led nowhere and connected to nothing, and that was why the general was arrested and brought before the Emperor of China on the charge of treason. When he told his tale the charge of treason was tossed out of court. Instead the general was sentenced to death for being drunk on duty, and desperation produced one of the loveliest excuses in history. That wall, the general said firmly, had been perfectly placed, but one night a dragon leaned against it and fell asleep, and in the morning it was discovered that the bulk of the beast had shoved the wall into its current ludicrous position.

Word of Dragon's Pillow swept through the delighted court, where the general had clever and unscrupulous friends. They began their campaign to save his neck by bribing the emperor's favorite soothsayer.

"O Son of Heaven," the fellow screeched, "I have consulted the Trigrams, and for reasons known only to the August Personage of Jade that strange stretch of wall is the most important of all fortifications! So important it is that it cannot be guarded by mortal men, but only by the spirits of ten thousand soldiers who must be buried alive in the foundations!"

The emperor was quite humane, as emperors go, and he begged the soothsayer to try again and see if there might not have been some mistake. After pocketing another bribe the soothsayer came up with a different interpretation.

"O Son of Heaven, the Trigrams clearly state that *wan* must be buried alive in the foundations, but while *wan* can mean ten thousand, it is also a common family name!" he bellowed. "The solution is obvious, for what is the life of one insignificant soldier compared to the most important wall in China?"

The Emperor still didn't like it, but he didn't appear to have much of a choice, so he ordered his guards to go out and lay hands on the first common soldier named Wan. All accounts agree that Wan behaved with great dignity. His family was provided with a pension, and he was told that Heaven had honored him above all others, and he was given a trumpet with which to sound the alarm should China be threatened, and then a hole was cut in the base of the wall and Wan marched dutifully inside. The hole was bricked up again, and a watchtower—the Eye of the Dragon—was placed upon the highest point of Dragon's Pillow where Wan's ghost could maintain its lonely vigil.

The emperor was so sick of the whole affair that he refused to allow that cursed stretch of wall, or anyone connected with it, to be mentioned in his presence. Of course that is what the clever fellows had been planning all along, and their friend the general was quietly set free to write his memoirs.

For nearly a century Dragon's Pillow was a favorite of sightseers. A small number of soldiers was detached to maintain the wall, but since it served no purpose except as a watchtower for a ghost it was eventually allowed to fall into decay. Even the sightseers lost interest in it, and weeds grew and rocks crumbled. It was a paradise for children, however, and for a few centuries it was the favorite playpen of the children of my village, but then something happened that left Dragon's Pillow abandoned even by children.

One evening the children of Ku-fu were beginning one of the games that had originated somewhere back toward the beginning of time, and suddenly they stopped short. A hollow, bodiless voice—one boy later said that it might have been echoing through two hundred miles of bamboo pipe—drifted down to them from the Eye of the Dragon. So strange were the words that every one of the children remembered them perfectly, even though they took to their heels as soon as their hearts resumed beating.

Was it possible that poor Wan, the most important of all sentinels on the most important of all watchtowers, was sending a message to China through the children of the humble village of Ku-fu? If so, it was a very strange message indeed, and sages and scholars struggled for centuries to wrest some meaning from it.

If my illustrious readers would care to take a crack at it, I will wish them the very best of luck.

> *Jade plate,*
> *Six, eight.*
> *Fire that burns hot,*
> *Night that is not.*
> *Fire that burns cold,*
> *First silver, then gold.*

2.
The Plague

My story begins with the silk harvest in the Year of the Tiger 3,337 (A.D. 639), when the prospects for a record crop had never seemed better.

The eggs that Ma the Grub handed out were quite beautiful, jet-black and glowing with health, and the leaves on the mulberry trees were so thick that the groves resembled tapestries woven from deep green brocade, and youngsters raced around singing, "Mulberry leaves so shiny and bright, children all clap hands at the sight!" Our village crackled with excitement. Girls carried straw baskets up the hill to the monastery, and the bonzes lined them with yellow paper upon which they had drawn pictures of Lady Horsehead, and the abbot blessed the baskets and burned incense to the patron of sericulture. Bamboo racks and trays were taken to the river and vigorously scrubbed. Wildflowers were picked and crushed, lamp wicks cut into tiny pieces, and the oldest members of each family smeared cloves of garlic with moist earth and placed them against the walls of the cottages. If the garlic produced many sprouts it would mean a bountiful harvest, and never in living memory had anyone seen so many sprouts. The women slept with the sheets of silkworm eggs pressed against their bare flesh, in order to hasten the hatching process through body heat, and the old ones tossed handfuls of rice into pots that bubbled over charcoal fires. When the steam lifted straight up, without a quiver, they yelled, "Now!"

The women brushed the eggs into the baskets with goose feathers. Then they sprinkled the crushed wildflowers and the pieces of lamp wicks on top and placed the baskets upon the bamboo racks. The goose feathers were carefully pinned to the sides of the baskets, and charcoal fires were lit beneath the racks. (The significance of wildflowers, lamp wicks, and goose feathers has been lost in antiquity, but we would never dream of changing the custom.) The families knelt to pray to Lady Horsehead, and in every cottage the eggs hatched right on schedule.

The Dark Ladies wriggled lazily, enjoying the heat of the fires, but they were not lazy for long. Unelss one has seen them, it is quite impossible to imagine how much silkworms can—must—eat, and their only food is mulberry leaves. It is not much of an exaggeration to say that the chewing sounds of ravenous silkworms are enough to waken hibernating bears, but sleep would be out of the question anyway. It takes thirty days, more or less, for silkworms to prepare to spin, and there are but three brief periods when they aren't eating: the Short Sleep, the Second Sleep, and the Big Sleep. After the Big Sleep silkworms will die if an hour passes without food, and we worked day and night stripping leaves from trees and carrying them to the cottages in basket brigades. The children were given regular rest periods, of course, but during the thirty days the rest of us were lucky to get sixty hours of sleep.

The old ones tended the fires, because silkworms must have steady heat, and the children who were too young to work in basket brigades were turned out to fend for themselves. In grove after grove we stripped the trees to the bare branches, and then we stumbled in exhaustion to the mulberry grove that belonged to Pawnbroker Fang. That cost us more IOUs, but they were the finest trees in the village. Gradually the silkworms changed color, from black to green, and from green to white, and then translucent, and the oldest family members erected bamboo screens in front of the racks, because silkworms are shy when they begin to spin and must have privacy.

The deafening feeding noises dropped to a roar, and then to a sound like distant surf, and then to a whisper. The silence that finally settled over our village seemed eerily unreal. There was nothing more to be done except to keep the fires going, and if fortune favored us we would pull the screens away in three days and see fields of snow: the white cocoons called Silkworm Blossoms, massed upon the racks and waiting to be reeled into spindles in continuous strands more than a thousand feet long.

Some of us made it to our beds, but others simply dropped in their tracks.

I awoke on the fifteenth day of the eighth moon, which happened to be my nineteenth birthday, to the sound of a soft pattering rain. The clouds were beginning to lift. Slanting rays of sunlight slid through silver raindrops, and a soft mist drifted across the fields like smoke. In the distance I could see the hazy outline of Dragon's Pillow, and nearby on the riverbank some boys were teasing Fang's Fawn, who was riding a water buffalo. I decided that the boys were following her around because the rain had plastered her tunic around small shapely breasts that the pretty little girl didn't have a month ago, and Fawn was enjoying the attention immensely. Bells were ringing from the monastery upon the hill.

I stretched lazily in bed, savoring the smells of tea and porridge from Auntie Hua's kitchen, and then I jerked upright. The boys at the riverbank were staring wide-eyed at Fang's Fawn, who had turned pale as death. She clutched her throat and gave a sharp cry of pain and toppled from the water buffalo to the grass.

I was out the door in an instant. Fawn's eyes were wide and staring, but she didn't see me while I tested her pulse, which was faint and erratic. Perspiration glistened on her forehead. I told the boys to run for her father, and then I picked her up and raced up the hill to the monastery.

The abbot was also our doctor, professionally trained at Hanlin Academy, but he was clearly puzzled by Fawn's sickness. Her vital signs had dropped so low that he had to hold a mirror to her lips to find a trace of condensation, and when he took a pin and pricked her flesh at various pain points there was no reaction. Her eyes were still wide and unseeing.

Suddenly the pretty little girl sat up and screamed. The sound was shocking in the hush of the monastery. Her hands clawed the air, fending off something that wasn't there, and she jerked convulsively. Then she fell back upon the bed and her eyes closed. Her body grew limp, and once more her vital signs dropped to almost nothing.

"Demons!" I whispered.

"I sincerely hope so," the abbot said grimly, and I later learned that he had begun to suspect rabies, and that he would prefer to confront the most hideous demons from the most horrible corners of Hell.

There had been noises swelling up in the village below the hill, a confusion of sounds, and now we began to hear curses from the men and wails and lamentations from the women. The abbot looked at me and raised an eyebrow. I was out the door and down the hill in a flash, and after that things got so confusing that I have difficulty sorting them out in my mind.

It began with Auntie Hua. She had been tending the fire at the silkworm rack in her cottage and she had smelled something that worried her. When she cautiously peered through a crack in the screen she had not seen a field of snow, but a black rotting mass of pulp. Her agonized wails brought the neighbors, who raced back to their own cottages, and as howls arose from every corner of the village it became apparent that for the first time in living memory our silk harvest had been a total failure. That was merely the beginning.

Big Hong the blacksmith ran from his house with wide frightened eyes, carrying his small son in his arms. Little Hong's eyes were wide and unseeing, and he screamed and clawed the air. The blacksmith was followed by Wang the wineseller, whose small daughter was screaming and clawing the air. More and more parents dashed out with children in their arms, and a frantic mob raced up the hill toward the monastery.

It was not rabies. It was a plague.

I stared in disbelief at two tiny girls who were standing in a doorway with their thumbs in their mouths. Mother Ho's great-granddaughters were so sickly that the abbot had worked night and day to keep them alive, yet they were completely untouched by the plague. I ran past them into their cottage. Mother Ho was ninety-two and sinking fast, and my heart was in my mouth as I approached her bed and drew back the covers. I received a stinging slap on my nose.

"Who do you think you are? The Imperial Prick?" the old lady yelled.

(She meant Emperor Wu-ti. After his death his lecherous ghost kept hopping into his concubines' beds, and in desperation they had recruited new brides from all over, and it was not until the total reached 503 that the exhausted spectre finally gave up and crawled back into its tomb.)

I ran back out and turned into cottage after cottage, where tiny children stared at me and cried, or laughed and wanted to play, and the old ones who wept beside the racks of rotting silkworms were otherwise as healthy as horses. Then I ran back up the hill and told the abbot what I had seen, and when we made a list the truth was indisputable, and it was also unbelievable.

Not one child under the age of eight and not one person over the age of thirteen had been affected by the plague, but every child—every single one—between the ages of eight and thirteen had screamed and blindly clawed the air, and now lay as still as death in the infirmary that the abbot had set up in the bonzes' common room. The weeping parents looked to the abbot for a cure, but he spread his arms and cried out in despair:

"First tell me how a plague can learn how to *count*!"

Auntie Hua had always been the decisive one in our

family. She took me aside. "Ox, the abbot is right, "she
said hoarsely. "We need a wise man who can tell us how
a plague can learn to count, and I have heard that there
are such men in Peking, and that they live on the Street
of Eyes. I have also heard that they charge dearly for
their services."

"Auntie, it will take a week to squeeze money out of
Pawnbroker Fang, even though Fawn is one of the victims," I said.

She nodded, and then she reached into her dress and
pulled out a worn leather purse. When she dumped the
contents into my hands I stared at more money than I
had ever seen in my life: hundreds of copper coins, strung
upon a green cord.

"Five thousand copper cash, and you are never to tell
your uncle about this. Not ever!" the old lady said fiercely.
"Run to Peking. Go to the Street of Eyes and bring a wise
man back to our village."

I had heard that Auntie Hua had been a rather wild
beauty in her youth and I briefly wondered whether she
might have reason to sacrifice to P'an Chin-lien, the patron of fallen women, but I had no time for such specu-
lations because I was off and running like the wind.

I share my birthday with the moon, and Peking was a
madhouse when I arrived. Trying to shove through the
mobs that had turned out for the Moon Festival was like
one of those nightmares in which one struggles through
quicksand. The din was incredible, and I forced my way
through the streets with the wild eyes and aching ears of
a colt at a blacksmith's convention, and I was quite terrified when I finally reached the street that I was looking
for. It was an elegant avenue that was lined on both sides
with very expensive houses, and above each door was
the sign of a wide unblinking eye.

"The truth revealed," those eyes seemed to be saying.
"We see everything."

I felt the first stirrings of hope, and I banged at the
nearest door. It was opened by a haughty eunuch who
was attired in clothes that I had previously associated
with royalty, and he ran his eyes from my bamboo hat to

my shabby sandals, clapped a perfumed handkerchief to
his nose, and ordered me to state my business. The eunuch didn't blink an eye when I said that I wanted his
master to explain how a plague could learn to count, but
when I said that I was prepared to pay as much as five
thousand copper cash he turned pale, leaned weakly against
the wall, and groped for smelling salts.

"Five thousand copper cash?" he whispered. "Boy,
my master charges fifty pieces of silver to find a lost dog!"

The door slammed in my face, and when I tried the
next house I exited through the air, pitched by six husky
footmen while a bejeweled lackey shook his fist and
screamed, "You dare to offer five thousand copper cash
to the former chief investigator for the Son of Heaven
himself? Back to your mud hovel, you insolent peasant!"

In house after house the result was the same, except
that I exited in a more dignified manner—my fists were
clenched and there was a glint in my eyes, and I am not
exactly small—and I decided that I was going to have to
hit a wise man over the head, stuff him in a bag, and carry
him back to Ku-fu whether he liked it or not. Then I
received a sign from Heaven. I had reached the end of
the avenue and was starting to go back up the other side,
and suddenly a shaft of brilliant sunlight shot through the
clouds and darted like an arrow into a narrow winding
alley. It sparkled upon the sign of an eye, but this eye
was not wide open. It was half-shut.

"Part of the truth revealed," the eye seemed to be
saying. "Some things I see, but some I don't."

If that was the message it was the first sensible thing
that I had seen in Peking, and I turned and started down
the alley.

3.
A Sage with a Slight Flaw in His Character

The sign was old and shabby, and it hung above the open door of a sagging bamboo shack. When I timidly stepped inside I saw smashed furniture and a mass of shattered crockery, and the reek of sour wine made my head reel. The sole inhabitant was snoring upon a filthy mattress.

He was old almost beyond belief. He could not have weighed more than ninety pounds, and his frail bones would have been more suitable for a large bird. Drunken flies were staggering through pools of spilled wine, and crawling giddily up the ancient gentleman's bald skull, and tumbling down the wrinkled seams of a face that might have been a relief map of all China, and becoming entangled in a wispy white beard. Small bubbles formed and burst upon the old man's lips, and his breath was foul.

I sighed and turned to go, and then I stopped dead in my tracks and caught my breath.

Once an eminent visitor to our monastery had displayed the gold diploma that was awarded to the scholar who had won third place in the imperial *chin-shih* examination, and in schoolbooks I had seen illustrations of the silver diploma that was awarded to second place, but never did I dream that I would be privileged to see the flower. The real thing, not a picture of it. There it was, casually tacked to a post not two feet from my eyes, and I reverently blew away the dust to read that seventy-eight years ago a certain Li Kao had been awarded first place among all the scholars in China, and had received an appointment as a full research fellow in the Forest of Culture Academy.

I turned from the picture of the rose and gazed with wide eyes at the ancient gentleman upon the mattress. Could this be the great Li Kao, whose brain had caused the empire to bow at his feet? Who had been elevated to the highest rank of mandarin, and whose mighty head was now being used as a pillow for drunken flies? I stood there, rooted in wonder, while the wrinkles began to heave like the waves of a gray and storm-tossed sea. Two red-rimmed eyes appeared, and a long spotted tongue slid out and painfully licked parched lips.

"Wine!" he wheezed.

I searched for an unbroken jar, but there wasn't one. "Venerable Sir, I fear that all the wine is gone," I said politely.

His eyes creaked toward a shabby purse that lay in a puddle. "Money!" he wheezed.

I picked up the purse and opened it. "Venerable Sir, I fear that the money is gone too," I said.

His eyeballs rolled up toward the top of his head, and I decided to change the subject.

"Have I the honor of addressing the great Li Kao, foremost among the scholars of China? I have a problem to place before such a man, but all that I can afford to pay is five thousand copper cash," I said sadly.

A hand like a claw slid from the sleeve of his robe. "Give!" he wheezed.

I placed the string of coins in his hand, and his fingers closed around it, taking possession. Then the fingers opened.

"Take this five thousand copper cash," he said, enunciating with a painful effort, "and return as soon as possible with all the wine that you can buy."

"At once, Venerable Sir," I sighed.

Having performed similar chores for Uncle Nung more times than I cared to count I judged it wiser to buy some food as well, and when I returned I had two small jars of wine, two small bowls of congee, and a valuable lesson in the buying power of copper coins. I propped the old man's head up and poured wine down his throat until he had revived enough to grab the jar and finish the rest of it at a gulp, and long practice enabled me to slip a bowl of congee into his fingers and get it to his lips before he realized that it wasn't wine. Two spots of color had appeared in his cheeks when he finished it, and after the second jar of wine he willingly attacked the second bowl of congee.

"Who you?" he said between slurps.

"My surname is Lu and my personal name is Yu, but I am not to be confused with the eminent author of *The Classic of Tea*. Everyone calls me Number Ten Ox," I said.

"My surname is Li and my personal name is Kao, and there is a slight flaw in my character," he said matter-of-factly. "You got a problem?"

I told him the whole story, and I was weeping at the end. He listened with interest, and had me go over it again, and then he pitched the empty bowl over his shoulder so that it smashed upon the rest of the crockery. When he hopped up from his mattress I was astonished to see that he was as spry as a goat.

"Number Ten Ox, eh? Muscles are highly overrated, but yours may come in handy," he said. "We will have to hurry, and for a variety of reasons you may be required to twist somebody's head off."

I could scarcely believe my ears.

"Master Li, do you mean that you will come to my village and find out how a plague can learn to count?" I cried.

"I already know how your plague learned to count," he said calmly. "Bend over."

I was so stunned that I bent over backward until he advised me to try it the other way around. Master Li hopped nimbly upon my back and wrapped his arms around my neck and stuck his tiny feet into the pockets of my tunic. He was as light as a feather.

"Number Ten Ox, I am no longer as fast on my feet as I used to be, and I suspect that time may be crucial. I would suggest that you take aim at your village and start running like hell," said the ancient sage.

My head was spinning, but my heart was wild with hope. I took off like a deer. Li Kao ducked as I bolted through the door and my head struck something, and when I skidded from the alley and glanced back I saw that my head had struck the bottom of an old shabby sign, and that a half-closed eye was spinning around and around as though it was peering at mysteries in every corner of the empire.

I have no idea whether or not it was premonition, but the image remained with me throughout our journey back to Ku-fu.

Auntie Hua looked somewhat askance at the sage I had brought back to our village, but not for long. That antiquated gentleman stank of wine, and his robe was as filthy as his beard, but such was his air of authority that even the abbot accepted his leadership without question, and Li Kao walked from bed to bed, peeling back the children's eyelids and grunting with satisfaction when he saw that the pupils of their eyes were not fixed and dilated.

"Good!" he grunted. "It is not a question of teaching a plague how to count, which is quite simple, but of which agent was used, and I had feared that there might be brain damage. Now I shall need samples of mulberry leaves from every grove, clearly labeled so that we will know where they came from."

We raced to do his bidding. Basket after basket of mulberry leaves was carried up the hill to the monastery, and Li Kao placed them in vials and added chemicals, while the abbot adjusted the fires beneath alchemists' stoves. When the eighteenth batch of leaves turned the chemicals pale orange Li Kao began to work with great speed, boiling the leaves to a pulp, adding more chemicals a drop at a time, increasing the heat and reducing the liquid. The pale-orange color began to turn green. When the liquid had been reduced to nothingness a tiny pile of black crystals remained in the vial, and Li Kao placed half of them into a new vial to which he added some colorless liquid. Then he straightened up and stretched wearily.

"Another minute and I will be sure," he said, and he walked over to the window. Some of the younger children who had escaped the plague were wandering disconsolately in the abbot's garden, and Li Kao pointed to a small boy. "Watch," he said.

We watched and nothing happened. Then the boy absentmindedly plucked a leaf from a tree, and he lifted it to his mouth and began to chew.

"All children do that," Master Li said quietly. "The children of your village who were old enough to work in basket brigades chewed mulberry leaves, but the older they were, the more self-conscious they became about doing childish things, and that is why the seizures were limited to children between the ages of eight and thirteen. You see, we are not dealing with a plague but with an agent that was deliberately designed to kill silkworms."

He turned and pointed to the vial. The liquid had the evilest color that I had ever seen: slick and green and slimy and garish, like gangrene.

"That is *ku* poison, for which there is no known antidote," he said grimly. "It was smeared upon the leaves in the mulberry grove that belongs to a certain Pawnbroker Fang."

A lynch mob poured down the hill, but the warehouse door was locked. "Ox!" the abbot snarled. I kicked the door halfway across the room, and a pathetic sight met our eyes. Ma the Grub was lying on his back. Traces of *ku* poison smeared his lips, and he was as dead as Confucious. Pawnbroker Fang was still alive, but barely. His glazed eyes tried to focus on us, and his lips moved.

"We never intended to...It was the silkworms," he whispered. "If they died...the IOUs...own everything...Now my daughter..."

He was almost gone. The abbot knelt and placed a small jade Buddha in the pawnbroker's hands and began to pray for his miserable soul. Fang's eyes opened one last time, and he looked blindly down at the jade Buddha, and he made a truly heroic effort.

"Cheap, very cheap," he sneered. "No more than two hundred..."

Then he too was dead.

Li Kao gazed down at the bodies with a rather strange expression on his face, and then he shrugged his shoulders.

"So be it," he said. "I suggest that we leave them here to rot and return to the monastery. We have far more important things to worry about."

Pawnbroker Fang and Ma the Grub had almost certainly killed the children of my village, but when I looked back at the bodies I could find no anger in my heart.

The abbot led the way. We lit candles, and our shadows loomed like twisted giants upon the gray stone walls as we trudged down the long winding flight of steps to the great vaulted cellar where the scrolls were stacked in long rows of wooden shelves. Our monastery is very old, and over the centuries the abbots had added to the library. The medical texts numbered in the hundreds, and I helped the novices bring scroll after scroll to the long tables where the abbot and his bonzes checked every reference to *ku* poison. The references were extensive, since the poison has been a favorite agent for assassination for nearly two thousand years, and the information was always the same: The victims' vital signs would drop so low that they expended almost no energy at all and could last for months, but nothing could restore them to consciousness, and death was inevitable. There was no antidote.

The poison was said to have been imported from Tibet.

Li Kao was the only scholar who was qualified to interpret the ancient Tibetan texts such as *Chalog Job Jad*, and he said that the abbot's copy of *Zaraga Dib Jad* was so rare that there might not be another one in existence. The rustle of the old parchment was punctuated by Master Li's soft curses. The Tibetan physicians had been magnificent at describing treatments but terrible at describing symptoms, and apparently it had been taboo to mention by name any agent whose sole purpose was murder—possibly, he pointed out, because the alchemists who invented such things belonged to the same monkish orders as the physicians. Another problem was the antiquity of the texts, which were faded and spotted to the point of illegibility. The sun had set and was rising again when Master Li bent close to a page in *Jud Chi, The Eight Branches of the Four Principles of Special Therapy*.

"I can make out the ancient ideograph for 'star,' and next to it is a badly spotted character that could mean many things, but among them is the ideograph for 'wine vessel,'" he muttered. "What would you get if you combined the ideographs of star and wine vessel?"

"You would get the logograph 'to awake from a drunken stupor,'" said the abbot.

"Precisely, and 'drunken stupor,' if used figuratively, is such a maddeningly vague description of symptoms that it could mean almost anything. The interesting thing is that the preceding text suggests seizures and clawing of air," said Master Li. "Can we say that the children are now lying in stupors?"

He bent close to the text and read aloud.

"To awake from a drunken stupor, only one treatment is effective, and this will succeed only if the physician has access to the rarest and mightiest of all healing agents. . . ." He paused and scratched his head. "The ancient ideograph for 'ginseng' is accompanied by an exceptionally elaborate construction that I would translate as 'Great Root of Power.' Has anyone ever heard of a ginseng Great Root of Power?"

Nobody had. Li Kao went back to the text.

"The Great Root must be distilled to the essence, and

three drops must be applied to the tongue of the patient. The treatment must be repeated three times, and if it is truly the Great Root, the patient will recover almost immediately. Without such a root no cure is possible...." Master Li paused for emphasis. "And while the patient may remain in his stupor for months, he cannot be awakened, and death is inevitable."

"*Ku* poison!" the abbot exclaimed.

Now the bonzes checked every reference to ginseng, which meant almost every page because at one time or another the plant had been prescribed for almost every ailment known to man, but nowhere was there a reference to a Great Root of Power. We had reached a dead end.

Li Kao suddenly smacked the table and jumped to his feet.

"Back to Pawnbroker Fang's office at the warehouse!" he commanded, and he started up the stairs at a trot, with the rest of us at his heels. "The Guild of Pawnbrokers represents the world's second-oldest profession, and their records are older than the oracle bones of An-yang. The Guild publishes lists of extremely rare and valuable items that might escape the untutored eye, and a Great Root of Power, if such a thing exists, will probably be worth ten times its weight in diamonds and will look like a dog turd," he explained. "A fellow like Fang would undoubtedly subscribe to the entire list, in hopes of swindling an heir who does not know the value of his inheritance."

He trotted rapidly down the path and through the door of the warehouse, and then he trotted right over the spot where two bodies should have been lying.

"Those fellows?" he said in answer to our stunned expressions. "Oh, they got up and took to their heels a long time ago."

I grabbed the abbot and held him, but Big Hong and a number of others were closing in on the ancient sage in a menacing manner.

"Do you mean that you knew all along that those murderers were faking their suicides?" the abbot roared.

"Of course, but one should be careful about charging them with murder. So far as I know, they haven't killed anyone yet, and they certainly never intended to," Master Li said calmly. "Reverend Sir, have you considered the plight of Pawnbroker Fang's children? His daughter will probably die, but even if she recovers, what sort of a life could she look forward to when she discovered that her father had been torn to pieces by the people of her own village? Her little brother would be condemned to a life of shame at the age of five, which seems a trifle unfair. Surely there is a family that will care for innocent children, and explain that their father was only trying to improve the silk, but that he made a mistake and ran away, and all is forgiven."

I released the abbot, who bowed to the sage, and Big Hong cleared his throat.

"My wife and I will take Fang's Flea," he said huskily. "Fawn, too, if she lives. They will have a loving home."

"Good man," said Master Li. "As for Pawnbroker Fang and Ma the Grub, why not let them punish themselves? Greed such as theirs gnaws at the vitals like packs of rats, day and night, never ceasing, and when they arrive in Hell they will have already experienced whatever torments the Yama Kings may decree. Now let's get to work."

Fang's files were so extensive that they filled two large cabinets and a trunk, and the abbot found the first reference to a Root of Power. We had no idea whether it was the same as a Great Root of Power. The bonzes found three other references, but only one of them was contemporary.

"Thirty years ago, at a price of three hundred talents, which I cannot possibly believe, a Root of Power was sold to the Ancestress," said the abbot, looking up from his lists. "There is no further mention of it, and I assume that it is still in the dear lady's possession."

Li Kao looked as though he had bitten into a green persimmon.

"If that woman laid eyes on me, she'd have my head in two seconds," he said sourly. Then he had second thoughts. "Come to think of it, it would be a miracle if she recognized me. She couldn't have been more than sixteen when I was summoned to the emperor's palace, and that was a good fifty years ago."

"Master Li, you were summoned by an emperor?" I asked with wide eyes.

"Several, but this particular one was old Wen," he said. "In the carefree days of my youth I once sold him some shares in a mustard mine."

We stared at him.

"A mustard mine?" the abbot said weakly.

"I was trying to win a bet concerning the intelligence of emperors," he explained. "When I was summoned to court I assumed that I was going to be rewarded with the Death of Ten Thousand Cuts, but Emperor Wen had something else in mind. Oddly enough, it was sericulture. Some barbarians were trying to learn the secret of silk, and the emperor thought that they might be getting close to the truth. 'Li Kao,' he commanded, 'sell these dogs a mustard mine!' It was one of the most ghastly experiences of my life."

Li Kao turned and trotted back out the door, and we followed like sheep as he started back toward the monastery. I was learning that there were many sides to Master Li, and I listened with fascination.

"I had to turn their brains to butter with strong wine, and every morning I pried my eyelids open and glared at red-bearded barbarians who were snoring in puddles of vomit," he said. "They had the constitutions of billy goats, and it was a month and a half before I was able to persuade them that silk is extracted from the semen of snow-white dragons that breed only in caverns concealed in the mysterious Mongolian glaciers. Before sailing away with the sad news, their leader came to see me. He was an oaf named Procopius, and the wine had not improved his appearance. 'O great and mighty Master Li, pray impart to me the Secret of Wisdom!' he bawled. A silly smile was sliding down the side of his face like a dripping watercolor, and his eyeballs resembled a pair of pink pigeon eggs that were gently bouncing in saucers of yellow wonton soup. To my great credit I never batted an eyelash. 'Take a large bowl,' I said. 'Fill it with equal measures of fact, fantasy, history, mythology, science, superstition, logic, and lunacy. Darken the mixture with bitter tears, brighten it with howls of laughter, toss in three thousand years of civilization, bellow *kan pei*—which means "dry cup"—and drink to the dregs.' Procopius stared at me. 'And I will be wise?' he asked. 'Better,' I said. 'You will be Chinese.'"

Li Kao led the way back to the infirmary and slowly walked up the long line of beds. Weariness bowed his shoulders, and in the bright morning sunlight his wrinkled skin was nearly transparent.

The children of Ku-fu looked like wax effigies. Fang's Fawn had always been pretty, but now the bone structure was showing beneath her smooth skin. She was exquisite as a carving in white jade is exquisite, without warmth or life. On the bed next to her was a woodcutter's daughter named Bone Helmet, a thin, plain girl who had been gentle and loving. Since she had been old enough to thread a needle, she had worked on her father's burial garment, and he had proudly worn it at every festival, and now the heartbroken father had dressed his daughter in his own garment. Bone Helmet looked incredibly small and helpless in a blue silk robe that was five times too big for her, and the irony of "longevity" that she had embroidered over it in gold thread was not very funny.

Favorite toys had been placed near each child's limp hands, and the parents sat silent and helpless beside the beds. Mournful howls drifted up from the village, where lonesome dogs were searching for their young masters.

Li Kao sighed and straightened his shoulders and beckoned for me to come closer. "Number Ten Ox, I have no idea whether or not a Root of Power is the same as a Great Root of Power, and for all I know the only use for such a thing is to mix it with glue and use it to repair sandals," he said quietly. "Two things I do know. Anyone who tries to steal a valuable item from the Ancestress is begging for an unpleasant death, and I am now too old to attempt it without having some muscle to back me up. I have accepted your five thousand copper cash, and you are my client, and the decision is yours."

"Master Li, when do we leave?" I asked eagerly.

I was ready to race out the door, but he looked at me wryly.

"Ox, if the children die suddenly there is nothing that we can do about it, and if the textbook prognosis holds true, they should last for months. The worst thing that we could do would be to arrive at our destination weary and unprepared," he said patiently. "I'm going to get some rest, and if you can't sleep, perhaps the abbot will be kind enough to expand your education on the subject of the quest. Ginseng is the most interesting as well as the most valuable plant in the whole world."

He yawned and stretched.

"We'll have to go back through Peking to pick up some money, and we'll leave at the first watch," he said.

Li Kao lay down in the bonzes' bedchamber. I had never been so wide awake in my life. The abbot took me into his study for instruction, and what I learned about ginseng was so interesting that I was almost able to forget the children for an hour.

4.
Root of Lightning

No medicinal plant is quite so controversial, the abbot explained. There are eminent physicians who swear that it is no more effective than strong tea, and there are those who swear that it is effective in treating anemia, cachexia, scrofula, gastrointestinal catarrh, and malfunctions of the lungs, kidneys, liver, heart, and genital organs. Long ago when the plant was plentiful, peasants would mix the ginseng root with owl brains and turtle fat and smear the mixture over the heads of patients to cure insanity, or blend it with the powdered horns of wapiti deer and sprinkle it over the patients' chests to cure tuberculosis. Strangest of all is the professional ginseng hunter, because for him it is not a plant but a religion.

The legends are quite marvelous. Ginseng hunters refer to the plant as *chang-diang shen*, "the root of lightning," because it is believed that it appears only on the spot where a small mountain spring has been dried up by a lightning bolt. After a life of three hundred years the green juice turns white and the plant acquires a soul. It is then able to take on human form, but it never becomes truly human because ginseng does not know the meaning of selfishness.

It is totally good, and will happily sacrifice itself to aid the pure in heart. In human form it can appear as a man or as a beautiful woman, but more often it takes the form of a child, plump and brown, with red cheeks and laughing eyes. Long ago, evil men discovered that a ginseng child can be captured by tying it with a red ribbon, and that is why the plant is now so hard to find, the hunters say. It has been forced to run away from evil men, and it is for that reason that ginseng hunting has become one of the most hazardous occupations upon the face of the earth.

The ginseng hunter must display the purity of his intentions right from the start, so he carries no weapons. He wears a conical hat made from birch bark, and shoes of tarred pigskin, and an oiled apron to protect him from dew, and a badger skin attached to his belt, on which he sits when the ground is wet. He carries small spades made from bone and two small pliable knives that are quite useless for defense. Along with a little food and wine, that is all he has, and his quest takes him into the wildest mountains where no men have dared to pass before. Tigers and bears are his companions, and the hunter fears strange creatures that are even more dangerous than tigers—such as the tiny owls that will call him by name and lead him into the Forest of Oblivion from which no man returns, and the bandits that are more brutal than savage bears and who crouch beside the few paths in order to murder an unarmed hunter and steal his roots.

Ginseng hunters, when they have thoroughly searched an area and found nothing, will mark the barks of trees with *kao chu kua*, which are tiny secret signs that tell other hunters not to waste their time there. Hunters would not dream of deceiving each other, because they are not competitors but fellow worshippers. Where a find has been made a shrine is raised, and other hunters who pass will leave offerings of stones, or scraps of cloth. If a hunter finds a plant that is not mature enough he will put stakes around it with his mark on them. If other hunters find the place they will pray and offer gifts, but they would rather cut their throats than take the plant for themselves. The behavior of a man who makes a find is very strange.

A weatherworn, clawed, half-starved ginseng hunter will occasionally have the good fortune to make his way through dense underbrush and come upon a small plant with four branches that have violet flowers and a fifth branch in the center that rises higher than the others and is crowned with red berries. The stalk is deep red, and the leaves are deep green on the outside and pale green on the inside. He will drop to his knees, his eyes streaming with tears, and spread his arms wide to show that he is unarmed. Then he will kowtow and bang his head three times upon the ground, and he will pray,

"O Great Spirit, do not leave me! I have come with a pure heart and soul, after freeing myself from sins and evil thoughts. Do not leave me."

Then the hunter covers his eyes and lies still for many minutes. If the ginseng plant does not trust him, and wishes to change into a beautiful woman or a plump brown child and run away, the hunter does not want to see where it has gone. At length he opens his eyes, and if the plant is still there his joy is not so much from the fact that he has found a valuable root as it is from the fact that he has been judged and found to be pure in heart.

He takes the seeds and carefully replants them so that the ginseng can grow again. The leaves and flowers are stripped and ceremoniously burned, with many prayers. The hunter's bone spades are used to dig up the root, which is forked and has something of a human shape—skeptics point to the shape as the basis of an ignorant folk religion—and the small pliable knives are used to clean the tiny tendrils called beards, which are supposed to be crucial to the curative powers. The root is wrapped in birch bark and sprinkled with pepper to keep insects away, and the happy hunter begins the long, dangerous trek back toward the safety of civilization.

"Where his throat will probably be slit by somebody like Ma the Grub," the abbot said sourly. "Who will be swindled by somebody like Pawnbroker Fang, who will sell the root to somebody like the Ancestress, who will squat like a huge venemous toad upon a folk deity whose sole purpose in life is to aid the pure in heart."

"Reverend Sir, I have never heard of the Ancestress," I said shyly.

The abbot leaned back and rubbed his weary eyes.

"What a woman," he said with grudging admiration. "Ox, she began her career as an eleven-year-old imperial concubine, and by the time she was sixteen she had Emperor Wen wrapped around her fingers to the point where he took her as his number three wife. The Ancestress promptly poisoned the emperor, strangled his other wives, decapitated all but the youngest of his sons, elevated that weakling to the throne—Emperor Yang—and settled down behind the scenes as the real ruler of China."

"Reverend Sir, I have heard all my life that Emperor Yang was a depraved and vicious ruler who nearly destroyed the empire," I exclaimed.

"That's the official version, with parricide tossed in," the abbot said drily. "Actually he was a timid little fellow, and quite likable. The real ruler was the Ancestress, which is a title that she awarded herself and which carries a certain Confucian finality. Her reign was brief, but gorgeous. She set about bankrupting the empire by decreeing that every leaf that fell in her imperial pleasure garden must be replaced by an artificial leaf fashioned from the costliest silk. Her imperial pleasure barge was 270 feet long, four decks high, and boasted a three-story throne room and 120 cabins decorated in gold and jade. The problem was finding a pond big enough for the thing, so she conscripted 3,600,000 peasants and forced them to link the Yellow and Yangtze rivers by digging a ditch 40 feet deep, 50 yards wide, and 1,000 miles long. The Grand Canal has been invaluable for commerce, but the important thing for the Ancestress was that three million men died during the construction, and a figure like that confirmed her godlike grandeur.

"When the canal was finished," the abbot said, "the Ancestress invited a few friends to accompany her on an important mission of state to Yang-chou. The fleet of pleasure barges stretched sixty miles from stem to stern, was manned by 9,000 boatmen, and was towed by 80,000 peasants, some of whom survived. The important mission of state was to watch the moonflowers bloom, but Emperor Yang did not watch the moonflowers. The excesses of the Ancestress were being performed in his name, so he spent the entire trip staring into a mirror. 'What an excellent head!' he kept whimpering. 'I wonder who will cut it off?' The chopping was performed by some friends of the great soldier Li Shih-min, who eventually took the imperial name T'ang T'ai-tsung and who sits upon the throne today. T'ang shows every sign of becoming the greatest emperor in history, but I will humbly submit that he made a bad mistake when he assumed that little Yang was responsible for the crimes of the Sui Dynasty and allowed the Ancestress to retire in luxury."

I suppose that I was pale as a ghost. The abbot reached out and patted one of my knees.

"Ox, you will be traveling with a man who has been walking into dangerous situations for at least ninety years, assuming that he began at your age, and he is still alive to tell about it. Besides, Master Li knows far more about the Ancestress than I do, and he is sure to exploit her weaknesses."

The abbot paused to consider his words. Bees droned and flies buzzed, and I wondered if the knocking of my knees was audible. A few minutes ago I had been ready to dash out like a racehorse, and now I would prefer to dart down a hole like a rabbit.

"You are a good boy, and I would not like to meet the man who can surpass you in physical strength, but you know very little about this wicked world," the abbot said slowly. "To tell the truth, I am not so worried about the damage to your body as I am about the damage to your soul. You see, you know nothing whatsoever about men like Master Li, and he said that he would stop in Peking to acquire some money, and I rather suspect..."

His voice trailed off, and he groped for the proper words. Then he decided that it would take several years to prepare me properly.

"Number Ten Ox, our only hope is Master Li," he said

somberly. "You must do as he commands, and I shall be praying for your immortal soul."

With that rather alarming blessing he left me to return to the children, and I went out to say farewell to my family and friends. Later I was able to catch some sleep. In my dreams I was surrounded by plump brown children as I attempted to tie a red ribbon around a root of lightning in a garden where three million fake silk leaves rustled in a breeze that stank of three million real rotting bodies.

5.

Of Goats, Gold, and Miser Shen

"A spring wind is like wine," wrote Chang Chou, *"a summer wind is like tea, an autumn wind is like smoke, and a winter wind is like ginger or mustard."* The breeze that blew through Peking was tea touched with smoke, and spiced with the fragrance of plum, poppy, peony, plane trees, lotus, narcissus, orchid, wild rose, and the sweet-smelling leaves of banana and bamboo. The breeze was also pungent with pork fat, perspiration, sour wine, and the bewildering odors of more people than I had dreamed there were in the whole world.

The first time I was there I had been too intent upon reaching the Street of Eyes to pay much attention to the Moon Festival, but now I gaped at the jugglers and acrobats who were filling the air with clubs and bodies, and at girls who were as tiny and delicate as porcelain dolls, and who danced on the tips of their toes upon enormous artificial lotus blossoms. The palanquins and carriages of the nobility moved grandly through the streets, and men and women laughed and wept in open-air theatres, and gamblers screamed and swore around dice games and

cricket fights. I envied the elegance and assurance of the
gentlemen who basked in the practiced admiration of sing-
song girls—or tiptoed into the Alley of Four Hundred
Forbidden Delights if they wanted more action. The most
beautiful young women that I had ever seen were pounding drums in brightly painted tents as they sang and chanted
the Flower Drum Songs. On almost every corner I saw
old ladies with twinkling eyes who sold soft drinks and
candied fruits while they cried, *"Aiieeee! Aiieeee! Come
closer, my children! Spread ears like elephants, and I
shall tell you the tale of the great Ehr-lang, and of the
time when he was devoured by the hideous Transcendent
Pig!"*

Master Li had sharp elbows. He moved easily through
the throngs, followed by yelps of pain, and he pointed
out the landmarks and explained that the strange sounds
of the city were as comprehensible to urban ears as barn-
yard sounds were to mine. The twanging of long tuning
forks, for example, meant that barbers had set up shop,
and porcelain spoons rapping against bowls advertised
tiny dumplings in hot syrup, and clanging copper saucers
meant that soft drinks made from wild plums and sweet
and sour crab apples were for sale.

As he moved toward his destination, I assumed in my
innocence that he was intending to acquire some money
by visiting a wealthy friend, or a moneylender who owed
him a favor. I blush to admit that not once did I pause to
consider the state of the bamboo shack in which I had
found him or the nature of friends that he was likely to
have. I was quite surprised when he turned abruptly from
the main street and trotted down an alley that reeked of
refuse. Rats glared at us with fierce glittering eyes, and
fermenting garbage bubbled and stank, and I stepped nervously over a corpse—or so I thought until I smelled the
fellow's breath. He was not dead but dead-drunk, and at
the end of the alley, the blue flag of a wine seller hung
above a sagging wooden shack.

I later learned that the wineshop of One-Eyed Wong
was the most notorious in all China, but at the time I
merely noticed that the low dark room was swarming with

vermin and flies, and that a thug with a jade earring that dangled from one chewed earlobe did not approve of the product.

"You Peking weaklings call this watery piss wine?" he roared. "Back in Soochow we make wine so strong that it knocks you out for a month if you smell it on somebody's breath!"

One-Eyed Wong turned to his wife, who was blending the stuff behind the counter.

"We must add more cayenne, my turtledove."

"Two hundred and twenty-two transcendent miseries!" wailed Fat Fu. "We have run out of cayenne!"

"In that case, O light of my existence, we shall substitute the stomach acid of diseased sheep," One-Eyed Wong said calmly.

The thug with the earring whipped out a dagger and lurched around the room, savagely slashing the air.

"You Peking weaklings call these things flies?" he yelled. "Back in Soochow we have flies so big that we clip their wings, hitch them to plows, and use them for oxen!"

"Perhaps a few flattened flies might add bouquet," One-Eyed Wong said thoughtfully.

"Yours is genius of the highest order, O noble stallion of the bedchamber, but flies are too risky," said Fat Fu. "They might overpower our famous flavor of crushed cockroaches."

The thug did not approve of Master Li. "You Peking weaklings call these midgets men?" he howled. "Back in Soochow we grow men so big that their heads brush the clouds while their feet are planted upon the ground!"

"Indeed? In my humble village," Master Li said sweetly, "we grow men so big that their upper lips lick the stars, while their lower lips nuzzle the earth."

The thug thought about it.

"And where are their bodies?"

"They are like you," said Master Li. "All mouth."

His hand shot out, a blade glinted, blood spurted, and he calmly dropped the thug's earring into his pocket, along with the ear that was attached to it. "My surname is Li and my personal name is Kao, and there is a slight flaw in my character," he said with a polite bow. "This is my esteemed client, Number Ten Ox, who is about to strike you over the head with a blunt object."

I wasn't quite sure what a blunt object was, but I was spared the embarrassment of asking when the thug sat down at a table and began to cry. Li Kao exchanged a bawdy joke with One-Eyed Wong, pinched Fat Fu's vast behind, and beckoned for me to join them at a table with a jar of wine that was not of their own manufacture.

"Ox, it occurs to me that your education may be deficient in certain basic aspects of human intercourse, and I suggest that you pay close attention," he said. He placed the thug's jade earring, which was quite beautiful, upon the table. "A lovely thing," he said.

"Trash," sneered One-Eyed Wong.

"Cheap imitation jade," sneered Fat Fu.

"Carved by a blind man," sneered One-Eyed Wong.

"Worst earring I ever saw," sneered Fat Fu.

"How much?" asked One-Eyed Wong.

"It is yours for a song," said Master Li. "In this case a song means a large purse of fake gold coins, two elegant suits of clothes, the temporary use of a palatial palanquin and suitably attired bearers, a cart of garbage, and a goat."

One-Eyed Wong did some mental addition.

"No goat."

"But I must have a goat."

"It isn't that good an earring."

"It doesn't have to be that good a goat."

"No goat."

"But you not only get the earring, you also get the ear that is attached to it," said Master Li.

The proprietors bent over the table and examined the bloody thing with interest.

"This is not a very good ear," sneered One-Eyed Wong.

"It is a terrible ear," sneered Fat Fu.

"Revolting," sneered One-Eyed Wong.

"Worst ear I ever saw," sneered Fat Fu.

"Besides, what good is it?" asked One-Eyed Wong.

"Look at the vile creature it came from, and imagine

the filth that has been hissed into it." Master Li bent over the table and whispered, "Let us assume that you have an enemy."

"Enemy," said One-Eyed Wong.

"He is a wealthy man with a country estate."

"Estate," said Fat Fu.

"A stream flows through the estate."

"Stream," said One-Eyed Wong.

"It is midnight. You climb the fence and cleverly elude the dogs. Silent as a shadow you slip to the top of the stream and peer around slyly. Then you take this revolting ear from your pocket and dip it into the water, and words of such vileness flow out that the fish are poisoned for miles, and your enemy's cattle drink from the stream and drop dead on the spot, and his lush irrigated fields wither into bleak desolation, and his children splash in their bathing pool and acquire leprosy, and all for the price of a goat."

Fat Fu buried her face in her hands.

"Ten thousand blessings upon the mother who brought Li Kao into the world," she sobbed, while One-Eyed Wong dabbed at his eyes with a filthy handkerchief and sniffled, "Sold."

In the country my life had been attuned to the rhythm of the seasons, and things happened gradually. Now I had entered the whirlwind world of Li Kao, and I believe that I was in a state of shock. At any rate, the next thing that I remember was riding through the streets with Li Kao and Fat Fu in a palatial palanquin, while One-Eyed Wong marched ahead of us and bashed the lower classes out of the way with a gold-tipped staff. One-Eyed Wong was dressed as the major-domo of a great house, and Fat Fu was attired as a noble nurse, and Master Li and I dazzled the eyes in tunics of sea-green silk that were secured by silver girdles with borders of jade. The jeweled pendants that dangled from our fine tasseled hats tinkled in the breeze, and we languidly waved gold-splattered Szech'uen fans.

A servant brought up the rear, dragging a cart filled with garbage and a mangy goat. The servant was a thug of low appearance with a bandage around his head, and he kept whimpering, "My ear!"

"The house of Miser Shen," said Fat Fu, pointing ahead to a large unpainted building in front of which cheap incense burned before the statues of the Immortal of Commercial Profits, the Celestial Discoverer of Buried Treasures, the Lord of Lucrative Legacies, and every other greedy deity in the Heavenly Ministry of Wealth. "Miser Shen owns eight flourishing businesses, six houses in six different cities, one carriage, one sedan chair, one horse, three cows, ten pigs, twenty chickens, eight savage guard dogs, seven half-starved servants, and one young and beautiful concubine named Pretty Ping," said Fat Fu. "He acquired all of them by foreclosing mortgages."

Ahead of us was an old peasant with a mule that was hauling a stone-wheeled cart that belonged in a museum.

"Manure!" he shouted in a quavering melancholy voice. *"Fresh manuuuuuuure!"*

Inside the house a rasping voice exclaimed, "Stone wheels? Stone wheels in Peking?" Shutters flew open and an extraordinarily ugly gentleman stuck his head out. "Great Buddha, they *are* stone wheels!" he yelled, and he vanished inside the house. A moment later I heard him scream, "Cook! Cook! Don't waste a second!" And then the front door crashed open and Miser Shen and his cook raced outside and fell in behind the ancient cart.

They were carrying armloads of kitchen cutlery, which they began to sharpen against the slowly revolving stone wheels.

"At least two copper coins saved, Master!" the cook cried.

"What a bonanza!" howled Miser Shen.

"Manure!" cried the peasant. *"Fresh manuuuure!"*

Another pair of shutters flew open, and Fat Fu pointed toward a heart-shaped face and a pair of luscious almond eyes.

"Pretty Ping," she said. "Pretty Ping owns one cheap dress, one cheap coat, one cheap hat, one pair of cheap sandals, one pair of cheap shoes, one cheap comb, one cheap ring, and enough humiliation to last twenty life-times."

"More cutlery!" howled Miser Shen. "Bring the hoes and shovels too!"

"One million mortifications," moaned Pretty Ping, and the shutters slammed shut.

"Manure!" the old peasant cried. *"Fresh manuuuure!"*

"The heat," Master Li panted, fluttering his fan in front of his face. "The stench. The noise!"

"Our lord is weary and must rest!" Fat Fu shouted to One-Eyed Wong.

"Even this pigpen will do," Master Li said weakly.

One-Eyed Wong rapped Miser Shen's shoulder with his gold-tipped staff.

"You there!" he bellowed. "A thousand blessings have descended upon you, for Lord Li of Kao has conde-scended to rest in your miserable hovel!"

"Eh?" said Miser Shen, and he gaped at the gold coin that One-Eyed Wong slapped into his hand.

"Lord Li of Kao shall also require a suite for his be-loved ward, Lord Lu of Yu!" bellowed One-Eyed Wong, slapping a second gold coin into Miser Shen's hand.

"Eh?" said Miser Shen, and a third gold coin smacked into his palm.

"Lord Li of Kao shall also require a suite for his goat!" bellowed One-Eyed Wong.

"Your master must be made of gold!" Miser Shen gasped.

"No," One-Eyed Wong said absentmindedly. "His goat is."

A few minutes later I found myself in Miser Shen's best room with Li Kao, the goat, and the garbage. The fake gold coins were concealed inside fish heads and mil-dewed mangoes, and Li Kao fed a shovelful of the stuff to the goat. This was followed by a pint of castor oil, and shortly thereafter he raked through the mess on the floor with a pair of silver tongs and extracted two glittering coins.

"What!" he cried. "Only two gold coins? Miserable beast, do not arouse the wrath of Lord Li of Kao!"

A dull thump from the hallway suggested that Miser Shen had toppled from a peephole in a dead faint. Li Kao gave him time to recover, and then tried again with the garbage and castor oil.

"Four? Four gold coins?" he yelled furiously. "Insolent animal, Lord Li of Kao requires four hundred coins a day to maintain the style to which he is accustomed!"

The dull thump shook the flimsy wall. After Miser Shen recovered, Master Li tried for a third time, and now his rage knew no bounds.

"Six? Six gold coins? Cretinous creature, have you never heard of geometric progression? Two, four, *eight*, not two, four, *six*! I shall sell you for dog food and return to the Glittering Glades of Golden Grain for a better goat!"

The sound of the thump suggested that Miser Shen would be unconscious for quite some time, and Master Li led me out into the hallway. As we stepped over the prostrate body he took my arm and said quite seriously, "Number Ten Ox, if we are to survive our visit to the Ancestress you must learn that a soldier's best shield is a light heart. If you continue with that long face and soggy soul you will be the death of us, and we will attend to the matter immediately." He trotted briskly up the stairs and opened doors until he found the right one.

"Who are you?" cried Pretty Ping.

"My surname is Li and my personal name is Kao, and there is a slight flaw in my character," he said with a polite bow. "This is my esteemed client, Number Ten Ox."

"But what are you doing in my bedchamber?" cried Pretty Ping.

"I am paying my respects, and my client is preparing to spend the night," said Master Li.

"But where is Miser Shen?" cried Pretty Ping.

"Miser Shen is preparing to spend the night with a goat."

"A goat?"

"It will be a very expensive goat."

"A very ex . . . *What are you doing?*" cried Pretty Ping.

"I am undressing," I said, because I had been well

brought up and I would never dream of contradicting so venerable a sage as Li Kao. Besides, I had been told to obey him by the abbot, who was praying for my soul.

"I shall scream!" cried Pretty Ping.

"I sincerely hope so. Ah, if I could only be ninety again," Master Li said nostalgically. "Ox, flex a few muscles for the young lady."

Pretty Ping stared at me, as Li Kao turned and trotted back down the stairs. I grinned back at a young lady whose family had fallen into the clutches of a usurer, and whose beauty had condemned her to the embraces of an elderly gentleman who was equipped with a pair of glittering little pig eyes, a bald and mottled skull, a sharp curving nose like a parrot's beak, the loose flabby lips of a camel, and two drooping elephant ears from which sprouted thick tufts of coarse gray hair. Her luscious lips parted.

"Help," said Pretty Ping.

The noises downstairs suggested that Miser Shen was acquiring a goat, some castor oil, and a load of garbage, and Pretty Ping and I took the opportunity to get acquainted. In China when young people wish to become acquainted they usually start by playing Fluttering Butterflies, because there is no better way to get to know somebody than to play Fluttering Butterflies.

"*Eat!*" Miser Shen screamed to the goat.

After young people have become acquainted it is customary to warm things up with the Kingfisher Union, because it is impossible to engage in the Kingfisher Union without becoming close friends.

"*Gold!*" screamed Miser Shen.

A cup of wine is then called for, and a discussion of relative merits that is usually resolved in favor of Hounds by the Ninth Day of Autumn.

"*Eat!*" screamed Miser Shen.

The young gentleman then plays the lute while the young lady dances in a manner that would cause a riot if performed in public, and they inevitably become entangled in Six Doves Beneath the Eaves on a Rainy Day.

"*Gold!*" screamed Miser Shen.

Now that friendship has been firmly established it is but a step and a jump to become soulmates, and the fastest way to become soulmates is Phoenix Sporting in the Cinnabar Crevice.

"Eat!" screamed Miser Shen.

This will lead to wine, love poems, and a return to Fluttering Butterflies, but slowly and drowsily, accompanied by giggles, and so it goes in China until the dawn, when somebody might calm down enough to consider testing the purity of gold coins.

"What is that appalling stench, O most perfect and penetrating of partners?" yawned Pretty Ping.

"I fear that it marks the approach of Miser Shen, O beauty beyond compare," I said sadly, as I climbed out of bed and pulled on my trousers.

"And what is that angry noise, O most tantalizingly tender of tigers?" asked Pretty Ping.

"I fear that Miser Shen is arming his seven half-starved servants with clubs, O rarest of rose petals." I sighed, as I collected my sandals, tunic, jade-embroidered silver girdle, fine tasseled hat, and gold-splattered Szech'uen fan.

"Merciful Buddha! What is the ghastly thing that is oozing obscenely through my doorway?" howled Pretty Ping.

"I fear that it is a mound of goat manure, beneath which you should find Miser Shen. Farewell, O seduction of the universe," I said, and I jumped out the window to the street below.

Li Kao was waiting for me, well rested after a pleasant night with Fat Fu and One-Eyed Wong, and he appeared to approve of the sparkle in my eyes. I bent over and he hopped up upon my back, and then I raced through the streets toward the city walls while behind us Miser Shen screamed, *"Bring back my five hundred pieces of gold!"*

6.

A Winsome Damsel

Our path toward the house of the Ancestress ran through steep mountains, and most of the time Master Li rode upon my back. Sea sounds filled the immense sky as the wind blew through tall trees—pine surfs, as the poets say—and the clouds looked like white sails that were gliding across an endless blue ocean.

One day we climbed down the last mountainside to a green valley, and Li Kao pointed ahead to a low hill.

"The summer estate of the Ancestress should be on the other side," he said. "To tell the truth, I'm rather looking forward to seeing her again."

He smiled at a memory of fifty years ago.

"Ox, I hear that she's put on a great deal of weight, but the Ancestress was the most beautiful girl that I have ever seen in my life, and the most charming when she felt like it," he said. "Still, there was something about her that rang warning bells in my mind, and I was quite fond of old Wen. I was in high favor after the affair of Procopius and the other barbarians—I was even allowed to approach the throne on an east-west axis, instead of groveling upon my knees from the south—and one day I sidled up to the emperor and said with a sly wink that I had arranged for us to spy upon some newlyweds who were about to consummate the happy union. Wen was something of a voyeur, so we tiptoed to my suite and I opened a small curtain and pointed a pedantic finger.

"O Son of Heaven," I said, "it would appear that marriage to a certain kind of female can have unfortunate side effects."

"The newlyweds happened to be praying mantises," said Master Li. "The groom was happily engrossed in copulation, and right on cue his blushing bride craned her pretty neck and casually decapitated him. The groom's hindquarters continued to pump away while the bride devoured his head, which says something about the location of his brains, and for a moment the emperor had second thoughts about wedding bells. But the Ancestress got to him and I was exiled to Serendip, which was quite fortunate because I wasn't around when she poisoned poor Wen and began massacring everyone in sight."

We reached the top of the hill and I stared down in horror at an estate that resembled a vast military fort. It covered almost an entire valley, and it was surrounded by high parallel walls. The corridors between them were patrolled by guards and savage dogs, and everywhere I looked I saw soldiers.

"I understand that her winter palace is really something," Master Li said calmly.

"Can we really get into her treasure chambers and steal the Root of Power?" I asked in a tiny frightened voice.

"I have no intention of attempting such a thing," he said. "We'll persuade the dear lady to bring the root to us. Unfortunately that means that we will have to murder somebody, and I have never truly enjoyed slitting the throats of innocent bystanders. We must pray that we will find somebody who thoroughly deserves it."

He started down the hill.

"Of course, if she recognizes me, the funeral will be ours, and for once she will abandon the axe in favor of boiling oil," he said.

In the last town of consequence Li Kao made certain arrangements, such as purchasing an elegant carriage and renting the largest suite in the inn, and then he went to the town square and tacked one of Miser Shen's gold coins to the message board. I assumed that it would be stolen as soon as we turned our backs, but he drew mysterious symbols around it, and the townspeople who approached the message board turned pale and backed away hurriedly, muttering spells to protect themselves from evil. I had no idea what was going on.

That evening the most alarming bunch of thugs that I had ever seen in my life paused at the message board, studied the coin and the symbols, and began trickling by twos and threes into the inn. Li Kao had set out jars of the strongest wine, which they swilled like hogs, growling and snarling and glaring at me with their hands on the hilts of their daggers. The animal noises stopped abruptly when Li Kao entered and climbed up upon a table.

It was as if hands had been clapped over their filthy mouths. Their eyes bulged, and sweat poured down their greasy faces. The leader of the thugs turned quite gray with terror, and I thought that he was going to faint.

Master Li was wearing a red robe that was covered with cosmological symbols, and a red headband with five loops. His right trouser leg was rolled up, and his left trouser leg was rolled down, and he wore a shoe on his right foot and a sandal on his left. He laid his left hand across his chest with the little and middle fingers extended, and he slid his right hand back inside the sleeve of his robe. The sleeve began to flutter in peculiar patterns as he wriggled the concealed fingers.

Four of the thugs grabbed their leader and forced him forward. Cut-Off-Their-Balls Wang was shaking so hard that he could barely stand, but he managed to slide his own right hand inside his sleeve, and the sleeve began to flutter in response. Master Li's sleeve moved faster and faster, Cut-Off-Their-Balls Wang replied in the same silent fashion, and so it went for many minutes. At last Li Kao extracted his hand from the sleeve and gestured dismissal, and to my astonishment the thugs and their leader backed out of the room on their knees, humbly banging their heads against the floor.

Li Kao smiled and opened a jar of better wine and motioned for me to join him at a table.

"The lower the criminal, the more impressed he is with the childlike mumbo-jumbo of the Secret Societies," he said complacently. "For some reason Cut-Off-Their-Balls Wang is under the impression that I am a great grand master of the Triads, and that I intend to cut his gang in for a share of the loot when I make my move against the Ancestress. In the latter respect," said Master Li, "he is absolutely right."

Two days later some aristocratic ladies who were returning to the estate of the Ancestress were ambushed by villains whose appearance was so terrifying that the guards fled and left the ladies to their fate. Things were looking very bad for them until two intrepid noblemen rode to the rescue.

"On your knees, dogs, for you face the rage of Lord Li of Kao!" Master Li yelled.

"Cower, knaves, before the fury of Lord Lu of Yu!" I shouted.

Unfortunately, our lead horse slipped in some mud, and our carriage crashed into the ladies' carriage, and we were pitched on top of half-naked females who were screaming their heads off. We gazed groggily at a pretty jade pendant that was dangling between a pair of pretty pink-tipped breasts, and it took a moment for us to remember what we were doing there. Then we jumped down to engage the ruffians.

Li Kao stabbed right and left with his sword, and I swung away with both hands—he was missing, of course, and I was pulling my punches short—and the thugs remembered that they weren't actually supposed to rob and rape anybody and began to do a very good job of acting. Once, when my foot slipped in the mud, a punch accidentally landed and sent the leader of the bandits sprawling. I forgot about the accident, and soon the bandits fled in terror and we turned to accept the gratitude of the rescued ladies.

Cut-Off-Their-Balls Wang had already lost his nose and both of his ears in back-alley battles, and he did not appreciate losing several teeth as well. He crept up behind me with a log in his hands.

"A present from Lord Lu of Yu!" he yelled, and he swung with all his might, and I saw a glorious burst of orange and purple stars, and then everything turned black.

I awoke in a very expensive bed surrounded by very expensive women who were battling for the honor of bathing the bump on my skull.

"*He wakes!*" they shrieked at the tops of their lungs. "*Lord Lu of Yu opens his divine eyes!*"

I had been brought up to be courteous, but there are limits.

"If you don't stop that infernal racket, Lord Lu of Yu will strangle you with his divine hands," I groaned.

They paid no attention to me, and the ear-splitting babble continued, and gradually I began to make some sense out of it. Our miraculous intervention had saved them all from rape and ruin, and the esteem in which we were held was not diminished by our fine tasseled hats, green silk tunics, jade-bordered silver girdles, Szech'uen fans, and money belts that bulged with Miser Shen's gold coins. This was all according to plan, but I was rather puzzled by repeated references to "the bridegroom," and I was trying to get up enough strength to ask a few questions when I began to realize that my wounds were far more serious than I had thought.

I was sick enough to imagine that the floor was shaking, and that my bed was starting to bounce up and down. The hallucination was accompanied by a dull, rhythmic, pounding noise that gradually increased in volume, and the ladies suddenly stopped babbling. They turned pale and tiptoed quietly from the room through a side door, and I began to smell a revolting odor of rotting flesh.

The bedroom door crashed open, and the woman who marched inside weighed approximately five hundred pounds. The floor shook as she marched toward my bed. The coldest eyes that I had ever seen, even in nightmares, glittered between puffy rolls of sagging gray flesh, and a massive swollen hand shot out and grabbed my chin. The icy eyes moved over my face.

"Satisfactory," she grunted.

She grabbed my right arm and probed the biceps.

"Satisfactory," she grunted.

She jerked the covers down and squeezed my chest.

"Satisfactory," she grunted.

She ripped the covers all the way down and prodded my private parts.

"Satisfactory," she grunted.

Then the creature stepped back and I stared pop-eyed at a leveled finger that resembled a gangrened sausage.

"They call you Lord Lu of Yu," she growled. "I know Yu well, and there is no Lord Lu. They call your antiquated companion Lord Li of Kao, and the province of Kao does not exist. You are frauds and fortune hunters, and your criminal activities do not interest me in the least."

She slapped her hands to her hips and glared at me.

"My granddaughter has taken a fancy to you, and I want great-grandchildren," she snarled. "The wedding will take place as soon as your wounds have healed. You will present me with seven great-grandchildren, and they will be boys. I intend to overthrow the T'ang Dynasty and restore the Sui, and boys are more suitable for the purpose. In the meantime you will not annoy me by showing your silly face any more than is absolutely necessary, and you will not speak unless spoken to. Insolence in my household is punishable by immediate decapitation."

The monster turned and plodded from the room, and the door slammed viciously behind her. For a moment I lay there paralyzed, and then I jumped from the bed and ran across the floor and started to climb out of the window. The view made me stop. That immense estate boasted no less than seven pleasure gardens, and one of them, in the tradition of great houses, was a pretty artificial peasant village. I gazed at simple thatched roofs, and crude water wheels, and green fields, and pigs and cows and chickens and water buffaloes. I felt tears well in my eyes and trickle down my cheeks.

My village was praying for a ginseng root.

I made my way back to the bed, and I lay there wrapped in misery and terror.

7.

A Great House

When I had recovered enough to take stock of my surroundings it gradually dawned on me that the monster had decided upon seven great-grandchildren some time ago, and that her granddaughter would be ordered to see to it that they were twelve years old at birth. I was lying in the dormitory of the boys who were going to aid in overthrowing the T'ang Dynasty, and I will confess that I wept when I considered the life that my poor children were to lead.

Seven small beds were aligned side by side with geometric precision. Seven small desks were placed precisely in front of them, and the writing brushes lay exactly three inches to the right of the inkstones. Nothing in that cold inhuman room was so much as an eyelash out of alignment, and that included the signs on the walls. Some were *kung kuo-yo*, Tables of Demerits, and I will give an example.

EACH DEMERIT IS TO BE PUNISHED
BY STROKES OF THE BIRCH ROD

Exciting lustful thoughts in oneself	5
Showing one's nakedness when easing nature at night	2
Lewd dreams	2
If such dreams occasion lewd actions	10
Singing frivolous songs	5
Studying frivolous songs	10
Not yielding the way to a woman	10
If at the same time one looks at the woman	20
If one looks longingly at her	30
If one conceives lewd thoughts about her	40
Insolence to a woman	50
Insolence to the Ancestress	500
If such insolence is recurrent	Decapitation

Other signs were lessons to be memorized, and my frightened eyes jerked from one to another. Now and then in my dreams I find myself in a classroom with fragments of lessons plastered all over it.

The effectiveness of the flame throwers known as *meng huo yu* may be enhanced by the addition of pulped bananas and coconuts to the oil, which will cause the fiery mixture to stick to the flesh...

The Fire Drug will release deadly gas upon explosion with the addition of five ounces of *langtu*, two and one half ounces of pitch, one ounce of bamboo fibers, three ounces of arsenic oxide...

An excellent poison can be swiftly produced under field conditions by boiling two baskets of oleander leaves, distilling the essence, and adding three ounces of dried aconite tubers. At sea a simple extraction of the sac of the blowfish...

A more subtle approach was employed by Wang Shihchen, who presented his victims with pornographic novels after smearing the edge of each page with arsenic, and when the victim licked his finger to turn the pages...

Testicle crushers are easily manufactured by . . .

Severed heads may be preserved for display by . . .

I slid down and pulled the covers over my head, and I did not emerge until I heard the door open and a familiar voice said, "What a stroke of luck! Your engagement is a godsend—incidentally, how did you like the winsome damsel who recently ruled China?"

I jumped up and embraced him. "Master Li," I sobbed, "if my fiancée resembles her grandmother in any way, I can never go through with this!" A happy thought suddenly occurred to me. "But if we're engaged, I won't see her until the wedding."

"Normally that would be the case, but an exception has been made because you've already seen almost all of her," he said. "She was the one in the carriage with the pretty jade pendant between the pretty breasts. Don't worry about it. All you have to do is to take an occasional stroll with her in the gardens, while I figure out whom we have to kill in order to get the Root of Power."

"But the Ancestress . . ." I quavered.

"Has not recognized me," said Master Li. "Her natural distaste for fortune-hunting criminals has been reinforced by my unfortunate habit of rolling my eyes, drooling saliva, giggling at inopportune moments, and popping my cheek with an unwashed finger. I doubt that she will seek out your company, and all you'll have to worry about will be your fiancée, her father, and the butler."

My future father-in-law turned out to be the sweetest and gentlest of men, and as a scholar he bowed only to Li Kao. Ho Wen had earned second place in the *chin-shih* examinations, and I would have had to enter Hanlin Academy to find two such minds under one roof. The contrast between them was fascinating.

Li Kao would toss an idea into the air and watch it sparkle, and then he would toss a second one, and then he would send handfuls of associated ideas spinning into space, and when they returned to earth they would be neatly linked into a necklace that fit perfectly around the throat of the subject. Ho Wen, on the other hand, was a plodding one-step-at-a-time scholar who never made a mistake, and whose memory was so prodigious that not even Li Kao could match it. I once asked him the name of a distant mountain, and this is the answer that I received.

"The sacred mountains are five in number: Hengshan, Changshan, Huashan, Taishan, and Sungshan, with Taishan leading in rank and Sungshan in the center. Mountains not sacred but very distinguished include Wuyi, Wutang, Tienmu, Tienchu, Tienmuh, Niushi, Omei, Shiunherh, Chichu, Chihua, Kungtung, Chunyu, Yentang, Tientai, Lungmen, Keuiku, Chiuyi, Shiherh, Pakung, Huchiu, Wolung, Niuchu, Paotu, Peiyo, Huangshan, Pichi, Chinshu, Liangfu, Shuanglang, Maku, Tulu, Peiku, Chinshan, Chiaoshan, and Chungnan. Since the mountain to which you refer is none of these—"

"Ho," I moaned.

"—it might not be too rash to conclude that it is Kuangfu, although I would not like to be quoted in the presence of the Ancestress because the slightest mistake can mean instant decapitation."

Li Kao immediately grasped the potential of Ho's memory. He told him to drop our titles when we were alone and address us as Li Kao and Number Ten Ox, and at the first opportunity he turned the subject to ginseng. Ho's eyes lit up, but before he could begin a discourse that might last several weeks Li Kao asked him if he had ever heard of a Great Root of Power. Even Ho Wen had to stop and think about that, and then he said, slowly and hesitantly,

"I was four years old, visiting a cousin at the Blessings of Heaven Library in Loyang." He paused for more thought. "Third basement, fifth row on the left, second rack from the top. Behind *Chou-pi Mathematics* I found Chang Chi's *Typhoid Fever and Other Diseases*, behind which I found the sixteen volumes in fifty-two rolls of Li Shih-chen's *Outline of Herb Medicine*, behind which I found a mouse's nest. I was chasing the mouse at the time. In the nest was a scrap of parchment with a pretty picture that was labeled 'Great Root of Power,' but the parchment had been so badly chewed that I could not make out what species the root belonged to."

He squinted and pursed his lips as he tried to visualize the picture.

"It was a very strange root," he said. "There were two tiny tendrils that were the Legs of Power, two more that were the Arms of Power, and a fifth tendril that was the Head of Power. The central mass of the root was the Heart of Power, which was labeled 'The Ultimate.' Unfortunately the mice had devoured everything else, so I do not know what the word 'ultimate' referred to. I very much doubt that the root was ginseng, because I have never heard of ginseng that resembled it."

His interest in ginseng had a specific origin. One day a grave was being dug in the family cemetery and a shovel had pitched out some fragments of clay tablets. Ho Wen had instantly recognized ideographs of immense antiquity. He had persuaded the workmen to gather every fragment that there was, and then he had settled down to an impossible task. The fragments were almost illegible, but he was determined to decipher the text or die in the attempt. His face was flushed with pride when he took us to his workshop and showed us the tiny clay fragments, and the theories of mathematical probability that he had devised to suggest the sequence of characters in the ancient script. He had been working on it for sixteen years, and already he had deciphered ten whole sentences, and if he lasted another sixteen years he hoped to have four whole paragraphs.

One thing he was sure of. It was a ginseng folk or fairy tale, and it was one of the oldest known to man.

Ho Wen had no money of his own. In my innocence I assumed that the distinction of his scholar's rank was worth more than money, but I soon learned otherwise. I suspect that the rich are the same in every country in that money is their sole standard of value, and was Ho Wen referred to as Master Ho? Venerable Scholar Ho? Second-Most-Learned-of-Mortals Ho? Not exactly. He was referred to as Henpecked Ho, and he lived in mortal terror of the Ancestress, his wife, her seven fat sisters, and his daughter. In a great house a poor scholar's status is just slightly higher than that of the boy who carries away the night soil.

There was no resemblance whatsoever between Henpecked Ho and his daughter. My bride-to-be was a startlingly pretty girl whose name was Fainting Maid. I assumed that the unusual name came from a line of poetry, but I learned better on our first stroll through the gardens when we were chaperoned by Li Kao and her father.

"Hark!" cried Fainting Maid, pausing on the path and pointing dramatically. "A cuckoo!"

Well, I am a country boy.

"Nay, my beloved," I chuckled. "It is a magpie."

She stamped a pretty foot. "It is a cuckoo!"

"Precious one, the magpie is imitating a cuckoo," I said, pointing to the magpie that was imitating a cuckoo.

"It is a *cuckoo*!"

"Light of my life," I sighed, "it is a magpie."

Fainting Maid turned red, turned white, reeled, clutched her heart, and screeched, "Oh, thou hast slain me!" Then she staggered backward, lurched to the left, and gracefully swooned.

"Two feet back, six to the left," her father sighed.

"Does she ever vary it?" Li Kao asked with scientific interest.

"Not so much as an inch. Precisely two feet back and six feet to the left. And now, dear boy, you are required to kneel and bathe her delicate temples and beg her forgiveness for your intolerable rudeness. My daughter," said Henpecked Ho, "is never wrong, and I might add that never in her life has she been denied anything that she wanted."

Is it possible that among my illustrious readers there may be one or two who are contemplating marriage for money? I have a very clear memory of a golden afternoon when the butler was instructing me in the etiquette of a great house, Henpecked Ho's beloved wife and her seven

fat sisters were sipping tea in the Garden of Forty Felic-
itous Fragrances, Fainting Maid was insulting the intelligence of her ladies-in-waiting in the Gallery of Precious
Peacocks, and the Ancestress was chiding a servant who
had dropped a cup on the Terrace of Sixty Serenities.

"The cook hands the guest a ladle with an engraved
handle and a stand which is placed west of the tripods,"
said the butler. "The guest takes the handle of the ladle
with his right hand, palm inward, and lays the ladle alongside the stand."

"Off with his head!" roared the Ancestress.

"Then," continued the butler, "he faces east, at the
west of the tripods, to receive the food that is his due and
that is determined by his attire, beginning with the state
umbrella that is displayed by his servants."

"Gabble-gabble-gabble-gabble-gabble!" squawked
Henpecked Ho's wife and her seven fat sisters.

"The umbrella of First and Second Rank officials have
yellowish-black gauze covers, red raw silk linings, three
tiers, and silver spires, and the umbrellas of the Third
and Fourth Rank officials are the same, except that the
spires are red."

"Forgive me, My Lady! Of course The Gentlewoman's
Guide to Needlepoint *was written by Confucius!"* wailed
a lady-in-waiting.

"The umbrellas of the Fifth Rank," said the butler,
"have blue gauze coverings, red raw silk linings, two tiers,
and silver spires, and those of the Sixth through Ninth
Rank have blue oiled, raw silk coverings, red raw silk
linings, one tier, and silver spires."

"Deposit the corpse in the pigsty!" roared the
Ancestress.

Enough.

8.
Dancing Girl

*One night Li Kao and I stopped by Henpecked Ho's work-*shop and found him in tears, holding a cheap silver comb in his hands while he wailed. When he had recovered enough to speak he asked us to hear his story, because he had no one else with whom to share joys or sorrow. Li Kao made him drink some wine, and then we sat down to listen.

"A few years ago I managed to please the Ancestress in some way," said Henpecked Ho. "She graciously al-lowed me to take a concubine, but I had no money of my own. I could not aspire to a lady of quality, or even the maid of a lady of quality, so I chose a dancing girl from Hangchow. Her name was Bright Star, and she was very beautiful and very brave, and I loved her with all my heart. She did not love me, of course, because I am old and ugly and something of a worm, but I never forced myself on her and I think that she was reasonably happy. I gave her this comb as a token of my love. As you can see, it is not a very good comb, but it was all that I could afford, and she wore it in her hair to please me. I had never been in love before, and in my foolishness I thought that my joy would last forever.

"One night the Ancestress entertained some officers from the fort, and among them was a young captain whose family was so distinguished that it was common knowledge that the Ancestress would choose him to wed Fainting Maid. For some reason the name of Bright Star was mentioned, and suddenly the captain was all attention. She was no common dancing girl, he said excitedly. Bright Star had become a living legend in Hangchow through her skill and courage at the Sword Dance, and the young captain, who was a very famous swordsman himself, said that he would give anything to meet such an opponent. Since no distinctions of rank are allowed in the Sword Dance, the Ancestress ordered Bright Star to perform. When she opened an old wicker case and took out two swords I could see that she kept her heart in those glittering blades. She allowed me to oil her body, and I marveled at the pride and happiness in her eyes, and my beautiful dancing girl walked out the door like a queen.

"Sword Dancers wear only loincloths, of course, and I could not bear to see Bright Star displayed like a piece of meat for the soldiers to leer at. I did not attend the dance, but I did not have to. The wind drifted down from the mansion and with it came a clash of steel blades that grew louder and louder and faster and faster. I heard cheering, and then I heard the audience roaring at the tops of their lungs. The drums pounded like thunder, and when the sand clock ran out the audience continued to cheer in delight and wonder for nearly ten minutes. The judges refused to declare a winner. Only gods, they said, had the right to choose between gods, and the palm was cut in two and half was given to each contestant.

"That night I lay in my bed and listened to the sobs of a dancing girl. She had fallen in love with the young captain, but what was she to do? Her social status was so low that it would be quite impossible for a gentleman of his rank to take her as a secondary wife, and she would be forced to see him as the husband of my daughter but never could she reach out and touch him. All night long she wept, and in the morning I made my way to the fort and had a long talk with a young captain who had not slept a wink, because whenever he closed his eyes he saw the face of Bright Star. When I returned that evening I clasped a gold chain around the throat of a dancing girl, and on the end of it was a beautiful jade pendant that was the token of the captain's love.

"Am I not a worm?" said Henpecked Ho. "I had so little pride that I would even play panderer for the woman I loved. All that mattered was her happiness, and I went about it quite methodically. I discovered that there were two brief periods when the corridor between the walls was unguarded. At sunset, when the guards went off duty, the men in the kennels waited for a few minutes to make sure that everyone was out before they released the dogs, and at sunrise the guards waited for a few minutes before entering the corridor, to make sure the dogs were safely locked up. There was a small door in the inner wall at the north end of the estate, and I stole the key and gave it to Bright Star. That evening at sunset I gave the signal that the corridor was clear, and the young captain scaled the outer wall and raced across, and Bright Star opened the door. At sunrise he was able to return to the fort in the same way.

"For nearly a month she lived in Heaven. I lived in Hell, of course, but that was scarcely important on the relative scale of things," said Henpecked Ho. "Then one evening I heard a terrible scream. I raced to the wall and found Bright Star frantically tugging at the door. She had just opened it, but somebody had approached and she had been forced to hide, and when she came back she discovered that the door had been closed and locked and that the key had been taken. I raced to the kennels to try to stop the men from releasing the dogs, but I was too late. The terrible baying pack raced down the corridor, and the young captain was able to kill a great many of them but he could not kill them all. As Bright Star desperately tugged at the door, she was forced to listen to the death of her captain. She could not stand it. When I ran back, I discovered that my beautiful dancing girl had thrown herself into an old well beside the wall.

"It was no accident. They knew at the fort that the captain was slipping away at night, and everyone who had attended the Sword Dance had seen the light in his eyes. From the joy in the eyes of Bright Star it was obvious that the captain had found a way to cross the corridor, but who could have been so cruel as to lock the door and take the key? It was the murder of two innocent young people."

Henpecked Ho began to weep again, and it was nearly a minute before he could continue.

"Bright Star may have wanted to die, but her fate was far worse," he sobbed. "So great had been her desire to reach the young captain that even in death she must continue to try to get through the door in time, but of course she cannot do it. The following night I returned to the well that had claimed her life, and I discovered that my beautiful dancing girl had been trapped in a ghost dance. Now I fear that she must suffer the agonies of the damned throughout eternity."

Li Kao jumped to his feet and clapped his hands sharply together.

"Nonsense!" he said. "There has never been a ghost dance that couldn't be broken, and there never will be. Ho, take us to the scene of the tragedy and you and I and Number Ten Ox will take care of the problem immediately."

It was almost the third watch, the hour of ghosts, when we walked through the garden in the moonlight. The breeze sighed sadly through the leaves, and a lonely dog barked in the distance, and an owl drifted down like a falling leaf across the face of the moon. When we reached the wall I saw that the door had been removed and the hole had been bricked up. The old well was covered over, and the path was overgrown by weeds.

Li Kao turned to me. "Ox, have you been taught how to see ghosts?" he asked quietly.

I blushed bright red. "Master Li," I said humbly, "in my village young people are not introduced to the world of the dead until they have become civilized enough to respect the living. The abbot thought that I might possibly be ready for instruction after the fall harvest."

"Don't worry about it," he said reassuringly. "The world of the dead is immensely complicated, but seeing ghosts is simplicity itself. Take a look at the wall where the door used to be. Take a very close look, and keep looking until you see something strange."

I stared until my eyeballs hurt.

"Master Li, I see something that puzzles me," I said finally. "That faint shadow above the rose bush cannot possibly be caused by branches, or by clouds passing the face of the moon. Where does it come from?"

"Excellent," he said. "You are looking at a ghost shadow. Ox, listen carefully because what I am about to say will sound silly, but it is not. Whenever you see a ghost shadow, you must realize that the dead are trying to show you something, and you must think of the shadow as being a soft comfortable blanket that you would like to pull over you. It is quite easy. Calm your heartbeat, and clear your mind of everything except a comfortable blanket. Now reach out with your mind and pull it toward you, and then up over your head. Gently...gently ...gently.... No. You are trying much too hard. It requires no effort at all. Think of the comfort and warmth. Gently...gently...gently.... Good. Now tell me what you see."

"Master Li, the patch in the wall is gone and the door is back in place!" I whispered. "It is standing open, and the well is uncovered, and the path is clear of weeds!"

And so it was, although it was like a picture with a hazy frame around it that flickered at the periphery of my vision. Faint in the distance I heard the watchman rap three times with his wooden knocker, and the three of us sat upon the grass beside the path. Henpecked Ho reached out and squeezed my shoulder.

"Dear boy, you are about to see something very beautiful, and you will learn that there is beauty that can break the heart," he said quietly.

The Great River of Stars was sparkling above us, like

a diamond necklace clasped around the black velvet throat of the sky. The cassia trees sparkled with dew, and the high brick wall appeared to be painted with silver, and bamboos lifted like long fingers that waved in a soft breeze as they pointed toward the moon. A flute began to play, but it was like no flute that I had ever heard before. The same few notes were repeated over and over, softly and sadly, but with subtle variations in pitch and tone that caused each note to flutter in the air like the petal of a flower. A strange flickering light moved slowly through the trees.

I caught my breath.

A ghost was dancing toward us to the hypnotic rhythm of the flute. Bright Star was so lovely that my heart felt as though a hand were squeezing it, and I found it difficult to breathe. She wore a long white robe that was embroidered with blue flowers, and she was dancing down the path with indescribable grace and delicacy. Every gesture of her hands, every movement of her feet, every subtle swirl of her robe gave meaning to the word perfection, but her eyes were wide and desperate.

Li Kao leaned over. "Look behind you," he whispered.

The door was closing. Closing very slowly, but just slightly faster than the unchanging song of the flute, and now I realized that the music was a chain that bound a dancing girl. Her eyes were agonized as she watched the door swing slowly shut, and two ghost tears trickled down her cheeks like transparent pearls.

"Faster," I prayed silently. "Beautiful girl, you must dance faster!"

But she could not. Bound to a rhythm that she could not break, she floated toward us like a cloud, feet barely touching the ground, whirling with exquisite grace and pathetic desire. Her arms and hands and long, flowing robe formed patterns that were as subtle as smoke, and even the fingers that reached toward the door were positioned in the pattern of the dance. She was too late.

The door closed tight, with a cold cruel click of a lock. Bright Star stood motionless, and a wave of agony flowed over me like a harsh winter wind. And then she was gone, and the music was gone, and the well was covered, and the path was overgrown by weeds, and I was staring with wet eyes at a bricked-up patch in a wall.

"Every night she dances, and every night I pray that she will be able to get through the door to her captain, but she cannot dance faster than the music allows," Henpecked Ho said quietly. "Thus Bright Star must dance until time comes to an end."

Li Kao was softly humming the flute song as he thought, and then he slapped a knee with a hand.

"Ho, the chain of a ghost dance is woven from the victim's own desire, but that magnificent young woman is ruled by more than one desire," he said. "No power in life or in death can prevent her from honoring her art and it is artistry that will free a dancing girl. Your job will be to steal two swords and a couple of drums. Ox, I'd do it myself if I could be ninety again, but it looks as though you can have the honor of chopping off your arms and legs."

"Of doing what?" I asked in a tiny voice.

"It is said that the challenge of the Sword Dance is stronger than death itself, and now is the time to prove it," said Master Li.

I quivered in my sandals, and I saw myself trundling upon a trolley with a begging bowl clutched in my two remaining fingers. "Alms for the poor! Alms for a poor legless cripple..."

Every year there are well-meaning officials who attempt to ban the Sword Dance on the grounds that it kills or maims hundreds, if not thousands, and though the dance will continue as long as the great T'ang sits upon the throne (the Son of Heaven devotes an hour a day to practice with the swords) I suppose that I should explain a "barbaric ritual" that may someday become as obsolete as scapulimancy.

There are two contestants, two drummers, and three judges. The drums set the pace, and once the dance begins it is forbidden to break the rhythm in any way. The contestants are required to perform six mandatory maneuvers in sequence, each with an increasing level of difficulty, and all maneuvers are performed while leaping—both feet must leave the ground—and require precise slashes with two swords over, under, and around the body, that are graded according to grace, accuracy, closeness of blades to the body, and elevation of leap. These mandatory maneuvers are very important because the judges must beware of mismatches, and if one of the contestants is clearly outclassed, they will refuse to allow the dance to continue.

The contestants begin quite far apart and move closer with each maneuver, and at the completion of the six mandatory maneuvers they are practically face to face. If the judges are satisfied they signal for the drummers to sound the beat of the seventh level, and now the dance becomes art, and occasionally it becomes murder.

Seventh-level maneuvers are free-form, and the only requirement is that they must be of the highest difficulty. The dancers attempt to express their souls, and the fun lies in the fact that once a maneuver has been completed the dancer is free to clip the hair from his opponent's head, if he can do so before his feet touch the ground. The opponent is free to parry and thrust, but only after his own maneuver has been completed and only before his own feet touch the ground. A dancer who attempts a stroke while so much as a toe is touching the earth is immediately disqualified. Masters disdain such easy targets as the hair on the head and attempt to barber their opponent's beard or mustache, if he wears such adornments, and the loss of noses and eyes and ears is considered to be an occupational hazard of no great importance. Of course if a dancer panics and breaks the rhythm he will probably be killed, because he will be leaping up when he should be coming down and his opponent will aim for his hair and cut off his head.

During the mandatory maneuvers the drummers play together, but with the seventh level they split, one for each dancer, and it is said that a truly great drummer is the equivalent of a third sword. Sample gymnasium conversation:

"I hear that Fan Yun has challenged you. Who's your drummer?"

"Blind Meng."

"*Blind Meng!* Great Buddha, I must sell my wife and wager the proceeds! Orderly, be so kind as to order flowers for Fan Yun's widow."

Of course that is at the master level, and the enemy of the raw amateur, such as Number Ten Ox, is not his opponent but he himself. The swords are as sharp as razors, and terrific force is required to whip them around the body in a seventh-level maneuver, and the amateur is likely to beam with pride after a successful maneuver only to discover that he has left one of his legs lying upon the ground.

It is quite impossible to describe the beauty of the Sword Dance in words. It is skill and pride and courage and grace and beauty rolled into one, and when two consummate masters go at it their bodies seem to float effortlessly into the air and hang suspended in space, and their swords are flashing blinding blurs—particularly at night, in the light of torches—and the clash of steel meeting steel is like the songs of gongs that thrill the heart as well as the ears. Each brilliant maneuver inspires a counter maneuver even more brilliant, and the drummers drive their rhythms into the hearts of their champions and force them past human limitations into the realm of the supernatural. The audience screams as a blade slips through and blood spurts, but the dancers laugh out loud, and then the sand clock runs out and the drums fall silent, and even the judges leap to their feet and cheer as the panting contestants drop their swords and embrace.

One might assume that this dangerous sport requires the strength of a man, but speed and suppleness can counterbalance strength. It is said that among the six greatest dancers of all time there was one woman, and I insist that the figure must be revised. Two of them were women, and I am in a position to prove it.

That night Li Kao carried two sharp swords up the path toward the wall. They had to be sharp because an expert would spot dull blades in a second. Henpecked Ho carried two drums, and I carried two thousand pounds of sheer terror. My flesh was all goose bumps as I stripped to my loincloth, and my fingers were like icicles as I took the swords from Li Kao. They hid in the shrubbery, and I have never known time that passed so slowly yet reached midnight with such appalling swiftness.

The watchman's knocker rapped three times, and I turned to see the faint outlines of a ghost shadow upon the patch where the door had been. The shadow blanket slipped easily over my head, and the door stood open and the well was uncovered and the path was clear of weeds. I walked up the path to meet Bright Star.

The flute began to play its haunting melody. A light moved toward me. The exquisite girl came dancing down the path, and again I caught my breath as I watched the agony of her perfection as she honored her art, even while her heart was breaking. She did not see me.

Henpecked Ho began pounding his drum, and at first I couldn't imagine what he was doing. He certainly wasn't sounding the challenge to the Sword Dance, but finally my pulse told me the answer. The gentle scholar was playing the song that he loved most on earth and that he had learned during the lovesick sleepless nights; the heartbeat of a dancing girl. He leaned over his drum and put his weight into it, and the insistent heartbeat thudded and thundered through the trees, and the first flaw in the dance of Bright Star was the faintly puzzled expression that began to appear in her eyes.

Li Kao's drum rang out with the challenge to the Sword Dance, weaving in and out and over and around the steady beat of a heart, and an awareness, a growing wonder, began to shine in the eyes of the dancing girl. I stepped forward and raised my swords in the salute, and then I knew that the legend was true, and that the challenge to the dance is stronger than death itself, because her eyes began to sparkle, and as the challenge and the heartbeat pounded louder and louder her hands lifted gracefully to the clasp of her throat and her robe fell to the ground, and she danced toward me in her loincloth, with the jade pendant that her captain had given her hanging between her small firm breasts on a golden chain, and Henpecked Ho's silver comb in her hair.

Then she saw me. She spread her hands wide and two ghost swords suddenly sparkled in the moonlight. The heartbeat thudded even louder, and Li Kao began to pound the command for the mandatory maneuvers.

A master would never consent to dance with an amateur. It would be murder. I plastered a silly smile on my face and pretended that I was making a joke of boring classroom exercises, and then I launched into the air with the Tiger, the Kingfisher, Dragon's Breath, the Swan, the Serpent, and Night Rain. Bright Star didn't suspect that I was doing the very best that I could. She laughed and promptly imitated me, even to the slight stumble that I made after Dragon's Breath. We were moving closer and closer together, and Henpecked Ho's drum joined Li Kao's as they thundered the command for seventh-level maneuvers.

I sent a fervent prayer to the August Personage of Jade, and then I leaped off the ground with Eighth Drake Under the River Bridge. The August Personage of Jade must have heard me, because I managed to complete the eight savage slashes around my body and between my legs without castrating myself, but when I saw Bright Star's response I nearly fainted. She lifted effortlessly into the air and floated like a leaf as she slashed her swords around her body in Ice Falling From a Mountaintop which is very nearly impossible—and still had time before her toes touched the ground to take a couple of playful swipes that would have neatly trimmed my eyebrows if her ghost swords had been real. I managed to complete Stallion Racing in the Meadow, and Bright Star tripled the level of difficulty with Storm Clouds, but her eyes narrowed suspiciously when she saw that I had left myself wide open.

It was now or never. I leaped into the air with Widow's Tears, and Bright Star turned pale with shock and horror. I was dancing *backward*, out of reach of her swords. The drums continued, and she almost lost her balance. My

cowardice was plain to see, but the judges had not stopped
the contest, and there could be only one explanation.
They had been bribed, and the Sword Dance had been
defiled, and her whole world was crashing down around
her ears.

"What? You break the rhythm of the dance?" I sneered.
"Are you afraid of me, base-born dancing girl?"

That did it. The beautiful ghost uttered a piercing scream
of rage, and her lithe body shot up into the air, and her
swords began to flicker around her body like tongues of
flame as she pursued me down that path, performing seventh-level maneuvers that I could not possibly believe,
even though the blades were flashing right in front of my
face. I puffed and panted and danced backward as fast
as I could, but nothing on earth could persuade a dancer
to continue if the opponent failed to complete a maneuver,
and now I was slicing myself to ribbons.

Henpecked Ho began to pound Bright Star's heartbeat
so powerfully that blood was spurting from the palms of
his hands, and Li Kao's drum was drowning out the ghost
flute as it commanded: *Faster! Faster! Faster!* I glanced
behind me. The door was already half-closed, and I danced
faster, but my lungs were filled with hot coals and there
were black spots before my eyes. Somehow I managed to
complete Eagle Screams without leaving my severed
feet upon the ground. Bright Star contemptuously count-
ered with Eagle Screams Above the Lamb—which has
been successfully performed no more than five times in
the two thousand years of the Sword Dance—and had
time for two swipes that would have removed my ears
and a third that was intended to emasculate me. Her eyes
were on fire and her hair was standing up like the fur of
a big beautiful cat. The ghost swords were whipping around
her leaping body with unbelievable force, and they slashed
out to remove my eyes and my nose, and her toes barely
touched the ground before she was airborne again.

Now and then she comes to dance for me in my dreams.
I do not believe that many men are so honored.

Faster! the drums thundered. *Faster! Faster!* I danced
faster, and then my swords got all tangled up as I at-

tempted Tenth Dive of the Blue Heron, and I backed into a log upon the path and tripped and fell. The beautiful ghost leaped over me and her swords flashed out to remove my hide from my nose to my toes, and she landed on the other side. The drums stopped instantly. Bright Star shook her head dazedly, and then her eyes widened with wonder and hope as she realized that the log that had tripped me had been placed directly in front of the door, and it was still partly open, and she had leaped right through the gap.

Li Kao and Henpecked Ho came running up the path as the dancing girl slowly turned to her captain. He was a tall, handsome ghost, and in life he must have been very heroic because he was able to turn from Bright Star and lift his clenched fist in the soldier's salute, and to hold it for the full seven seconds before he swept his dancing girl into his arms. Then the ghosts faded away, and the flute faded away, and the door faded away, and the cover returned to the well, and the weeds returned to the path, and we were looking at a bricked-up patch in a wall.

The hands of Master Li and Henpecked Ho were dripping with blood, and I looked like something that the cat had dragged from a slaughterhouse. We made a rather bedraggled group for such solemn ceremonies, but we doubted that anyone would mind. At Henpecked Ho's workshop we cut paper silhouettes of the happy couple. We burned paper money for the dowry and food for the guests, and we spilled wine upon the ground. Henpecked Ho spoke for the bride, and I spoke for the groom, and Li Kao chanted the wedding vows, and when the cock crowed we thanked the newlyweds for the banquet and let them go at last to the bridal bed. Thus Bright Star married her captain, and Henpecked Ho's gentle heart was finally at rest.

"All in all," said Master Li as he helped me limp down the path, "it has been a rather satisfactory evening."

9.
A Brief Interlude for Murder

As soon as my wounds had healed, Master Li suggested that I should take another stroll through the gardens with Fainting Maid, with her father and himself as chaperones, and Ho and I were quite surprised when he led the way up the path toward the old well and the bricked-up patch of wall. Fainting Maid was in good form.

"Roses! My favorite flowers!" she squealed, pointing to some petunias.

Master Li's voice was as sweet and smooth as warm honey. "Beautiful roses indeed," he cooed, "but as Chang Chou so charmingly put it, women are the only flowers that can talk."

Fainting Maid simpered coyly.

"Stop!" cried Master Li. "Stop right here, with your exquisite feet against this mark in the path! Here the light strikes you perfectly, and never has your beauty been more breathtaking."

Fainting Maid posed prettily.

"Absolute perfection," Master Li sighed happily. "A lovely lady in a lovely setting. One can scarcely believe

that so tranquil a spot could have been the scene of tragedy, yet I have heard that here a door was locked, and a
key was stolen, and a handsome young man and the girl
who loved him lost their lives."

"A stupid soldier and a slut," Fainting Maid said coldly.

Her father winced, but Li Kao at least partially agreed.

"Well, I'm not so sure about the slut, but the soldier
was stupid indeed," he said thoughtfully. "He was honored with the opportunity of marrying you, O vision of
perfection, yet he dared to prefer a lowly dancing girl.
Why, he even gave her a valuable jade pendant that should
rightfully have been yours!"

I was beginning to sense a certain menace behind Li
Kao's beaming smile.

"I would imagine that it was the first time in your life
that you had been denied something that you wanted,"
said Master Li. "You know, I find it rather odd that Bright
Star wasn't wearing the captain's pendant when they fished
her body from the water. She would scarcely have paused
to take it off before seeking a watery grave, unless, of
course, she wasn't seeking a watery grave at all. Meaning
that somebody hired a pack of thugs to lock a door and
steal a key and murder a dancing girl."

His hands shot out and jerked a gold chain from Fainting Maid's neck, and up over her head. At the end of the
chain was a jade pendant, which he bounced in the palm
of his hand, and I realized with a sick sense of shock that
I had seen it twice before. First between Fainting Maid's
breasts in the carriage, and then in ghost form between
the breasts of Bright Star.

"Tell me, dear child, do you always wear this next to
your sweet little heart?" Master Li asked, smiling as
warmly as ever.

Henpecked Ho was staring at his monstrous daughter
with horror and revulsion, and I suppose that the expression on my face was similar. Fainting Maid decided that
Li Kao was the safest.

"Surely you do not mean to suggest—"

"Ah, but I do."

"You cannot possibly suspect—"

"Wrong again."

"This incredible nonsense—"

"Is not nonsense."

Fainting Maid turned red, turned white, clutched her chest, reeled, and screeched, "Oh, thou has slain me!" Then she lurched two steps back and six to the left and disappeared.

Li Kao gazed at the spot where she had vanished. "Captious critics might tend to agree with you," he said mildly, and then he turned to her father. "Ho, you are perfectly free to hear whatever you choose, but what I hear is a magpie that is imitating the sounds of a scream and a splash."

Henpecked Ho's face was white, and his hands trembled, and his voice was unsteady, but he never flinched.

"Clever little creature," he whispered. "Now it is imitating the sound of somebody screaming 'Help!'"

Li Kao linked arms with Henpecked Ho, and the two of them strolled up the path while I trotted nervously behind.

"What a talented magpie," Master Li observed. "How on earth can it manage that sound of thrashing in the water, and the gurgle that sounds strikingly like somebody sinking down into a deep pool?"

"Nature is full of remarkable talents," Henpecked Ho whispered. "Yours, for example."

"There is a slight flaw in my character," Master Li said modestly.

When we returned an hour later I judged from the silence that the talented magpie was no longer with us.

"I think that I had best remove this mark from the path, lest busybodies wonder why it is precisely two feet in front and six feet to the right of an old well from which somebody has rashly removed the cover," said Master Li. "Ready?"

"Ready," I said.

"Ready," said Henpecked Ho.

We rent our garments and tore our hair as we raced back toward the mansion.

"Woe!" we howled. *"Woe! Woe! Woe! Poor Fainting Maid has fallen into a well!"*

Li Kao and I were viewed with suspicion, but since the girl's own father had been with us there could be no question that it had been an accident.

10.

It Was a Grand Funeral

Li Kao was delighted that he had been able to murder somebody who thoroughly deserved it, and his reason for murder was that the Ancestress, in her own inimitable way, was deeply religious. An example of her piety was the immense mausoleum that she had erected for herself, assuming that someday she would condescend to join the gods. It was a giant iron pillar more than a hundred feet high, with the burial chamber in the center and the message that she wished to preserve for posterity engraved in huge characters above the entrance. If the history of the Ancestress is lost in the passage of time, I imagine that the scholars of the future will be rather puzzled by her epitaph.

HEAVEN PRODUCES MYRIADS OF THINGS TO NOURISH
    MAN;
MAN NEVER DOES ONE GOOD TO RECOMPENSE
    HEAVEN.
KILL! KILL! KILL! KILL! KILL! KILL! KILL!

Another example of her piety was her fondness for lohans. I don't mean the statues of Buddhist saints, such as the 142,289 that can be found in Lung-men. I mean real lohans.

A real lohan is a saintly monk who has given up the ghost while seated in the meditative mudra. This is considered to be a sign from Heaven, and when the deceased is discovered contemplating his navel, with his legs crossed, the soles of his feet turned up, and his hands lying limply upon his lap with the palms up, his body is carefully wrapped in layers of burlap. The burlap is treated with successive coats of lacquer and the finished product is a real saint whose preserved body will last for centuries. (If the lacquer is properly applied and the body is placed in water, it will last forever.) Such lacquered lohans are extremely rare, but the Ancestress possessed no less than twelve of them. Those with nasty minds suspected that more than one of the saints had been peacefully contemplating when an agent of the Ancestress slipped a knife between his ribs. This may or may not have been true, but the Ancestress was unquestionably proud of them and brought them out for all great ceremonial occasions.

In the days that followed the demise of Fainting Maid mourners gathered from all over, and the most illustrious erected sacrificial tents along the road that the funeral procession would take to the cemetery. They brought private orchestras, and even troupes of actors and acrobats, and there was a great deal of socializing among the nobility. More and more people poured into the estate, including countless bonzes who were employed by the Ancestress to pray day and night for her soul, and the affair rather resembled a festival.

The great day dawned with a drizzle. Clouds hovered overhead throughout the morning and early afternoon, and it was hot and humid with a sulphurous smell in the air. Henpecked Ho, who had willingly agreed to help us, muttered grim warnings about evil signs as he walked from count to marquis to duke. Shaggy black beasts with eyes like fire had been seen in the woods, said Henpecked Ho. Servants had seen two ominous ghosts—"A woman in

white and a woman in green!"—who had warned of demons, and when a search was made of the pleasure pavilions the carving of a demon had indeed been found,
with an iron band around its head and a chain around its
neck. A bronze candelabrum had floated through the air
beside the Lake of the Fifth Fragrance: "With seven
flames!" hissed Henpecked Ho, and I hope that no one
will judge that sweet old man rashly when I report that
at the funeral of his daughter he was having the time of
his life.

A great roll of drums signaled the approach of the
funeral procession. First came outriders in double rows,
followed by servants waving phoenix banners and musi-
cians playing mournful music. They were followed by long
lines of priests who swung lighted censers of gold, and
then by the coffin with the sixty-four bearers that desig-
nated a princess. As the bereaved fiancé I had the place
of honor, wailing and tearing my hair as I walked beside
the coffin. Next came soldiers from the army of the Ancestress who carried an immense canopy of phoenix-
embroidered yellow silk, and beneath the canopy were
bonzes who pulled twelve bejeweled carts. In each cart,
seated in the meditative mudra, was a lacquered lohan.

The saints were looking down approvingly at the visible signs of the piety and grief of the Ancestress. She
had opened her treasure chambers to provide suitable
offerings to the spirit of the departed, and items of immense value were placed at the lohans' feet. Of course
everyone understood that the Ancestress had no intention
of burying her wealth with Fainting Maid, but the display
was customary, and it was also designed to make lesser
mortals turn green with envy. After the burial gifts came
four soldiers who were carrying the state umbrella of the
Ancestress, and beneath the umbrella marched her chief
eunuch, who was carrying the great crown of the Sui
Dynasty upon a silken pillow. Then came the great lady
herself. An army of servants groaned beneath the crushing
weight as they carried her sedan chair, which was covered
with a canopy of phoenix-embroidered yellow silk, with
silver bells at the sides and a golden knob in back.

In case anyone wonders why she used the phoenix symbols of an imperial consort rather than the dragon symbols of an emperor, the answer is simple. The imperial dragons were embroidered all over a large silken pillow, and the Ancestress was sitting on it.

I will not describe the ceremony of the burial in detail because I would have to begin with the 3,300 rules of *chu* etiquette, which would send my readers screaming into the night, but I will mention that the body of my beloved had been covered with quicksilver and "Dragon's Brains," and that I had been quite disappointed when I had discovered that the latter were merely Borneo camphor.

Fainting Maid could not presume to share the mausoleum with the Ancestress. Like all other family members, she was buried in the common dirt, in order to spend eternity at the great lady's feet, and I was required to pour handfuls of dirt over my head and wail like a man demented as I flung myself upon the grave, while the aristocracy made critical comments concerning the artistry of my performance. Hooded monks surrounded the grave, banging bells and gongs and spraying incense in all directions. Their leader had his hands clasped piously in prayer, or so I thought until his real hands slipped slyly from his robe and neatly picked the pockets of the Marquis of Tzu.

Henpecked Ho ran around with wild eyes, babbling about evil spirits and demons, and who could doubt it? Lightning flickered evily in the distance, and terrible things began to happen. Prince Han Li, for example, was engrossed in a profound theological discussion with one of the hooded monks, and when the prince was next seen he was lying in a ditch with a large bump on his head, divested of his purse, jewelry, red leather belt studded with emeralds, silver-winged cap with white tassels, and knife-pleated white mourning garment with a gold-threaded design of five-clawed dragons. Screams and roars of rage were lifting from the pavilions of the wealthy, whose valuable funeral gifts had miraculously disappeared. Lady Wu, whose beauty was said to rival that of the semilegendary Queen Feiyen, was carried into the bushes by a creature who had no ears or nose, and whose eyes were as yellow as his teeth.

We all have our little weaknesses, but I must question the judgment of Cut-Off-Their-Balls Wang when he abandoned his fellow hooded monks to disport in the bushes with Lady Wu. He missed a great deal of excitement.

It was obvious that Henpecked Ho's warning had been correct, and that the funeral of Fainting Maid had been attacked by demons. Only an immediate exorcism could save the lives of one and all, and Henpecked Ho was nothing less than magnificent as he led the Grand Master Wizard and the forty-nine assistants—who had fortuitously arrived with the hooded monks—and soon the cemetery was shrouded by rolling clouds of incense. Henpecked Ho bravely waved the banners that represented the five directions of Heaven, while wizards who wore cosmological mantles and seven-starred tiaras sprayed the graves with holy water. Drums nearly deafened us as Ho and the wizards grappled with invisible demons, swinging peachwood whips and swords that were engraved with the Eight Diagrams and the Nine Heavenly Spheres. They stuffed the nasty demons into jars and bottles, which were stoppered and sealed and stamped with closure decrees that forbade them to be opened throughout all eternity.

In the middle of all this a miracle occurred that could have converted the most stubborn atheist in the whole world.

An exceptionally saintly lacquered lohan was admiring the diamond-encrusted imperial sceptre that the Ancestress had placed at his feet, and apparently he feared that the other funeral gifts might be defiled by demons. So he stood up from the meditative mudra and began making a tour of inspection. Bonzes screamed and fainted in droves, and even the Ancestress, who had been screaming "Off with their heads!" turned pale and drew back in fear. The lacquer glinted like dull gold in the sultry light, and the saint appeared to be floating through the clouds of incense as he drifted among his fellow lohans and inspected each gift to make sure that it was safe. The last gift was inside a small jade casket, which the saint picked up and opened.

"Got it!" he exclaimed happily.

Unfortunately the light coat of lacquer had wiped fifty years of wrinkles from the lohan's face, and the Ancestress sat up straight.

"You!" she screamed. "You and your damned praying mantises nearly ruined me with Emperor Wen! Soldiers, seize this fraudulent dog!"

Master Li took to his heels, clutching the jade casket, and I hopped up from Fainting Maid's grave and raced in pursuit. The army of the Ancestress ran after us, and the diversion was a godsend to Cut-Off-Their-Balls Wang, who emerged from the bushes and gathered his men and began stealing everything in sight, and confusion degenerated into chaos. Then the storm that had been hovering all day broke with a bang, and lightning and thunder joined the drums of the wizards and the howls of the victims, and blinding rain became an even better cover than rolling clouds of incense. We escaped quite easily and reached our hiding place, a small natural cave in the riverbank. Then we stripped and dried off, and Li Kao opened the casket and held it out to me.

Inside was the most magnificent ginseng root imaginable. No wonder the Ancestress had included it among her most valuable possessions, as Master Li had foreseen, and the aroma that came from it was so powerful that it made my head spin.

"Ox, this is truly extraordinary, but the Root of Power in no way resembles the Great Root that Henpecked Ho described," said Master Li. "Of course Ho doubts that his root was ginseng, and we must pray that this will do the job."

I was convinced that the children were as good as cured, and I cannot describe the joy in my heart. The rain soon ceased and the clouds drifted away, and we tiptoed through a thick swirling mist. Henpecked Ho was waiting for us at the entrance to the cemetery, and his eyes were sparkling as they had been when Bright Star passed safely through the door. We started off through the graves, and as we approached the mausoleum of the Ancestress we heard the faint sound of shovels.

"Ho, I rather suspect that some of the scum of the earth that Cut-Off-Their-Balls Wang recruited are digging up your daughter," Master Li said thoughtfully. "Do you have any objection to having her coffin plundered?"

"None whatsoever," said Henpecked Ho. "My beloved wife and her seven fat sisters provided some rather expensive jewelry, and I seriously doubt that my dear daughter deserved to take it with her."

There was a good deal of iron beneath his meek exterior. We heard the sound of shovels striking the coffin, and then the sound of the lid being removed.

"This stuff any good?" asked a voice that was oddly familiar.

There was a pause for inspection, and then another oddly familiar voice answered, "First-rate."

The mist cleared enough so that I could see a blade glint in the moonlight.

"You use the knife," said the first voice. "I'm scared of corpses."

"Ho, we can't let them desecrate your daughter's body!" I whispered.

"Hair and fingernails," he whispered back.

"What?"

"Hair and fingernails," Master Li said quietly. "It's a very ancient practice. Grave robbers dig up the bodies of ladies of quality and clip their silken tresses and flawless fingernails, which they sell for a high price to an expensive courtesan. The courtesan claims the hair and fingernails to be her own, and gives them as a fidelity gift to a wealthy lover. The lover assumes that the lovesick lady has handed him the power of life and death—any decent witch could use such things to destroy the donor—and is inspired to reply in kind with immensely valuable fidelity gifts, and thus many a departed beauty has continued to bankrupt lovers long after her demise. A rather interesting form of immortality," said Master Li.

The shovels were pitching earth back into the grave, to delay discovery and pursuit, and I stuck my head through some bushes. My eyes very nearly popped out of their sockets.

"Who, pray tell, is shoveling earth so that it piles up neatly on the other side of the hole?" snarled Pawnbroker Fang.

"In answer to your question, my esteemed colleague," hissed Ma the Grub, "I would advise you to piss upon the ground and examine your reflection in the puddle!"

Li Kao stuck his head out beside me, and his eyes narrowed as he examined the unlovely pair.

"Strange," he said thoughtfully. "Destiny, perhaps, since Pawnbroker Fang is not the sort of man who would write down all he knows in his files. How do I look?"

"Look?" I asked stupidly.

"Lacquer holding?"

I examined him with a slight shudder. The lacquer was cracking, and he resembled a six-month-old corpse.

"You look ghastly," I whispered.

"Careful with that shovel!" yelped Ma the Grub, leaping back in fear. "You almost trapped my shadow inside the grave!"

"Why don't you tie your shadow to your body with a cord, like a sensible person?" Pawnbroker Fang grumbled.

"Splendid. Superstition has its uses," Master Li said happily.

Li Kao slipped from the bushes, and a lacquered lohan drifted eerily through the mist. "Oooooooooooooooooooo-ooo," the horrible spectre moaned.

Ma the Grub toppled upon the half-covered coffin in a dead faint, and Pawnbroker Fang dropped to his knees and covered his eyes, and a hollow haunted voice with a thick Tibetan accent vibrated through the night.

"I am Tso Jed Chonu, the Patron of Ginseng. Who dares to steal my Root of Power?"

"Spirit, spare me!" howled Pawnbroker Fang. "I knew that the Ancestress possessed such a root, but I swear that I did not know where it was hidden!"

"Not the lesser root!" roared the Patron of Ginseng. "I mean the Great Root!"

"O Spirit, only one Great Root of Power exists in all

the world, and no lowly pawnbroker would dare to touch it," Fang sobbed.

"Who has my root? Where has he hidden it?"

"I dare not say!" Fang wailed.

Tso Jed Chonu lifted his horrible face to Heaven and extended his hand for a lightning bolt.

"The Duke of Ch'in!" screamed Pawnbroker Fang. *"It's hidden in his labyrinth!"*

The terrible lohan stood lost in thought for nearly a minute. Then he flicked a finger.

"Begone!"

Ma the Grub's faint was not what it appeared to be. He vaulted from the coffin and passed Pawnbroker Fang in twenty steps as they raced away into the mist. Li Kao was looking thoughtfully down into the grave, and then he got down on his knees and reached for something. He stood up with an object in his hands, which he turned this way and that in the moonlight, and then he walked back and handed it to Henpecked Ho, who yelped in delight. It was a fragment of a clay tablet, and it was covered with the same ancient ideographs as the fragments that Ho had been working on for sixteen years, but it was big enough to contain whole paragraphs.

In the distance we could hear that his wife and her seven fat sisters had joined the Ancestress. "Off with their heads!" they howled, and Henpecked Ho wondered whether his joy might be made complete.

"Li Kao, in your journeys around the estate did you happen to encounter any more old wells?" he asked hopefully.

"I would advise using an axe," said Master Li.

"An axe. Yes, an axe by all means."

We started off again, toward the wall beside the old well. Li Kao hooted like an owl, and a dog replied with three yelps and a howl. We said our farewells to Henpecked Ho, rather tearfully on my part, and Li Kao climbed upon my back. The patch in the wall was now a cleverly painted piece of canvas, and I pulled it aside and raced across the empty corridor. As I began to climb a rope ladder up the side of the opposite wall I glanced back and

saw that Henpecked Ho was holding the precious clay
tablet in one hand while his other hand wielded an imag-
inary axe.

"Chop-chop!" he chanted happily. "Chop-chop-chop-
chop-chop!"

The mist swallowed him up, and I swung down the
other side to Cut-Off-Their-Balls Wang and his scum of
the earth. It had been twenty years since they had enjoyed
a windfall like the funeral of Fainting Maid, and they
begged Master Li to stay as their leader. We had other
things to do. I was off like the wind, racing across the
hills toward the village of Ku-fu, while Master Li rode
upon my back clutching the Root of Power.

11.
A Tale I Will Thee Tell

It was early afternoon, and dust danced in the sunlight that filtered into the monastery. The only sounds came from Li Kao and the abbot as they prepared the essence, and from bird songs that drifted with the breeze through the windows. The children had not moved so much as an eyelash since we had left, and the bonzes had been able to do no more for them than to bathe them and move them to different positions at regular intervals. It was hard to believe that the small pale bodies could still show faint vital signs, and the parents were as silent as the children.

An alchemist's stove burned beneath a bubbling vial of sugared water, in which Master Li had placed the Root of Power. The water began to turn orange, and the ginseng root took on a copperish-orange color that was almost translucent, like amber. Master Li moved the root to a fresh vial that was filled with mild rice wine. The abbot heated the liquid, and as it slowly bubbled down Master Li replaced it with the orange liquid from the first vial. Then the level of the liquid lowered until the root was barely covered, and the liquid turned saffron, and Master

Li sealed the vial and placed it in a pan of boiling water. Both the liquid and the root began to turn orange-black, and then jet-black. Only a small puddle of liquid remained, and Master Li removed the vial from the pan and opened the seal. An incredible fresh and pungent aroma filled the room, like a whole forest of mountain herbs just after a rain.

"That's all there is to it, and now we will see what we will see," he said calmly.

The abbot and Li Kao walked from bed to bed. The abbot parted the children's lips and Li Kao dipped the blackened root into the liquid and carefully applied three drops to each tongue. Three times the treatment was repeated, and there was just enough of the ginseng essence to go around.

We waited while the sounds of chickens and cows and water buffaloes drifted upon the breeze, and willows brushed their branches against the gray stone walls, and a woodpecker hammered in the garden.

Color was returning to the pale faces. The bedcovers began to lift and fall with strong regular breathing, and warmth flushed the cold limbs. Fang's Fawn sighed, and a wide smile spread across the face of Bone Helmet. All the children began to smile happily, and with a sense of humble awe I realized that I had witnessed a medical miracle. Parents wept for joy as they embraced their sons and daughters, and the grandparents danced, and the bonzes ran to the ropes and swung lustily up and down as they rang every bell in the monastery. The abbot was dancing a jig while he bellowed, *"Namo Kuanshiyin Bodhisattva Mahasattva!"* which is how good Buddhists say "hallelujah."

Only Li Kao remained unmoved. He walked from bed to bed, examining each child with analytical coldness, and then he signaled for me to pry Big Hong loose from his son. He bent over the boy and began testing his pulse: first the left wrist for the functions of the heart, liver, kidneys, small intestine, gall bladder, and ureter; then the right wrist for the lungs, stomach, parta ulta, large intes-

tine, spleen, and vital parts. He beckoned for the abbot
to come and repeat the same process and compare results.

The abbot's face turned puzzled, and then anxious,
and then desperate. He ran for his pins and began testing
acupuncture and pain points, with no reaction whatsoever
from the children. Little Hong's color remained high, and
his pulse remained strong, and the happy smile remained
on his lips, but when Master Li lifted one of his arms and
released it, the arm remained suspended in air. He moved
the arm to different positions, and it stayed precisely where
he placed it. The abbot grabbed Fawn and shook her
violently, and she did not even register a change in her
pulse.

Li Kao straightened up and slowly walked back to the
table and stared blankly down at the empty alchemist's
vial. All eyes were fixed on him. He was immeasurably
weary, and I could tell that in his tiredness he was strug-
gling to think of words that would soften the fact that
there is no such thing as an almost miracle. The Root of
Power had almost done it, but it simply wasn't strong
enough.

I couldn't bear it if his eyes turned to mine. I knew
that he had only one thing to tell me, and the words of
the ancient Tibetan text echoed in my mind. "Only one
treatment is effective, and this will succeed only if the
physician has access to the rarest and mightiest of all
healing agents, the Great Root of Power." I saw the terrified face of Pawnbroker Fang as he swore that only one
Great Root existed in all the world, and I heard him scream,
"The Duke of Ch'in! It's hidden in his labyrinth!" Even
an ignorant country boy knew that the Duke of Ch'in was
ten thousand times more dangerous than the Ancestress,
and that copper coins do not purchase suicide. If I went
after the Great Root, it would be on my own, and never
in history had anyone returned alive from the duke's labyrinth.

I turned and walked rapidly out the door and down the
maze of corridors that I knew like the back of my hand,
and then I jumped from a low window to the grass below
and began running across the hills.

I had no goal or purpose whatsoever, or perhaps I did in that I was subconsciously saying farewell to the village of Ku-fu. All I knew was that when I am depressed or frightened, I must do something physical, which is all I am good at, and if I keep at it long enough, I can usually forget my cares. I ran for hours through the hills and fields and forest, and lonely dogs began to follow me. I had quite a pack of them at my heels when my feet took me up a tiny winding path to a dense clump of shrubbery on a hillside, and I got down on my knees and wriggled through a tunnel into a small cave. The dogs squeezed in after me, and we sat down upon piles of bones.

They were called dragon bones, because it had once been believed that dragons periodically shed their bones as snakes shed their skins, but they actually were the shoulder bones of domestic animals that had been used for prophecy. Scapulimancy is very ancient, and the abbot had told me that the oracle bones of An-yang are the only solid proof that the semi-mythological Shang Dynasty had actually existed.

Do other people revert to childhood when they are frightened? I know that I did. The cave had been head-quarters for youthful desperadoes when I was a small boy, and we had brought all important questions to the infal-lible dragon bones. Now I lit a fire in the old brazier and placed the poker in it. The dogs crowded around me and watched with interest while I searched for a bone with a smooth unmarked side. I wrote Yes on the left and No on the right, and I cleared my throat.

"O Dragon, will I find the Great Root of Power in the labyrinth of the Duke of Ch'in and get out of there alive?" I whispered hoarsely.

I wrapped my hand in an old piece of horsehide and picked up the hot poker. The point sizzled as it bored into the bone, and the crack started slowly, lifting toward the answer. Then it split neatly in half, and the left crack shot up and speared Yes while the right half impaled No. I stared at the message. I would find the root, but wouldn't live to tell the tale? I would live to tell the tale, but wouldn't find the root? I was quite upset until it occurred to me that I was no longer ten years old, and I blushed bright red.

"Idiot," I muttered.

The sun had set. Moonbeams reached into the cave and touched my left hand, and the small scar on my wrist gleamed like silver. I threw back my head and laughed. The childhood friends who had passed the knife around the circle as we became blood brothers would have died from envy had they known that the skeleton of Number Ten Ox was destined to rattle in the duke's mysterious labyrinth, and I hugged a few dogs as I solemnly chanted the sacred vow of the Seven Bloody Bandits of the Dragon Bones Cave.

"Bat shit, rat shit, three-toed-sloth shit, bones and blades and bloody oath writ—"

"Now that has real merit," a voice said approvingly. "It beats the scholar's oath by a mile and a half."

The dogs barked excitedly as Master Li crawled into the cave. He sat down and looked around.

"Scapulimancy was a racket," he observed. "With a little practice a soothsayer could make a bone crack any way he wanted to, or jump through a hoop, for that matter. Did you ever cheat when you were a boy?"

"It would have spoiled our games," I mumbled.

"Very wise," he said. "The abbot, who is also very wise, told me that I would find you here, and if not, I should simply sit and wait. Don't be ashamed of reliving your childhood, Ox, because all of us must do it now and then in order to maintain our sanity."

He was carrying a large flask of wine, which he extended to me.

"Have a drink, and a tale I will thee tell," he said.

I sipped and choked on the fiery liquid. Li Kao reclaimed the flask and swallowed about a pint.

"It was a dark and stormy night," he said, wiping his mouth with the back of his hand. "A cold wind howled, and lightning flickered across the sky like the tongues of snakes, and thunder roared like dragons, and rain fell in torrents. Piercing through the gale came the sound of wheels and hoofbeats, followed by the most dreaded sound

in all China: the high-pitched hunting horns of the soldiers
of the Duke of Ch'in.''

This time I choked without benefit of wine, and Li Kao
pounded my back in a kindly fashion.

"A mule was pulling a buggy down a mountain path at
a suicidal rate, and a man and a woman were bouncing
upon the seat," he said. "The woman was nine months
pregnant, and she clutched a large burlap bag while the
man wielded a buggy whip. Once more the terrible horns
sounded behind them, and then a volley of arrows shot
into the night. The mule staggered and fell, and the buggy
crashed into a ditch. Apparently the soldiers were after
the bag that the woman carried, because the man tried to
take it from her so that the soldiers would attack him
while she escaped, but the woman was equally brave and
refused to relinquish the bag, and they were tugging back
and forth when the second volley of arrows reached them.
The man fell back mortally wounded, and the woman
staggered away with the shaft of an arrow protruding from
beneath her left shoulder blade, and the rain mercifully
covered the small determined figure as she crawled up
the winding path that led to the Monastery of Sh'u.''

Master Li hoisted the flask and drank thirstily. I had
no idea why he was telling me the story, but at least he
was taking my mind off my troubles.

"The arrow was her passport," he said. "It was stamped
with the tiger emblem of the Duke of Ch'in, and the Monastery of Sh'u hated the Duke of Ch'in. They did all they
could for her, and with the first faint light of dawn the
tiny wail of a newborn babe lifted above the walls. The
abbot and the midwife had worked a small miracle to save
the child, but nothing could be done for the mother.

"'Brave Soul,' the abbot whispered, wiping the sweat
from her fevered brow. 'Brave rebel against the evil Duke
of Ch'in.'

"The midwife lifted the wailing child. 'A thousand
blessings, my lady, for you have given birth to a healthy
son!' she said.

"The dying woman's nostrils twitched, and she opened

her eyes. With an immense effort she lifted a hand and pointed to the midwife.

"'Kao,' she panted. 'Li...Li...Li...Kao...'"

I jerked up my head and looked wide-eyed at Master Li, who winked at me.

"Tears blurred the abbot's eyes. 'I hear, my daughter,' he sniffled. 'Your son shall be named Li Kao.'

"'Kao!' the woman gasped. 'Li...Li...Li...Kao...'

"'I understand, my daughter,' the abbot sobbed. 'I shall raise Li Kao as my own son, and I shall place his tiny feet upon the True Path. He shall be instructed in the Five Virtues and Excellent Doctrines, and at the end of his blameless life his spirit shall surely pass through the Gates of the Great Void into the Blessed Regions of Purified Semblance.'"

Master Li swallowed another pint and offered me another sip, which produced the same choking result.

"The woman's eyes blazed with a strong emotion that strangely resembled fury," he said, "but her strength was spent. Her eyes closed, and her hand fell limply to her side, and her soul departed to the Yellow Springs Beneath the Earth. The midwife was greatly moved, and when she whipped a small goatskin flask from her robe and drank deeply, the smell of the stuff brought a cold chill to the abbot's heart. That revolting odor could only come from the finest paint remover and worst wine ever invented: Kao-liang. Repeat: *Kao-li*ang. Was it possible that the dying woman had not been naming a baby but demanding a snort? It was indeed possible, and it further developed that she had not been pursued by the duke's soldiers because she was an heroic rebel, but because she and her husband had stolen the regimental payroll. My parents were the most notorious crooks in China, and my mother could have escaped quite easily if she had not tried to battle my father for the loot."

Master Li shook his head wonderingly.

"Ox, heredity is a remarkable thing. I never knew my parents, yet at the tender age of five I stole the abbot's silver belt buckle. When I was six I made off with his jade inkstone. On my eighth birthday I stole the gold tassels from the abbot's best hat, and I still take pride in the feat because he happened to be wearing the hat at the time. When I was eleven I exchanged the abbot's bronze incense burners for a couple of jars of wine and got royally drunk in the Alley of Flies, and at thirteen I borrowed his silver candlesticks and tiptoed into the Alley of Four Hundred Forbidden Delights. *Youth*!" cried Master Li. "How sweet yet sadly swift pass the halcyon days of our innocence."

He buried his nose in his wine flask again, and burped comfortably.

"The abbot of the Monastery of Sh'u was truly heroic," he said. "He had vowed to raise me as his own, and he kept his word, and so well did he pound an education into my head that I eventually did quite well in my *chin-shih* examination. When I left the monastery, it was not in pursuit of scholarship, however, but in pursuit of an unparalleled career in crime. It was quite a shock for me to discover that crime was so easy that it was boring. I reluctantly turned to scholarship, and by the accident of handing in some good papers I was entombed in the Forest of Culture Academy as a research fellow, and I escaped from that morgue by bribing the court eunuchs to get me an appointment as a military strategist. I managed to lose a few battles in the approved manner, and then I became one of the emperor's wandering persuaders, and then Governor of Yu, and it was in the last occupation that the light finally dawned. I was trying to get enough evidence to hang the loathsome Dog-Meat General of Wusan, but he was so slippery that I couldn't prove a thing. Fortunately the Yellow River was flooding again, and I managed to convince the priests that the only way to appease the river god was through the custom of the ancients. So the Dog-Meat General disappeared beneath the waves tied to a gray horse—I was sorry about the horse, but it was the custom—and I tendered my resignation. Solving crime, I had belatedly discovered, was at least a hundred times more difficult than committing it, so I hung the sign of a half-closed eye above my door and I have never regretted it. I might add that I have also never left a case half-finished."

I gulped noisily, and I suppose that the hope in my eyes was shining as brightly as the moon.

"Why do you think I've been telling you this?" said Master Li. "I have a very good reason to be angry at the Duke of Ch'in, since one of his ancestors killed my parents, and if nothing else, my various careers have uniquely prepared me for the task of stealing ginseng roots."

He patted my shoulder.

"Besides, I'd take you for a great-grandson any day," he said. "I would never dream of allowing you to go out on your own to be slaughtered. Get some sleep, and we'll leave at dawn."

Tears blurred my eyes. Master Li called to the dogs and crawled from the cave, and they gamboled happily around him as he danced down the path toward the monastery, waving his wine flask. The high-pitched four-tone liquid-voweled song of High Mandarin drifted back upon the night breeze.

> *Among the flowers, with a flask of wine,*
> *I drink all alone——no one to share.*
> *Raising my flask, I welcome the moon,*
> *And my shadow joins us, making a threesome.*
>
> *As I sing, the moon seems to sway back and forth;*
> *As I dance, my shadow goes flopping about.*
> *As long as we're sober, we'll enjoy one another,*
> *And when we get drunk, we'll go our own ways.*
>
> *Thus we'll pursue our own avatars,*
> *And we'll all meet again in the River of Staaaaaaars!*

I wished that I could have seen him when he was ninety. Even now his leaps and capers were magnificent in the moonlight.

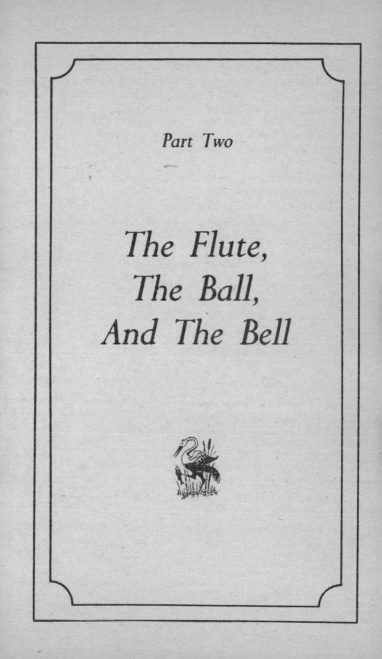

Part Two

The Flute,
The Ball,
And The Bell

12.
Of Castles and Key Rabbits

At the suggestion of the abbot I will explain for the benefit of barbarians that my country is Chung-kuo, which can mean Central Country or Middle Kingdom, whichever one prefers. The point is that it is the country in the exact center of the world, and the only country that lies directly beneath Heaven. "China" is a barbarian invention that was coined in awe and honor of the first Duke of Ch'in, who took over the empire in the Year of the Rat 2,447 (221 B.C.). He was a remarkable reformer. Mass murderers are usually reformers, the abbot tells me, although not necessarily the other way around.

"We are being strangled by our past!" roared the Duke of Ch'in. "We must make a new beginning!"

What he had in mind was the suppression of every previous philosophy of government and the imposition of one of his own, called Legalism. The abbot says that the famous first sentence of the Book of Legalism is, "Punishment produces force, force produces strength, strength produces awe, awe produces virtue; thus virtue has its origin in punishment," and that there is little need to read the second sentence.

The duke began his reforms by burning every book in the empire, with the exception of certain technical and divinatory works, and since the scholars were burned along with the books, there were vast areas of knowledge that vanished from the face of the earth. He disapproved of certain religions; temples and priests and worshippers went up in flames. He disapproved of frivolous fables; professional storytellers were beheaded, along with vast numbers of bewildered grandmothers. The leading Confucianists were decoyed into a ravine and crushed by falling boulders, and the penalty for possession of one line of the Analects was death by slow dismemberment. The problem with burning and beheading and crushing and dismembering is that it is time-consuming, and the duke's solution was a masterstroke.

"I shall build a wall!" cried the Duke of Ch'in.

The Great Wall of China did not begin with the duke, nor did it end with the duke, but it was the duke who first used it for the purpose of murder. Anyone who disagreed with him was marched away to the desolate north, and men died by the millions as they labored on the public-works project that insiders call the Longest Cemetery in the World. More millions died as they built the duke's private residence. The Castle of the Labyrinth covered seventy acres, and it was actually thirty-six separate castles connected by a labyrinth of underground passageways. (The idea was that he would have thirty-six imperial bedrooms to choose from, and assassins would never know where he slept.) Beneath the artificial labyrinth was a real one, running deep through a sheer cliff, and it was said that it was the home of a horrible monster that devoured the screaming victims of the Duke of Ch'in. True or not, the thousands of people who were tossed into it were never seen again.

The duke produced another masterstroke when he had the finest craftsmen in the empire fashion a great golden mask of a snarling tiger, which he wore on all public occasions. His successors continued to wear it for more than eight hundred years. Did a duke have watery eyes, a weak chin, and facial tics? What his subjects saw was a terrifying mask, "the Tiger of Ch'in," and the abbot explained that the barbarian rulers of Crete had used the mask of a bull for the same reason.

Mystery and terror are the bulwarks of tyranny, and for fourteen years China was one vast scream, but then the duke made the mistake of raising taxes to the point where the peasants had to choose between starvation or rebellion. He had confiscated their weapons, but he was not wise enough in the ways of peasants to confiscate their bamboo groves. A sharpened bamboo spear is something to avoid, and when the duke saw several million of them marching in his direction he hastily abandoned the empire and barricaded himself in the Castle of the Labyrinth. There he was invulnerable, and since he still controlled the largest private army in the country it was tacitly agreed that Ch'in would exist as a state within the state.

Emperors came and emperors went, but the Dukes of Ch'in seemed destined to go on forever, crouched and snarling in the most monstrous monument to raw power known to man.

The Castle of the Labyrinth lies in ruins now, a great gray mass of shattered slabs and twisted iron scattered across the crest of a cliff overlooking the Yellow Sea. There the tide is the strongest in China, and the tumbled stones shudder with the force of the waves. Vines have covered the splintered steel gates, and lizards with rainbow bellies and turquoise eyes cling to the fragments of walls, and spiders scuttle through the eternal shadows cast by banana and bamboo. The spiders that currently occupy the castle are huge, hairy, and harmless. The previous occupants were equally grotesque but not so harmless, and when I first saw the Castle of the Labyrinth it was standing in all its glory.

The barge that we traveled on was inching through a dense morning fog toward the junction with the Yellow Sea, and harsh commanding voices seemed to be shouting right in my ears. The air vibrated with great metallic crashes and the clash of a thousand weapons, and the heavy tread of marching feet. Then the fog began to lift, and my eyes lifted with it up the side of a sheer cliff to the most powerful fortress in the world; vast, moated, turreted, impregnable. I stared in horror at towers that scraped the clouds, and at immense steel gates that glittered like terrible fangs, and at a central drawbridge that could accommodate four squadrons of cavalry riding abreast. The great stone walls were so thick that the men who patrolled on top on horseback looked like ants riding small spiders, and ironshod hooves dislodged rocks that tumbled down the cliff and splashed in the water around the barge. One of them banged upon the roof of the cabin where Li Kao was sleeping off an overdose of wine, and he stumbled out on deck and gazed up, rubbing his eyes.

"Revolting architecture, isn't it?" he said with a yawn. "The first duke had no aesthetic sense whatsoever. What's the matter, Ox? A slight hangover?"

"Just a mild headache," I said in a tiny terrified voice.

As the fog continued to fade away, I gazed fearfully toward what must surely be the gloomiest and ghastliest city on earth, and I began to question my sanity when I heard the happy songs of fishermen and sniffed a breeze that was fragrant with a billion blossoms. And then the fog lifted completely and I stared in disbelief at a city so lovely that it might have been the setting of a fairy tale.

"Strange, isn't it?" said Master Li. "Ch'in is beautiful beyond compare, and it is also the safest city in all China. The reason, oddly enough, is greed."

He took a morning-after sip of wine and belched contentedly.

"Every single one of the first duke's successors has lived only for money, and at first their methods of acquiring it were crude but effective," he explained. "Once a year the reigning duke would choose a village at random, burn it to the ground, and decapitate the inhabitants. Then the duke and his army would set forth upon the annual tax trip. The severed heads led the way, mounted upon pikes, and the eagerness with which peasants lined up to pay taxes was a source of great gratification to the Dukes of Ch'in. Sooner or later an enlightened duke was bound to appear, however, and it is said that the one who has gone down in history as the Good Duke suddenly jumped to his feet during a council with his ministers, shot a hand into the air, and bellowed, 'Corpses cannot *pay* taxes!' This divine revelation produced a change of tactics."

Li Kao offered me some wine, but I declined.

"The Good Duke and his successors continued to murder peasants for fun and profit, and the annual tax trip continues to this day, but the wealthy were allowed to fill the dukes' coffers as a matter of free choice," he explained. "The Good Duke simply transformed his gloomy coastal town into the greatest and most expensive pleasure city on earth. Ox, every luxury and vice known to man is available at Ch'in at exorbitant prices, and the cost is more than offset by the fact that the dukes will not tolerate crime, which might divert coins from their own pockets. As a result the rich do not have to hire large private armies of guards, and in Ch'in and in Ch'in alone a wealthy man can lead a carefree existence. So long as a man spends freely, he has nothing to fear from the rulers of the Castle of the Labyrinth, and it is only a slight exaggeration to say that you and I are about to enter Paradise on Earth."

I will describe the city later on, but our first task was to find out who might be able to get us into the labyrinth and out again, and we discovered him inside an hour after we docked.

Every place of business was equipped with an iron chest with the duke's tiger emblem stamped upon it. Half of the coins from every transaction went into the chest and half into the proprietor's cash box, and somebody had to collect the duke's share. The position of Assessor of Ch'in had to rank very high among the most miserable occupations on earth, and the fellow who was stuck with it was universally known as the Key Rabbit—inescapably so, because he was a cringing little man with pink-rimmed eyes and a long pink nose that twitched in permanent terror, and as he pattered through the streets he was festooned with jangling chains of keys.

"Oh dear, oh dear, oh dear!" the poor fellow whimpered as he trotted into wineshops and brothels and gambling dens. "Oh dear, oh dear, oh dear!" he wailed as he trotted back out again.

He was followed by a platoon of soldiers and two carts, one to hold the loot and the other to hold the massive scrolls that listed every rule and regulation in the duke's domain. Magistrates could impose sentences, but only the Assessor could impose fines, and it was generally agreed that if the Key Rabbit missed a point of law that cost the duke one penny he would shortly be missing his head.

"Oh dear, oh dear, oh dear!" he whined as he trotted into the Lucky Gambler Cricket Fighting Arena. He searched through his thousands of keys for the right one, unlocked the chest, counted the coins, checked the records to see if the amount was suspiciously low, conferred with spies to confirm that no cheating had taken place, relocked the chest, and pattered down the street to the next place of business. "Oh dear, oh dear, oh dear!" he whimpered, which was a reasonable comment because if the duke's share was off by a penny, his head would also be off.

As the sun set over the Castle of the Labyrinth the Key Rabbit pattered up the path to the duke's treasure chambers, where clerks counted the coins, and then as often as not he would be forced to spend the night recounting the loot to make sure that the clerks hadn't pocketed a penny. Who had to accompany the Duke of Ch'in on the annual tax trip and determine how much was owed by each village? The Key Rabbit, of course, and it was common knowledge that if he failed to squeeze the final grain of rice from the peasants he would fail to keep his head.

That should have been enough grief for anyone, but not for the Key Rabbit. In a moment of raving insanity, he had married.

"Don't misunderstand me," said the old lady who was filling our ears with the gossip of the town. "Lotus Cloud is a dear, sweet country girl with the kindest heart in the world, but she was not prepared for the seductions of city life, and she has fallen victim to insatiable greed. Her husband, who has not one penny to call his own, cannot even relax when his wife takes a wealthy lover, because she is sure to bankrupt the fellow in a week. The Key Rabbit has decided that he committed some horrible crime in a previous incarnation, and he is being punished by marriage to the most expensive woman in the whole world."

For once my ignorant mind was keeping pace with that of Li Kao.

"The key to the labyrinth is the Key Rabbit, and the key to the Key Rabbit is his wife," said Master Li as we strolled away. "I'd do it myself if I were ninety, but it appears that Lotus Cloud will be your department. You may console yourself with the thought that the most expensive woman in the world is likely to be the most beautiful."

"Master Li, I shall do my duty," I said bravely.

"Yes indeed," he sighed. "Ox, you aren't going to make much of an impression upon a walking case of insatiable greed with what's left of Miser Shen's gold coins. We must get our hands on a fortune."

13.

The Art of Porcupine Cookery

Li Kao led the way to the customs shed, and an hour later he found what he wanted. Everything that was shipped in or out of the port of Ch'in was heavily taxed, and an enormously fat merchant was paying an export tax that amounted to an emperor's ransom. A small army of guards—a rare sight in Ch'in—was positioned around four rectangular wooden cases, and since it would be several hours before his ship sailed, the merchant waddled away to enjoy a light lunch.

"Ox, follow that fellow and come back and tell me what he eats," said Master Li.

"What he eats?"

"What he eats."

When I returned I was rather shaken. "Master Li, you won't believe this, but that merchant began with four large tureens of pimento and dumpling soup," I said. "Then he devoured three bowls of mussel stew, a pound of pickled mallows, two pounds of steamed snails, three servings of soft-shelled crabs, two plates of sweetmeats, ten honey cakes, and a watermelon. The proprietor wondered whether the esteemed guest might care for six or seven quarts of peaches in heavy syrup, but the merchant explained that he was on a diet and would be forced to settle for a gallon of green tea flavored with pine kernels."

"Where is he now?"

"He's having a steam bath and a massage, while two waiters from the restaurant stand ready with a stomach pump."

"Splendid," Master Li said happily. "Come along, Ox. We have to find the most unscrupulous alchemist in town and procure a jar of the Elixir of Eighty Evil Essences, and then we have to buy a coffin."

When the merchant waddled back from the massage parlor a truly pathetic sight met his eyes. I was draped over a coffin, sobbing my heart out, while Li Kao wailed and tore his hair.

"Woe!" I howled.

"The bride of my beloved great-grandson is dead!" howled Master Li.

"Speak to me, my beloved!" I screamed, pounding the coffin lid.

"Ten million maledictions upon the chef who persuaded me to serve porcupine at my great-grandson's wedding feast!" shrieked Master Li.

The merchant was at his side in an instant.

"Porcupine? Did you say porcupine?"

"Porcupine," Master Li sobbed.

"But, Venerable Sir, were you not aware that porcupine can be fatal unless properly prepared?"

Li Kao drew himself up affronted. "Do you take me for a fool?" he snapped. "I myself supervised the preparations, and every step was taken according to the instructions of Li Tsening."

"Surely not!" the merchant gasped. "Why, the great Li Tsening wrote *The Book of Porcupine Cookery*!"

"Why do you think I followed his instructions, you idiot?" Master Li shouted.

The merchant's eyes were glazed, and saliva flowed in streams. "Was it young, fresh porcupine?" he whispered.

"Barely one year old, and trapped the day before," Master Li sniffled.

A mighty spasm shook the merchant's vast belly. "From Yushan?" he whispered.

"Straight from the river," sobbed Master Li.

That was too much for the merchant. He tottered over to his guards, opened a large sack, extracted a pickled carp, devoured it noisily, and tottered back.

"The paste!" he gasped. "The paste was made one year before?"

"One year precisely," said Master Li. "Only the purest yellow beans were used."

"You are positive that all black and brown beans were removed? The slightest trace of such imperfection can be fatal!"

"All black and brown beans as well as those with purple markings were removed by hand," Master Li said huffily. "The remainder was sifted fifteen times, and carefully scrutinized. I was perfectly aware of the danger!"

"Venerable Sir, I am not accusing you," the merchant said contritely. "But I need scarcely point out that some error must have been made, since your great-grandson's poor bride . . . ah . . . Is it possible that rice flour was used?"

"Don't be an ass, young man!" Master Li said angrily. "Rice flour would have assassinated every single guest at the banquet! Only the purest Hua wheat flour was used, mixed with a little salt and exposed precisely six hours to the sun."

"With a veil to keep out the dust! Dust can be fatal!"

"With a veil to keep out the dust. Then the flour and beans were mixed into the paste and placed into a jar, which was in turn covered by an earthenware basin and sealed with lime, and I need not mention that only pure river water was used, since the slightest trace of well water would have been fatal."

"I cannot understand it," the merchant whispered. "Everything done properly, yet . . . Wait! What month was it?"

"Are you a raving lunatic? To prepare porcupine paste

in any month but June is to commit suicide!" Master Li
yelled.

The merchant had turned very pale. It was dawning
on him that unless a flaw could be found, he himself could
never safely enjoy the delicacy of all delicacies.

"Extraordinary," he whispered. "Everything done according to the instructions of the great Li Tsening, yet
the porcupine proved fatal after all. We must find the
error! Venerable Sir, I beg you to describe the precise
method by which your chef cooked the porcupine."

It occurred to me that I had become too interested in
porcupine cookery to mourn my departed bride properly.
"Woe!" I shrieked. "Woe! Woe! Woe!"

Li Kao patted my shoulder. "To think that such tragedy
should strike the only one of the great-grandsons who is
neither mentally deficient nor morally degenerate," he
sniffled. "But you are right; the error must be found. My
chef began by removing the eyes, stomach, internal organs, and embryos, if any were present. While he cut the
meat into pieces, my poor great-grandson cleaned every
clot of blood from each piece with his own noble hands.
Then the chef boiled the meat in pure river water—"

"With the skin still attached?"

"With the skin still attached. He then removed the meat
from the pot and placed it upon a cutting board—"

"A wooden cutting board?"

"Merciful Buddha, I am perfectly aware of the fact that
a metal or ceramic cutting board can be fatal!" Master Li
snarled. "My chef picked out every bristle and quill with
fine pincers, cut the flesh into smaller pieces—and I as-
sure you that they were square pieces—and sautéed them
in pork fat. Then and only then did he mix in the bean
paste and fry the mixture in hot oil. He took infinite care
to keep dust from the pot, and when he judged the meat
to be done, he dipped a paper roll into the sauce and held
it to the flame of a candle. Not until the paper caught fire
easily did he remove the porcupine from the pot and serve
it to the guests."

Not a flaw. Not one single error. The merchant's gluttonous world was crashing around him, and he buried his

face in his hands—oddly enough he reminded me of Bright
Star when she thought that the Sword Dance had been
defiled. His passion was not so noble, but it was equally
sincere. Li Kao took the opportunity to lift me to my feet,
and I wept upon his shoulder while he patted my back.

"How many died?" the merchant whispered.

"Only my bride!" I howled. "Woe! Woe! Woe!"

"She alone among two hundred," Master Li sobbed.
"And I myself selected the porcupines! I myself made the
bean paste! I myself supervised the preparation of the
meat! My beloved great-grandson removed the clots of
blood with his own hands! It was he who selected the
choicest piece to present to his bride! It was I who—"

"Wait!" cried the merchant. He grabbed my shoulders.
"My dear tragic boy," he whispered, "when you cleaned
the blood from the meat, what kind of pin did you use?"

I was really quite touched. Li Kao had done all the
work to bring the whale alongside, and now he was letting
me use the harpoon.

"What kind of . . . why, I don't remember!" I said.

"You must remember!" the merchant howled. "Was it
or was it not a silver pin?"

"Yes, it was," I said thoughtfully. "Now I remember
clearly. It was a pin of the purest silver, although it fell
to the ground as I came to the final piece of meat, so of
course I had to use another one."

"Silver?" he asked breathlessly.

I let the tension mount while I wrinkled my brow in
thought. "Gold," I finally said.

The abbot had always warned me against judging by
appearances, and the merchant was a classic example.
His hoggish appearance suggested self-indulgence at the
expense of all else, yet he did not rejoice because his
gluttonous world had been saved. Tears streamed down
his cheeks and his belly shook with sobs.

"Oh my boy, my poor tragic boy, the slightest contact
between porcupine and gold is fatal," he wept. "By the
evil curse of some malign spirit, you used gold for that
one last piece, and then with loving hands you placed it
upon the plate—"

"Of the woman I loved!" I shrieked. "My stupidity has slain my beautiful bride!"

I fell over the coffin in a faint, which allowed me to open the jar of the Elixir of Eighty Evil Essences that was concealed on the other side.

"To think that my beloved great-grandson could have been responsible for such a ghastly death!" Master Li gasped.

"I have often heard of porcupine poisoning, but I confess that I have never seen it," the merchant said in a tiny voice. "Is it very terrible?"

The guards and customs officials had been edging closer, with quivering ears, and they glanced nervously at the coffin.

"She began by breaking out in red spots, which spread until every inch of her skin was covered," Master Li whispered. "Then the red began to turn green."

The Elixir of Eighty Evil Essences was performing splendidly, and an unbelievable stench was lifting from the coffin.

"Gllgghh!" gagged the Chief of Customs.

"Then the ghastly glaring green began to turn black," Master Li whispered.

"Black?" the merchant said, waving fumes from his face.

"Well, to be pedantically accurate, it was a greenish-purplish yellowish black that tended to run at the edges," Master Li said thoughtfully. "Then the smell began."

"Smell?" said the Chief of Customs, gagging through the noxious cloud.

"I cannot describe that loathsome smell!" Master Li wept. "Guests began to run for their lives, and my beloved great-grandson reached out to touch his bride—oh, how can I describe the horror of that moment? *His fingers actually entered her body, for her smooth and supple skin had become soft jelly from which green and yellow corruption oozed. And the smell, the smell, the hideous toxic stench that caused dogs to collapse in spasms and birds to topple lifelessly from trees . . .*"

For some reason we appeared to be alone.

A few minutes later we staggered from the customs shed and joined the others, who were heaving their guts out over the rails of the pier. Allow me to inform you that the Elixir of Eighty Evil Essences can make a stone vomit. The merchant, the guards, and the customs officials held a conference and voted to toss us, along with the coffin, into the sea before corruption killed them all, but Li Kao appealed to their patriotism by pointing out that if my bride landed in the sea, she would destroy the Chinese fishing industry for at least three thousand years. A compromise was reached, and they provided us with a wheelbarrow for the coffin, a couple of shovels, and a terrified bonze who led the way to the lepers' cemetery, banging upon a gong and bellowing "Unclean! Unclean!" The bonze took to his heels, and we watched the sails of the merchant's ship disappear in the mist as he sped away with his four wooden cases, one of which was a coffin from which the funeral decorations had been removed.

We ripped the funeral decorations from the merchant's case and I pried the lid open. Inside I found a small bag lying upon a canvas cover, and I dumped the contents into my hand and stared in disbelief.

"Pins? Master Li, why would that merchant hire an army of guards to protect some cheap iron pins?"

"Great Buddha, that fellow couldn't possibly have been working alone. He must be the representative for a consortium of the richest companies in China!" Master Li gasped.

I didn't know what he was talking about. Li Kao jerked the canvas cover aside and scooped up a strange object from a pile—we later discovered that there were 270 of them—and began attaching pins to it. The iron practically jumped to the surface, and the next pin stuck to the end of the first one.

"Ten pins," he prayed. "If it will hold ten pins! Seven ... eight ... nine ... ten ... eleven ... twelve ... thirteen ... fourteen ... fifteen ... sixteen ... seventeen ..."

The eighteenth pin fell to the ground, and Li Kao turned to me with wonder in his eyes.

"Number Ten Ox, barbarian merchants and navies will

sell their very souls for Chinese magnetic compasses that are pure enough to hold ten inch-long pins attached end to end, and we have hundreds that are pure enough to hold seventeen! My boy, I have made some hauls in my day, but this is ridiculous," he said gravely. "You and I have just become the two wealthiest men in all China."

14.
Lotus Cloud

The first order of business was to establish our credentials as gentlemen of vast wealth and generosity, and I have a blurred memory of flowers and gongs and incense and silver bells, boat races and dice games and cricket fights, brawls and banquets and tangles of luscious bare limbs. We sailed upon brightly painted brothel barges that floated over azure lakes—and docked at artificial emerald islands where pallid priests with flabby faces and twitching hands sold the strangest things in peculiar pagodas—and we rode through the streets in a palanquin so huge that it was carried by sixty swearing servants. Naked dancing girls were draped around us, and we scooped handfuls of silver coins from a brass-bound chest and hurled them to the adoring mobs that followed our every step.

"Buy clean clothes!" we yelled. "Sweeten your foul breaths with decent wine! Get rid of your loathsome lice! Bathe!"

"*Long Live Lord Li of Kao!*" the mobs howled. "*Long Live Lord Lu of Yu!*"

I have probably given the impression that I had forgotten the importance of our quest. Such was not the case. Every night I dreamed of the children of Ku-fu, and I began to be tortured by guilt, and it was with immense relief that I heard Master Li say that our status was well enough established and it was time to make our move. He decided that the fastest way to get to the Key Rabbit would be to burn our palace to the ground, since it was rented from the Duke of Ch'in at a ruinous rate, and I was roasting a goose over the embers when the little fellow pattered up.

"Oh dear, oh dear, oh dear!" he wailed. "Regulation 226, paragraph D, subsection B: palaces, rented, accidental destruction thereof—"

"Willful. I found the view boring," Master Li yawned.

"Subsection C: palaces, rented, willful destruction thereof. Full value plus fifty percent, plus firefighting costs, plus wreckage removal costs, plus triple the normal fine for disturbing the peace, plus fifty percent of the total for defaming the view provided by the dukes, plus—"

"Stop babbling, you idiot, and give me the grand total!" Master Li roared.

I thought that the little fellow was going to die. He rolled his pink-rimmed eyes toward Heaven and screamed: "Nineteen thousand seven hundred and sixty-two pieces of gold!"

Li Kao shrugged and pointed toward a long row of chests. "Take one of the blue ones," he said indifferently. "Actually the blue ones each contain twenty thousand pieces of gold, but Lord Li of Kao and Lord Lu of Yu can scarcely be bothered with change."

The Key Rabbit toppled over backward. It took a few minutes to revive him, but he grasped the possibilities instantly.

"Alas!" he panted. "Lord Li of Kao and Lord Lu of Yu have no place in which to spend the night, and while my humble abode is scarcely suitable... You see, I will probably have to stay in the castle all night counting the duke's money, and my dear wife will be all alone and unprotected. Women require protection, among other things."

He fell to his knees and began kissing the tips of our sandals. *"Such as pearls!"* he wailed. *"Jade!"* he howled.

"May we offer you some roast goose?" Master Li said not unkindly. "It is Lord Lu of Yu's own recipe, marinated twenty-four hours in the lees of fine wine, with honey and crushed apricots. Lord Lu of Yu, incidentally, is a disciple of Chang Chou, who said that he preferred his own cooking, but other people's wives."

"Joy!" shrieked the Key Rabbit.

That night I prepared to meet the most expensive woman in the world. The moon was playing tag with fingers of clouds, and the breeze was warm and fragrant with flowers, and crickets chirped in the shadows of the Key Rabbit's garden. The path of pearls and jade that I had strewn upon the grass sparkled like a reflection of the Great River of Stars, and I found it difficult to breathe as I watched a young woman trot toward me, exclaiming with wonder as she picked up each glittering bauble. Then she got close enough so I could see her clearly.

"Number Ten Ox," I said to myself, "you have been robbed!"

She wasn't even pretty. Lotus Cloud was pure peasant, with big feet, short thick legs, large square hands, and a plain flat face. She stopped short and examined me with her head cocked at an angle, and she looked for all the world like a country girl who was trying to decide whether or not to buy a pet at a fair. I could almost hear her think, Yes, I'll take this cute thing home with me. And then she grinned.

I cannot describe that grin. It was as though all the hope and joy and love and laughter that there was in the whole world had gathered into a fist that reached out and belted me in the heart, and the next thing I knew I was on my knees with my arms wrapped around her legs and my head pressed against her thighs.

"My surname is Lu and my personal name is Yu, but I am not to be confused with the eminent author of *The Classic of Tea*, and everyone calls me Number Ten Ox," I moaned.

She laughed softly, and her fingers played with my hair. "I shall call you Boopsie," she said.

The measure of my enchantment may be judged from the fact that I enjoyed being called Boopsie. In fact, I felt like wagging my tail whenever Lotus Cloud came into view.

"Key Rabbit," I said a couple of days later, "your beloved wife is not witty, and she is not wise, and she cannot read or write, and she has no social graces what soever, and she isn't even pretty, and I worship the very ground that she walks on."

"That," sighed the Key Rabbit, "is what all her protectors say."

"Master Li, have I lost my mind?" I asked.

"Well, beauty is a ridiculously overrated commodity," he said. "Over the past eighty or ninety years I have known a great many beautiful women, and they've all been the same. A beauty is forced to lie late in her bed in the morning in order to gather strength for another mighty battle with nature. Then, after being bathed and toweled by her maids, she loosens her hair in the Cascade of Teasing Willows style, paints her eyebrows in the Distant Mountain Range style, anoints herself with Nine Bends of the River Diving-Water Perfume, applies rouge, mascara, and eye shadow, covers the whole works with two inches of the Powder of the Nonchalant Approach, squeezes into a plum-blossom-patterned tunic with matching skirt and stockings, adds four or five pounds of jewelry, looks into the mirror for any visible sign of humanity and is relieved to find none, checks to make sure that her makeup has hardened into an immovable mask, sprinkles herself with the Hundred Ingredients Perfume of the Heavenly Spirits who Descended in the Rain Shower, and minces with tiny steps toward the new day, which, like any other day, consists of gossip and giggles."

"That's part of it!" I cried. "Lotus Cloud hops out of bed and plunges her head into a pail of cold water, bellows *'Aaarrrggghhh!'* runs a comb through her hair, and looks around to see if there's anyone handy who feels like making love. If such is the case, she hops back into bed. If not, she jumps into whatever clothes are lying around and leaps out the door—or window, it doesn't matter—to see what wonders the new day will bring, and since she views the world with the delighted eyes of a child, the day is bound to be marvelous."

"That," sighed the Key Rabbit, "is what all her protectors say. How I wish that I could afford my dear wife for myself."

"*Nobody* can afford your dear wife," Master Li snarled.

He had a point, although Lotus Cloud was not promiscuous in her greed. At an early age the dear girl had become a specialist. Diamonds did not interest her. Emeralds bored her to tears. I once gave her a casket filled with gold, and she promptly handed it to a friend.

"Why did you do that?" I asked.

"Because she wanted it, Boopsie," said Lotus Cloud, and it was clear that she thought I was an idiot to ask such a stupid question.

Ah, but fill that same casket with pearls and jade! Never before or since have I known anything to match Lotus Cloud's reaction to a gift of pearls and jade. Her eyes grew wide with wonder, and her hands reached out reverently. A soul-shaking desire wracked her whole body, and her face was transfigured by indescribable longing. The sheer force of her greed would practically knock you off your feet, and she would fling herself into your arms and vow to adore you throughout eternity.

A man will do practically anything to get a reaction like that, and that was the trouble. Within ten minutes Lotus Cloud would forget all about your wonderful gift, and if you wanted to produce another reaction, you had to produce another casket of pearls and jade.

"Like all classic swindles it is simplicity itself," Master Li said with grudging respect.

"I greatly admire her technique, even as it drives me toward bankruptcy," I said.

"That," sighed the Key Rabbit, "is what all her protectors say."

Li Kao was making splendid progress with the Key Rabbit. It was only a matter of time before he would be able to persuade the duke's assessor to sneak us into the labyrinth and get us out again, but in the meantime I had to keep Lotus Cloud supplied with pearls and jade. Our chests of gold were melting like snow in August, and one terrible morning I stared in disbelief at the tiny handful of coins that was all that remained of the largest private fortune in China.

"Ox, don't look so guilty," Master Li said comfortingly. "The dear girl's pigeon-plucking technique is quite remarkable. Let's go pluck a few pigeons ourselves."

Not long afterward a splendid fellow named Liverlips Loo, who was attired as the major-domo of a great house, banged a gold-tipped staff against the door of the stingiest miser in town. Behind Liverlips Loo was a palatial palanquin, upon which rode two elegant aristocrats, a cart loaded with garbage, and a goat.

"Throw open the doors!" roared Liverlips Loo. "Ten thousand blessings have descended upon you, for Lord Li of Kao and Lord Lu of Yu have condescended to rest in your miserable hovel!"

I have decided that the problem with poetic justice is that it never knows when to stop.

The door crashed open and we stared at a gentleman who owned six different houses in six different cities, and who was blessed with a pair of glittering little pig eyes, a bald and mottled skull, a sharp curving nose like a parrot's beak, the loose flabby lips of a camel, and two drooping elephant ears from which sprouted thick tufts of coarse gray hair.

"*What have you done with my five hundred pieces of gold?*" screamed Miser Shen.

Liverlips Loo escaped quite easily, but when Li Kao and I jumped from the palanquin we landed on top of the Key Rabbit and his platoon of soldiers. Somehow we became entangled in a chain that was around the Key Rabbit's neck, and he tugged frantically at his end. "Oh dear, oh dear, oh dear!" he wailed, and I assume that he thought that we were trying to steal the key to the duke's front door. The single key on the end of the chain was shaped like a flower, with sixteen tiny points that had to

make contact with precisely the right amount of force
before the lock would open, and a pressure lock costs
several fortunes. The soldiers descended upon us. We
were hauled off to court, but since Liverlips Loo had
taken the cart and the goat with him, there was no evidence. Miser Shen could do little more than bellow ac-
cusations, but Miser Shen wasn't the problem. The
problem was that we were no longer in a position to pay
the mandatory fine for disturbing the peace, and the penalty for not paying a fine in the duke's city was death.

"Woe!" wailed the Key Rabbit. "Woe! Woe! Woe! To
think that I should be partly responsible for the decapitation of my dearest friend and the most generous protector that my dear wife has ever had!"

Eventually he calmed down enough to find a bright
side.

"Do not worry about Lotus Cloud," he told me comfortingly. "I have discovered that Miser Shen is the
wealthiest man in town. I will invite him to tea, and unless
my dear wife has suddenly lost her touch, she will be
rolling in pearls and jade."

"Splendid," I said.

There was no room in my heart for any more misery.
Whenever I closed my eyes I saw the children on Ku-fu
lying as still as death, and the abbot praying, and the
parents telling each other not to worry because Master
Li and Number Ten Ox were sure to return with the
wonderful root that could cure *ku* poisoning.

15.
The Labyrinth

I was to see Lotus Cloud one more time before we faced the headman's axe. We were chained to a long line of condemned convicts and marched through the streets, and the mobs that had sung the praises of Lord Li of Kao and Lord Lu of Yu gathered around us once more, to jeer and throw garbage. Lotus Cloud somehow made her way through the crowd. She slipped past the soldiers and ran up to me and tossed something that settled around my neck. I couldn't see what it was, and the jeers were so loud that I could only hear part of her message.

"Once when he was drunk, my miserable husband told me...Boopsie, I stole this because if the duke is playful..." Soldiers were dragging her away. "Follow the dragon!" Lotus Cloud yelled. "You must follow the dragon!"

Then she was gone, and I had no idea what she was talking about. The soldiers lashed the mob out of the way, and we were marched up the hill to the Castle of the Labyrinth.

I was so terrified that I have no memory at all of ap-

proaching the castle. Gradually I became aware of the
fact that we were crossing the great drawbridge and passing through immense steel gates, and we entered a courtyard that was vast enough to hold several thousand
soldiers. The murderous iron bolts of countless crossbows
pointed at us through slits in the massive walls, and above
us smoke and flames were lifting from vats of boiling oil.
The clash of weapons and the roar of harsh voices and
the tramp of marching feet was deafening, and when we
entered a maze of long stone tunnels an infinity of echoes
battered my ears. Ten times we reached checkpoints where
guards demanded secret signs and passwords, and then
iron gates crashed open and whips lashed us as we marched
through. A dull gleam of light was ahead of us, and soldiers lined the walls, and I realized that we were approaching a door of solid gold.

It swung silently open. The soldiers prodded us across
an acre of polished lapis lazuli toward a huge golden throne,
and I trembled with fear as I approached the Duke of
Ch'in. The hideous mask of a snarling tiger loomed larger
and larger, and the duke was so big that the breadth of
his shoulders matched the bulk of his mask. He wore
gloves of gold mesh and a long cloak of feathers, and I
saw with a shudder that the feathers at the bottom of the
cloak were darkly stained. The chopping block and the
basin that caught the heads and blood were almost directly
at his feet, and apparently he enjoyed the view.

Soldiers lined all four walls, and two rows of dignitaries
flanked the throne. The executioner was a huge Mongol
who was stripped to the waist, and his glittering axe was
almost as big as he was. A bonze administered the last
rites, and it seemed to me that the ceremony was pro-
ceeding with unseemly haste. The chain that linked the
convicts together was unlocked, although our hands remained manacled behind us, and the first condemned man
was shoved forward. The sergeant at arms bellowed the
charge against him and the death sentence, and soldiers
neatly kicked the poor fellow's feet out from under him
so that he fell with his neck stretched across the chopping
block. The bonze muttered the shortest prayer that I had

ever heard, and the sergeant at arms asked if the victim
had any last words. The condemned man began a desperate plea for mercy, which the bonze cut short by nodding to the executioners.

The great axe lifted, and the vast room was hushed.
There was a metallic blur and a dull thud, and blood
spurted and a head landed in the stone basin with a sickly
wet splash. The dignitaries applauded politely, and the
Duke of Ch'in uttered a little whinny of pleasure.

To my amazement Li Kao fainted, or so I thought until
I realized that he was using the opportunity to reach his
left sandal. He slid half of the heel aside and came up
with a couple of lockpicks, and then the swearing soldiers
jerked him back to his feet. Li Kao managed to slip one
of the tiny picks into my hands.

"Ox, we can't possibly escape from here," he whispered. "I'm afraid that we can do nothing for the children
of your village, but one of the Dukes of Ch'in killed my
parents, and if you have no objection, we will try to slit
this bastard's throat."

I had no objection, but the lockpick was a bit too small
and it was very difficult to work with it while my hands
were manacled behind my back. Again and again the great
axe flashed through the air, and the applause of the dignitaries was nearly continuous, and the line of condemned
men was steadily moving toward the throne. The duke
was laughing as the heads splashed into the basin, and
the soldiers joked with the sergeant at arms as they carried
the carcasses away. Sometimes the legs were still twitching, and spurts of blood from the severed necks caused
sticky red puddles to slide across the floor, joined by dark
trickles from the overflowing basin. The feathers at the
bottom of the duke's robe were dripping with scarlet.
Then only one prisoner stood between me and the axe.
He was a middle-aged man, slim and slightly stooped, and
he had been viewing the massacre with an air of ironic
calm.

"Chin Shengt'an, who dared to protest the peasant
taxes imposed by the Duke of Ch'in. The sentence is
death!" roared the sergeant at arms.

That must have taken incredible courage. I was later to learn that Chin Shengt'an was one of the greatest writers and critics in the empire, and that his name meant "Sigh of the Sage," because when he was born a deep sigh was heard from the Temple of Confucius. His feet were kicked out from under him. His neck lay on the block, and the bonze mumbled a prayer, and the sergeant at arms asked if he had any last words. The ironic eyes lifted.

"Eat pickled turnips with yellow beans," he said politely. "It gives the taste of walnut."

I deeply regret that I never had the opportunity to know him. The axe flashed through the air, and the head of the man who had dared to protest an unfair tax joined the others in the basin. The soldiers shoved me forward.

"Lord Lu of Yu, who failed to pay his fine for disturbing the peace. The sentence is death!" roared the sergeant at arms.

My feet were kicked from under me and my neck landed neatly upon the block. The ironic eyes of Shengt'an looked up at me from the basin, and while the bonze mumbled the prayer I tried to think of an exit line that would be worthy of his.

"Any last words?" asked the sergeant at arms.

I was only Number Ten Ox, so I lifted my head to the Duke of Ch'in. *"I hope I splatter blood all over you, you son of a sow!"* I yelled. Oddly enough I felt much better, and I stopped gagging at the thick sweet smell of blood.

To my astonishment the duke lifted a hand and stopped the executioner. He beckoned, and soldiers lifted me and dragged me so close to the throne that my face was almost touching the tiger mask. Surely the great and powerful Duke of Ch'in could not be interested in Number Ten Ox! He wasn't. He was interested in whatever it was that Lotus Cloud had tossed around my neck, and the gold-meshed fingers of his right hand reached out and touched it. Then he leaned forward, and I felt the eyes behind the slits in the mask boring into mine, and with a sick sense of terror I realized that he was looking right through my eyes into my brain! The voice that came through the mouthpiece was a voice of metal.

"So, the wife of my Assessor gave you this," the duke whispered. "He shall be punished for his careless words." I could feel his mind crawling over mine, probing and peering and searching. "You do not know what it means," he whispered. "You know nothing of importance. I see a foolish abbot, and I see children whose deaths will serve to decrease the surplus population, and I see a ghost who dances with swords, and I see your antiquated companion dancing and singing songs. I can find no awareness of meaningful things, and although you seek the right ginseng root, you do so for the wrong reason." The terrible tiger mask lifted. "Soldiers, continue with the execution," ordered the Duke of Ch'in.

My fingers had automatically continued to fumble with the pick, and suddenly I felt it turn in the lock.

"Master Li!" I yelled, as I jerked by hands apart and lashed out at the soldiers with the manacles. His hands were already free, and he used the chain of his manacles to trip the executioner, who toppled toward me. "Get him, Ox!" Master Li roared.

I grabbed the axe and whirled to the throne and struck with all my might, and to my astonishment that huge blade bounced off the flimsy cloak of feathers as though it had hit the strongest steel. My hands turned numb with the shock, and I swore and swung again. This time the duke was not so lucky. The blade plunged right through his chest to his heart, and I turned to die like a gentlemen at the hands of the soldiers. What I saw made me doubt my sanity.

The soldiers were laughing. The dignitaries were laughing. The bonze was laughing. The executioner got to his feet and began laughing. I turned dazedly to the throne, and there sat the Duke of Ch'in with the huge axe buried in his heart. He was laughing.

"Both the young fool and the old fool are fit for nothing more serious than bouncing balls and playing games! Very well, we will play a game," he chortled. His fingers closed around an ornament on the arm of his throne. The soldiers next to us scrambled hastily away. "You seek the Great Root of Power? It can indeed be found, so find it."

The floor suddenly dropped out from under us.

Down, down, down, plunging head over heels into darkness—just when I felt that I might fall forever, I landed with a shock in icy water, and I popped up to the surface and spat out a mouthful of brine.

"Maser Li!" I cried.

"Right behind you," he panted.

Li Kao grabbed my belt. A light was flickering in the distance. The pool in which we had landed was about fifty feet in circumference, and I swam across and climbed up upon a flat rock ledge. The light was coming from a single torch, and Li Kao lifted it from the brackets and swung it around.

We were in a large cavern carved from black stone. The air was moist and heavy, and it reeked of something unpleasant. Ahead of us was an archway, and when Master Li lifted the torch we saw that the first duke's famous maxim had been chiseled in the stone above the curve of the arch:

PUNISHMENT PRODUCES FORCE, FORCE PRODUCES
    STRENGTH,
STRENGTH PRODUCES AWE, AWE PRODUCES VIRTUE;
THUS VIRTUE HAS ITS ORIGIN IN PUNISHMENT.

We stepped through the archway and saw that an infinity of narrow tunnels branched out from the central path. We were walking upon human bones, and the reek came from decaying flesh, although I saw no recent bodies. I stared at shattered skulls, and at thigh bones that had been snapped like bamboo twigs.

"Master Li, the thing that did this had to be stronger than twenty dragons," I whispered.

"Oh, far stronger than that." He reached out and touched his finger to the wall, and when he held it to my nose I smelled seaweed. Then he lifted his torch high above his head, and when my eyes lifted with it I saw the corpses that were causing the horrible smell. They were crammed into crevices in the stone ceiling. Half of a face looked down at me, and a dangling leg dripped blood.

"The monster that stalks the labyrinth is simply the tide," Master Li said calmly, "and if the tide can get out of it, so can we. Ox, was that some sort of trick axe, like the fake swords used in carnivals?"

"No, sir," I said firmly. "That was a real axe, and it really entered the duke's heart."

He scratched his head thoughtfully. "Strange," he muttered. "If we get out of here alive, we most certainly must take another crack at killing him, purely in the interest of science."

"Master Li, the duke can read minds," I whispered, trembling all over. "He looked through my eyes, and I could feel his brain crawling over mine. It was wet and clammy, and it was like being nuzzled by cold, slimy lips."

"Your powers of description are commendable," he said, but I could tell that he didn't believe a word of it. "What was he so interested in?"

I had almost forgotten it, but now I lifted the thing that Lotus Cloud had tossed around my neck. It was a silver chain with a large piece of coral at the end of it. The coral was a beautiful deep-red, and a cleverly carved green jade dragon was winding through the holes. I wondered how the Key Rabbit had managed to acquire such a beautiful pendant, because it must be very expensive. I searched for some sort of a message that might be written on it, but there wasn't one.

Li Kao shrugged. "Well, at any rate we've arrived in the labyrinth, which is what we intended all along. Getting out may be a bit of a problem, however, and I suggest that we start immediately."

He strode forward, ignoring the side tunnels. The main passageway led on and on through the dank dripping rock, and finally I saw something gleam ahead of us. As we came closer, I saw that it was a huge copy of the tiger mask, perhaps ten feet tall, and it was set into a wall that formed a dead end. The mouth gaped wide, and the glittering teeth were solid steel, and behind them was a black hole. Li Kao moved the torch over a curious network of metal baffles that surrounded the tiger's mouth.

"Sound effects," he finally said. "The tide, or part of it, pours through this hole and shoots through the baffles, and as the tide increases, the noise gets louder. I would imagine that it is the scream of a raging tiger, and we had better find another exit before we hear it."

He started back, studying the rock walls for smooth worn surfaces that would indicate the passage of the water, and then he turned and darted into a side tunnel. The torchlight flickered over more bones, and the ceiling was so low that I had to duck not to strike my head against a corpse that was plastered above me in a crack. The reek of rotting flesh was indescribable. Li Kao turned into another low tunnel, and then another, and we twisted and turned until I had lost all sense of direction. He strode confidently ahead, however, following minute signs that indicated water rushing toward an exit, and finally he grunted in satisfaction.

The low tunnel was widening and rising, and ahead of us loomed a large black archway. Master Li trotted through it and stopped dead in his tracks, and I stared in horror at a large cavern and a pool of water that was about fifty feet in circumference. In the ceiling high above that pool was the trapdoor that led to the throne room of the Duke of Ch'in. We were right back where we had started, and the hair lifted upon my head as I heard a faint snarling growl in the darkness behind us. Slim dark shapes were sliding across the stone floor like snakes. It was water, and the tide was coming in.

Li Kao stood quite still, with his forehead wrinkled in thought. "Ox, what did Lotus Cloud say to you when she gave you that dragon pendant?" he asked quietly.

I repeated the fragmentary words that I had heard, and they still didn't make any sense to me. The water was rising with terrible swiftness, lapping my ankles, and the tiger at the end of the tunnel was beginning to roar.

"The Duke of Ch'in lives only for money," Master Li said slowly, thinking out loud. "He piles the stuff in treasure troves, and who beside the duke must have access to them? The man who has to collect the loot and count it, that's who, and Lotus Cloud happens to be married to him. Apparently he made an indiscreet remark about the pendant, and it might explain why the Key Rabbit was allowed to keep something so valuable. Ox, bend over."

I bent over and he climbed upon my back. With one hand he held the torch and with the other he lifted the dragon pendant.

"Lotus Cloud said that if the duke was playful you should follow the dragon, and when the duke dropped us into his labyrinth he said that we would play a game. Since we have no other hope, we will assume that the Key Rabbit indiscreetly told his wife that the locket enabled him to get to the duke's treasure troves."

He held the torch close.

"The dragon skips the first two holes in the coral and winds through the third hole on the left," Master Li said grimly. "Start through the archway, take the third tunnel to the left, and run like hell."

I ran as fast as I could, but the water was almost up to my knees. I darted into the third tunnel on the left, and Li Kao held the flickering torch close to the pendant. "Take the second tunnel on the right!" he yelled. The tide was rushing in so swiftly that shattered bones were flying across the boiling surface, and the tiger was roaring so loudly that I could barely hear Master Li. "Third left!... First right!... Second right!... Fourth left!"

The tiger was screaming in lunatic rage. The water was rising over my chest as I squeezed through another narrow opening, and then I collided with a blank wall. "Master Li, we must have made a wrong turn!" I shouted. I tried to turn and go back, but it was hopeless. Water had reached my chin, and the tide shoved like a giant hand and plastered me against the wall. Flying bones were smashing around my head, and one of them knocked the torch from Li Kao's hand. Now we were in total darkness, and the boiling water lifted over my mouth.

Li Kao's fingers found what his eyes had not. "Ox, the dragon goes straight up!" he yelled in my ear. "Don't fight the tide. Let it carry you to the ceiling!"

The tide scraped me against the wall as I lifted with it, and Li Kao's hands reached high and groped for an opening. He found it. A narrow chimney wound up from the ceiling through solid rock, and I barely managed to squeeze into it. I braced my feet against the sides and started to climb, but the tide was climbing faster than I was, boiling up over my head while my shoulders tried to wriggle through narrow openings, and my lungs were bursting. I had nearly lost consciousness when the tide reached its peak and my head broke through the water. I gulped air and climbed, and it seemed that hours had passed when the first faint light appeared in the pitch-blackness. A small glowing circle appeared high above us, and I used the last of my strength to reach it and to climb over the edge of the opening to the floor of a small cave.

The sun had set and the light came from the rising moon. A small opening looked out over the sea, and as the moon lifted higher, its pale rays reached farther and farther back into the blackness of the cave, and something began to glitter.

"Great Buddha, how Lotus Cloud would love this place!" I yelped.

She would not have been interested in the gold, or the diamonds and emeralds and rubies that were heaped in mounds, but most of all there were pearls and jade. Tons of them, and I do mean tons. As the moon lifted even higher and the whole incredible mass of loot appeared I decided that no single duke could possibly have piled up so much wealth. This had to be the collective effort of all the Dukes of Ch'in, right back to the first one, and they had not been snobbish when it came to money.

Cheap copper coins rubbed cheeks with gold, and semiprecious stones were piled with the choicest gems. A broken wooden doll was gazing with tiny turquoise eyes at a sceptre that would have bankrupted most kingdoms, and beside a huge jeweled crown was a set of false teeth carved in ivory. Li Kao was gazing at that incredible monument to greed with narrowed eyes, and he reached out and squeezed my shoulder.

"I would hate to think how many corpses this stuff

cost, and I rather believe that one of them wants to say something about it," he whispered.

I followed the direction of his eyes, and finally I saw it. At the top of the pile was a shadow where no shadow should be. Li Kao continued to hold my shoulder.

"Ox, don't move so much as an inch until we see what lies behind the ghost shadow. It may be a very important warning," he whispered.

I tried to calm the beating of my heart. I closed my mind to everything except a nice warm comfortable blanket, and then I reached out gently with my mind and drew it over my head. What happened then was very strange.

I was gazing at a girl who had almost certainly been murdered, because blood stained her dress where a blade had pierced her heart. Her clothes were in the style of a thousand years ago, and I sensed with every nerve in my body that she was making a terrible effort to appear before us. Her gaze was beseeching, and when she parted her lips I felt a hot searing wave of agony.

"Take pity upon a faithless handmaiden," she whispered. "Is not a thousand years enough?" Two transparent ghost tears slid slowly down her cheeks. "I swear that I did not know what I had done! Oh, take pity, and exchange this for the feather," she sobbed. "The birds must fly."

And then she was gone. Li Kao relaxed his grip on my shoulder. I could not possibly have heard correctly, and I sat up and tilted my head and pounded water from my left ear.

"Exchange something for a feather?"

"Oddly enough, I heard the same thing," said Master Li. "Also something about birds that must fly, which doesn't make much sense unless she was referring to travelers' tall tales about flightless birds, such as penguins and ostriches and other mythological beasts."

"I think that she was cupping something in her hands," I said.

I climbed to the top of the pile, slipping and sliding over sapphires, and slid back down with a tiny jade casket in my hands. Li Kao took it and turned it this way and that in the moonlight, and when he opened the lid I cried out in joy. A powerful fragrance of ginseng reached my nostrils, but Li Kao's exclamation was not joyful. He tilted the casket and two tiny tendrils with rather familiar shapes fell into the palm of his hand.

"Legs, bent at the knees," he sighed. "According to Henpecked Ho, these would be the Legs of Power, and we must pray they will be strong enough to carry the children to safety. I assume that the duke broke up the Great Root, and that pieces are hidden in treasure troves all over China."

He turned the casket upside down and one other object fell into his hand. It was a miniature tin flute, not much bigger than his thumbnail.

"What did she want us to exchange for a feather, the root or the flute?" I asked.

"How would I know? Ox, did the Duke of Ch'in really read your mind?"

"Yes, sir," I said firmly.

"I don't like this at all," Master Li said thoughtfully. He stared at the place where the ghost had been. Nearly a minute passed in silence. "Perhaps we'll figure it out in two or three hundred years," he finally said. "Let's get out of here."

It was easier said than done. It would be suicide to go back into the labyrinth, and the only other exit was the small mouth of the cave. We stood there and gazed down a hundred feet of sheer cliff that could not possibly be negotiated without ropes and grappling hooks at an angry sea where waves smashed against jagged rocks that lifted through the foam like teeth. There was one small calm pool almost directly beneath us, but for all I knew it was six inches deep. The moon was reflected in it, and I gazed from the moon to Master Li and back again.

"My life has been rather hectic, and I could use a long rest," he sighed. "When I get to Hell to be judged, I intend to ask the Yama Kings to let me be reborn as a three-toed sloth. Do you have any preference?"

I thought about it. "A cloud," I said shyly.

He was wearing a smuggler's belt that was studded

with fake seashells, and he snapped one of them open and put the Legs of Power inside. On second thought he took the tiny flute as well, and I filled my pockets with pearls and jade on the odd chance that I might live long enough to give them to Lotus Cloud. Li Kao climbed up upon my back and wrapped his arms around my neck, and I discovered that I was beginning to feel undressed unless I wore my ancient sage like a raincoat. I perched on the edge and took aim.

"Farewell, sloth."

"Farewell, cloud."

I held my nose and jumped. The wind whistled around our ears as we plunged toward the pool, and toward a jagged rock that we hadn't noticed.

"Left! Left!" Master Li yelled, pulling on my pendant chain like the reins of a bridle.

I frantically flapped my arms, like a large awkward bird, and the reflected moon grew larger and larger, and then so huge that I almost expected to see Chang-o and the White Rabbit stick their heads out and shake their fists at us. We missed the rock by six inches. The moon appeared to smile, and the warm waters of the Yellow Sea opened to embrace us like long-lost friends.

16.
Children's Games

The monastery was hushed and the tension was such that the warm air crackled as though touched by invisible lightning. The color of the liquid in the alchemist's vial had changed from saffron to black, and the essence was almost ready.

Li Kao lifted the vial from the pan of boiling water and removed the stopper, and when he and the abbot emerged from the cloud of steam they both appeared to have been reborn, with rosy cheeks and sparkling eyes, and the ginseng aroma was so strong that my heart began to pound furiously. I remembered that even the most skeptical physicians admitted that ginseng could have an astonishing effect upon the cardiovascular system, and my eyes were wide with hope as the abbot and Master Li moved down the line of beds. Three drops upon each tongue, repeated three times. The parents held their breaths.

The effect of the Legs of the Great Root of Power was quite extraordinary. The pale faces of the children flushed, and the heartbeats strengthened, and the covers lifted with deep easy breathing, and then the parents cried out in joy as child after child sat up and opened his eyes! They began to laugh and giggle, and then all the boys began to shake their shoulders up and down and make quick snatching gestures. When the girls began to make swooping pulling gestures I realized with a sudden shock of recognition that I was watching a ritual that I had performed at least a hundred times myself.

Li Kao strode up to Bone Helmet and waved a hand in front of her face. Her wide bright eyes never moved. He snarled and snatched a candle from a holder and lit it, but when he thrust it forward so that it was almost touching her nose the pupils of her eyes did not constrict. The abbot grabbed a boy called Monkey and shook him vigorously and got no reaction whatsoever. The children of Ku-fu continued to laugh and giggle and swoop and shake and snatch, completely unaware of their surroundings. They had awakened, but into a world of their own.

Bone Helmet suddenly stopped her swooping pulling gestures and sat silently, with the happy smile still on her face. Girl after girl, and a few boys, followed her example. Finally only Fang's Fawn continued her gestures, and the boys redoubled their efforts, and at last Fawn stopped and sat still. The children made a muffled sound that might have been a cheer, and then all of them except Fawn and Little Hong closed their eyes tightly. Little Hong's lips began to move, slowly and rhythmically, and the others started giggling again and began feeling the air with their fingers, with their eyes still closed. Only Fawn sat as before, completely still and silent.

I said that I recognized the ritual, but what happened next was totally unexpected. All the children suddenly stopped feeling the air, and all the heads jerked to the east. They were still and intent, and I sensed that they were listening to a sound that only they could hear. Bone Helmet parted her lips. When her small thin voice lifted through the hush of the monastery every one of us, including Master Li, who was an authority on the folklore of every corner of China, jerked our heads toward the windows and stared with wide eyes at the distant looming outline of Dragon's Pillow.

"Jade . . . plate . . ." she whispered.

"Six . . . eight . . ." whispered Little Hong.

"Fire that burns hot . . ." Monkey whispered.

"Night that is not . . ." whispered Wang Number Three.

"Fire that burns cold!" all the boys said together.

"First silver, then gold!" all the girls said together.

Little Hong turned back and resumed moving his lips rhythmically, and the animation returned tenfold as the others resumed groping through the air with their fingers. Only Fang's Fawn continued to sit silently. The giggles and laughter grew louder, and they chanted happily, over and over: *"Jade plate, six, eight, fire that burns hot, night that is not, fire that burns cold, first silver, then gold!"* Monkey lifted his right arm and began to swing it back and forth through the air. One of his fingers touched Fawn's forehead, and instantly Little Hong stopped moving his lips. The others opened their eyes and began to cheer, and a wide happy smile spread over Fawn's face. She yawned drowsily. Her eyes closed. Fawn sank back upon her bed, and child after child followed her example, and the weeping of parents again filled the monastery of Ku-fu as the children once more lay as still as death.

The Legs of Power had almost done it, but those two tiny tendrils could not carry the children to safety. The abbot took the arms of Li Kao and myself and led us into his study and slammed the door upon the sounds of grief. His wrinkles and worries had returned, and his hands were shaking, and he took a deep breath and turned to Master Li.

"Will you continue?" he asked quietly.

"Well, I don't seem to have anything else to do at the moment," Master Li said with a shrug of his shoulders. Then he smiled wryly. "No, the truth is that I'm becoming fascinated with this weird case, and if somebody tries to pull me off it, I will scream like a baby who has been robbed of a bright shiny new toy. It would help if I could figure out what those children were doing in there."

"They were playing the Hopping Hide and Seek Game," I said.

"The what?"

"The Hopping Hide and Seek Game," said the abbot.

The monastery supported itself by manufacturing a very good brand of wine, although the abbot and the bonzes were forbidden to touch it themselves, and he poured cups for Li Kao and me.

"It's a sex and courtship game, and it's been played by the children of Ku-fu for as long as anyone can remember," the abbot explained. "The object is to get possession of the girls' red hair ribbons. A large circle is drawn upon the ground, or perhaps natural barriers are used. The boys try to snatch the ribbons from the girls, but they must hop on one leg, which is what they were doing when their shoulders shook up and down. The girls try to trip the boys with the ribbons, thus the swooping pulling gestures. A boy who is tripped becomes the girl's prisoner and drops out of the game, and a girl who loses her red ribbon becomes the boy's prisoner and drops out of the game."

Li Kao was far more interested than I would have expected. "Considering the boys' one-legged handicap, the girls should win easily," he said.

"They should, except that they instinctively know that the best way to begin a long campaign in the battle of the sexes is to surrender, and the real point of the game is that there is a great deal of giggling and grappling and feeling of bodies," the abbot said drily. "Thus its longevity. Eventually only one girl will be left, and when she is captured she becomes the queen, and the boy who gets her ribbon becomes the king. In this case it was Fang's Fawn and Little Hong. The other children put on blindfolds. The king hides the queen somewhere inside the circle, and the others must try to find her by touch. This leads to more giggling and grappling and feeling of bodies, but there is a time limit. When Little Hong moved his lips, he was slowly counting to forty-nine."

"Is the count ever changed?" Master Li asked.

"No, sir," I said.

"Do they have formal titles, such as King of X and Queen of Y?"

"No, sir," I said.

"The peculiar thing," said the abbot, "was that suddenly they broke off and listened, and then they repeated that ancient nonsense rhyme that is said to have come from Dragon's Pillow. That is *not* part of the Hopping Hide and Seek Game."

Li Kao helped himself to more wine, and then he walked to the window and gazed out at the strange stretch of wall where the ghost of Wan was said to keep watch.

"Yet when they repeated that rhyme, they were able to find the queen," he said thoughtfully.

"Yes, sir," I said. "Monkey touched Fawn before the count reached forty-nine, and she smiled because she had won the game."

Li Kao swallowed his wine at a gulp and turned back to the room.

"Those children were completely unconscious. Then they had one tiny taste of the Great Root, and how did they react? Every single one of them instantly started playing the Hopping Hide and Seek Game, and every single one of them recited a nonsense rhyme that children from this village had first heard many centuries ago at Dragon's Pillow. I am beginning to suspect that the simple quest for a ginseng root is wrapped in more riddles than that Mysterious Mountain Cavern of Winds, where the White Serpent crushes heroes in the cold coils of enigmas, and while I am probably hallucinating, I am willing to bet that the ghost of a murdered maiden fits in here somewhere."

He turned to the abbot. "Reverend Sir, in your studies of myth and folklore, have you ever encountered a ghostly handmaiden who pleads that birds must fly?"

The abbot shook his head negatively.

"Or ghosts who beg people to exchange things for feathers? Possibly things like this?"

He took the tiny flute from his smuggler's belt. The abbot studied it with interest but without recognition, and Li Kao sighed and lifted it to his lips and blew gently into the mouthpiece. Then he hurled the flute to the floor, and all three of us jumped back and stared at it as one might view a cobra.

No flute sound came from that incredible thing. Instead we heard an old woman whose voice was so rich and warm that she might have been the grandmother of the entire human race.

"*Aiieeee! Aiieeee! Come closer, my children! Spread ears like elephants, and I will tell you the tale of a girl named Beauty, and of her wicked stepmother and her good fairy godmother, and of the magic fishbone and the carriage and the little slipper that fell from Beauty's foot and led her to a handsome prince!*"

Li Kao lunged. He grabbed the flute and covered the first of four tiny fingerholes and the voice stopped abruptly. He covered the second fingerhole and blew lightly into the mouthpiece.

"*Aiieeee! Aiieeee! Come closer, my children! Spread ears like elephants, and I will tell you the tale of the old woman and her little boy, and of the cow and the corn and the peddler, and of the beanstalk that grew to the clouds, and what happened when the little boy climbed it into a world of wonders!*"

Li Kao tried the other fingerholes, and each one produced a tale that had been delighting Chinese children for at least two thousand years, and which have even spread to the barbarian tribes. He stopped the last tale and glowered at the marvelous thing.

"Master Li, we could exchange that flute for ten thousand tons of feathers," I whispered.

"With the island of Taiwan tossed in for good measure," the abbot said shakily.

Master Li looked from the flute to the infirmary where the children lay, and back to the flute.

"That does it!" he snarled. "Ox, we have an evil duke who reads minds and laughs at axes, treasure troves that are hidden in labyrinths that are supposedly guarded by monsters, flutes that tell fairy tales, an incomprehensible ghost who might have come from one, an ancient children's game, and a ghostly message from Dragon's Pillow. If you're wondering about the wicked stepmother, just wait, because she's bound to turn up."

He replaced the flute in his belt, and shook a finger in front of my nose.

"Nothing on the face of this earth—and I do mean nothing—is half so dangerous as a children's story that happens to be real, and you and I are wandering blind-folded through a myth devised by a maniac. Mark my words!" he shouted angrily. "If the Key Rabbit can slip us into another one of the duke's treasure troves, we will most certainly shake hands with a two-hundred-foot armor-plated winged water moccasin that can hit the eye of a gnat with a spit of venom from twenty miles away, and that can only be slain by a hero who was born inside a knitting needle during a total eclipse of the moon on the thirty-first day of February."

I flushed, and looked down at my toes.

"If it's all right with you, I'd rather worry about real heads splashing into real basins filled with real blood," I said meekly.

"You have a point." He sighed.

Master Li looked wryly at the abbot and shrugged his shoulders.

"The supernatural can be very annoying until one finds the key that transforms it into science," he observed mildly. "I'm probably imagining complications that don't exist. Come on, Ox, let's go out and get killed."

The Duke of Ch'in had left on his annual tax trip, with the Key Rabbit and Lotus Cloud, and we caught up with them in Chuyen. Unfortunately, the Key Rabbit's apart-ment was high in an unclimbable tower in the palace of the duke's provincial governor. There were no vines to cling to, and no foot- or handholds, and every entrance was guarded by soldiers. Master Li did not appear to be greatly disturbed.

"Ox, I learned a valuable lesson in natural history when I was exiled to Serendip," he said. "When a foraging ant discovers something of value, it grabs a sample and dashes back to the colony screaming, 'Awake! Arise! Beat the drums! Sound general quarters! I have discovered wealth beyond the dreams of avarice!' Then the whole colony follows the ant back to the treasure, but are they content to take what they see? Not if it is a trail of something. Ants that find trails of something they like will follow those trails to the source, even if it means crossing half of the world. Do you see the significance of that?"

"No, sir," I said.

"You will," said Master Li.

In the marketplace he bought a large jar of honey and a box that contained a colony of ants. Then he bribed a maid to bring a message to Lotus Cloud, and on the first cloudy night we scaled the outer walls of the governor's palace, slipped past the guards, and made our way to the tower. I hooted three times like an owl. Lotus Cloud, who was enjoying the game immensely, opened her window and poured the jar of honey that the maid had brought down the wall, and when the thick sweet trickle reached us Li Kao opened the box and released the ants. They plunged into the honey with bulging squeals of delight, discovered that it was a trail, and started to climb.

The last ant was the biggest, and it was towing a gauze thread that was lighter than a feather. It scrambled over Lotus Cloud's windowsill, and she detached the thread and tugged three times. Li Kao tied a fine length of string to his end of the thread and tugged back, and Lotus Cloud began pulling it up. Then came a cord tied to the end of the string, and a rope tied to the end of the cord, and Lotus Cloud tied her end of the rope to something sturdy inside the apartment. Li Kao hopped upon my back and in a matter of minutes I had climbed an unclimbable wall and flopped over the windowsill.

"Boopsie!" Lotus Cloud squealed happily.

I dumped my pearls and jade at her feet. "Do I have a story to tell you!" I panted.

"Later," Li Kao said warningly.

Footsteps were approaching the door. I took Master Li on my back and swung back out the window, and then I clung to the rope and lifted my eyes back up over the windowsill. A pasty-faced lout crashed through the door, staggered across the room, dumped an armload of pearls and jade on top of *my* pearls and jade, fell to his knees, wrapped his arms around Lotus Cloud's legs, and buried his face against her thighs.

"My surname is Chia and my personal name is Chen and it is my unhappy lot to serve in this miserable rathole as the duke's provincial governor, and I have worshipped you ever since you grinned at me in the garden this morning," he moaned.

Lotus Cloud laughed happily; her fingers played with his hair.

"I shall call you Woofie," she said.

I sighed and sadly climbed back down the wall.

"Woofie?" said Master Li. "Ox, far be it for me to interfere with your affairs, but there would appear to be certain drawbacks in forming a close relationship with Lotus Cloud."

"I love her as much as ever." I sighed.

He patted my shoulder comfortingly. "At least you will never be lonely," he said. "You and her other admirers can hold annual conventions. Perhaps the imperial elephant stables might be large enough for the purpose, and if not, you can rent an impoverished province. I hear that the grain harvest in Hua has been miserable this year, and the peasants should be delighted to entertain sixty or seventy thousand visitors with money in their pockets. Although I am talking nonsense, since every one of you will be bankrupt."

"Great Heavens!" the lout yelled above us. "There is a rope tied to your bed!"

"Rope? What rope?" said Lotus Cloud.

The pasty-face peered over the windowsill, and under the circumstances there was little that we could do except smile in a friendly fashion and wave. The provincial governor pointed down at us and squawked.

"*Burglars*! Fear not, my beloved, I have my trusty sword!"

And then the bastard cut the rope.

We had ample time to survey the landscape as we plunged toward the courtyard. In another part of the palace a banquet was breaking up and the departing guests were climbing into carriages and sedan chairs. We were

plunging straight toward one of the later, and we landed
upon the vast belly of an enormously fat fellow. I bounced
off to the cobblestones, but Li Kao was much lighter and
he continued to bounce up and down like a ball while the
fat fellow's dinner sprayed into the air.

Pigeon-egg soup, with lotus roots and dumplings and
crushed pine kernels was followed by ducks's tongues
cooked in sesame oil with mushrooms and bamboo shoots,
which were followed by the ducks themselves—at least
three—which had been stuffed with shellfish and steamed
inside a cover of hardened bean curd, which were followed by spider crabs simmered in sweet white wine,
which were followed by lamb kidneys sautéed with minced
walnuts, which were followed by honeycakes, which were
followed by candied fruits, which were followed by sweet-
meats, which were followed by green tea, which was followed by plum wine, which was followed by Daffodil
Digestive Tonic, which was followed by Seven Spirits
Regulating Tonic, which was followed by Fragrant Fire
Vitality Tonic, which was followed by hiccups, which
were followed by a pair of hands that clamped around Li
Kao's throat.

"*What have you done with my case of compasses?*"
screamed our porcupine merchant.

17.

A Miraculous Transformation

In a way we were quite lucky. The Duke of Ch'in was
continuing his tax trip with the Key Rabbit—Lotus Cloud
was to rejoin them in a week or so—and in his absence
we received a very considerate death sentence from the
provincial governor, who was understandably annoyed
because we had delayed his entrance into Lotus Cloud's
bed.

"You may choose your own method for departing this
earth!" he yelled.

Then we were marched up to the roof of the tallest
tower and the door was bricked up. This left us the choice
between slowly starving to death or jumping to the cobblestones one hundred feet below, and I sat down miserably and buried my head in my hands. How much longer
could the children last? Two months? Three? The keen-
eyed bonzes that the abbot had posted would stare in vain
from the roof of the monastery, because Master Li and
Number Ten Ox were not going to return with the rest of
the Great Root of Power. I wept until I realized that some
of the sounds were coming from below me, and with a

startled sense of hope I saw that the soldiers were un-
sealing the door.

Hope faded quickly when I understood that they were
merely opening the door in order to shove another condemned prisoner up upon the roof, and as they bricked
it up again Master Li took note of a pair of little pig eyes,
a bald and mottled skull, a sharp curving nose like a parrot's beak, the loose flabby lips of a camel, and two drooping elephant ears from which sprouted thick tufts of coarse
gray hair.

"Would you care to buy a goat?" he said with a polite
bow.

To our astonishment Miser Shen ran to embrace us
with cries of joy.

"What good fortune!" he cried. "I had feared that I
would never have the opportunity of thanking my benefactors in person!"

"Benefactors?" I said.

"Thanking us?" said Master Li.

"For saving my life!" cried Miser Shen. "If it had not
been for you, the Key Rabbit would not have determined
the extent of my wealth, and if he had not determined the
extent of my wealth he would not have invited me to tea,
and if he had not invited me to tea I would still be the
stingiest and most miserable miser in China. Lotus Cloud,"
he said proudly, "made a new man of me."

"Let me guess," Li Kao said. "She bankrupted you in
a week?"

Miser Shen drew himself up proudly.

"Great Buddha, no! Why, such was the extent of my
wealth that it took the dear girl almost a month to reduce
me to abject poverty. Of course I owe a good deal to
luck," he added modestly. "After Lotus Cloud ran through
my countless chests of buried gold I was able to get very
good prices for my eight businesses, my six houses, my
carriage, my sedan chair, my horse, my three cows, my
ten pigs, my twenty chickens, my eight savage guard dogs,
my seven half-starved servants, my—Dear boy, do you
happen to remember my young and beautiful concubine?"

"Vividly," I said.

"I was very lucky there, because I was able to buy three more days of Lotus Cloud by selling Pretty Ping to an up-and-coming young fellow in the brothel business. Lucky for Pretty Ping too, because one of her customers fell in love with her and made her his number-three wife, and now he showers her with the gifts and affection that she never received from me. Poor girl, I treated her terribly." Miser Shen sighed. "But then I was not truly human, because I had not yet met Lotus Cloud."

"I am finding this fascinating," said Master Li. "What did you do when you had nothing left to sell?"

"Why, I turned to crime, of course," said Miser Shen. "I am particularly proud of my performance during the Dragon Boat Festival. It occurred to me that the boats originally raced to sacrifice to the spirit of Ch'u Yuan, who drowned himself as a protest against corrupt government, but that the festival has degenerated into little more than a professional boat race upon which vast sums are wagered. Well, there was the betting boat with the bookmakers and other dignitaries on board, and there came the dragon boats skimming across the water, and there I came, walking upon the surface. I was on stilts, of course, and I wore an exact copy of the ancient ceremonial costume of Ch'u Yuan, and I had a long staff and a big black beard.

"'Insolent dogs!' I roared. 'You dare to turn the occasion of my honorable death into a sporting event? I shall smite you with pestilence, typhoons, and earthquakes!'

"It was very effective because I had covered my head with protective ointment and my false beard with pitch, and at that moment I set fire to the beard," said Miser Shen. "When Ch'u Yuan came striding across the waves with a halo of flames around his head, the people on the betting boat dived into the water and swam for their lives, and I cut the anchor rope and climbed on board and sailed away with all the money. I spent every cent on pearls and jade, but the soldiers caught me before I could give it to Lotus Cloud, so here I am."

Li Kao turned and stared at me.

"This happy, vibrant fellow with an admirable t. for crime is Miser Shen?" he said incredulously. "Ox, . transformation is nothing short of miraculous!"

He turned back to Miser Shen and bowed.

"We must dispense with titles," he said. "My surname is Li and my personal name is Kao, and there is a slight flaw in my character, and this is my esteemed client, Number Ten Ox. We have something important to do, so we must escape from this tower as soon as possible, and we would be honored if you would care to accompany us."

Miser Shen wiped tears from his eyes. "It has been forty years since anyone wanted me to accompany them anywhere," he sniffled. "Unfortunately there is no way to escape from this tower."

"Something will turn up," Master Li said confidently.

He was right, although when it turned up he was as astonished as I was. There was a loud commotion at the gates and a mob burst into the courtyard and demanded to see the governor. The governor stepped out, along with our porcupine merchant, and the mob parted to reveal a furious farmer, a cow, and two gentlemen of low appearance. A babble of voices drifted up to us, and we were able to piece together the following account:

The farmer had heard a commotion in his pasture and he had rushed out to discover that a bald gentleman was down on his knees with his arms wrapped lovingly around the legs of one of the farmer's prize cows. A fat gentleman, who was carrying a small funeral urn, was weeping his eyes out, and he turned and wept on the farmer's shoulder for a while. Then he recovered enough to relate a marvelous tale.

The bald fellow's beloved mother had expired some time ago, and her son had honored her rather unusual request to be cremated. One night the ghost of his mother came to see him in a dream, and she expressed the wish to have her ashes placed among the lohans at Lung-men. So the bald fellow and his dear friend had set forth with the ashes on the pious pilgrimage, only to discover that the ghost had something else in mind. The road to Lung-

passed by the farmer's pasture, and the cow had
waiting for them. The bald fellow had recognized
soft brown eyes immediately.

"Mother!" he screeched. "My beloved mother has been
eborn as a cow!"

The reunion had been emotional, and the farmer was
forced to shed a few tears himself as he watched it. The
cow's eyes were streaming with tears of joy as she lovingly licked the bald fellow's skull. "Mother! What joy to
see you again!" he sobbed, kissing her hairy legs.

What choice did the farmer have? He felt the warm
glow of a deed well done as he watched his cow dwindle
in the distance with the arms of the two gentlemen wrapped
around its neck. He was only a gentleman farmer, and he
was quite surprised when he was informed that cows always weep when they lick salt.

"And that includes salt that has been sprinkled upon
a bald skull!" the farmer yelled.

"How dare you accuse us of fraud?" screamed
Pawnbroker Fang.

"We shall sue!" howled Ma the Grub.

When the farmer took off in pursuit he was joined by
neighbors who had also experienced the wiles of Ma and
Fang, and now they wanted the governor to hang these
crooks from the highest tree.

"Lies, all lies!" screamed Pawnbroker Fang.

"We demand compensation for slander!" howled Ma
the Grub.

"Ox, you know these creatures well. What will they
do now?" asked Master Li.

"They will go on the offense," I said firmly. "I don't
know how, but they'll manage it."

"Splendid. Gentlemen, let's get out of here."

There was a huge silk flag with the duke's tiger emblem
fluttering from a pole on top of the tower, and the soldiers
were too interested in Ma and Fang and the lynch mob
to notice when I cut it loose and hauled it down. From
the wreckage of an old bamboo pigeon coop we made a
basket to stand in, and the lanyard from the pole attached
the basket to the flag.

"The principle is the same as that of a falling leaf, which drifts down gently because the air that pushes up against its surface almost counterbalances the weight that pushes it down," Master Li explained. "This flag may just be large enough to hold enough air, although I would be happier if the tower were another hundred feet high."

We tiptoed back to the other side of the tower to see how Ma and Fang were coming along. Bees were droning beside the wall, and Ma the Grub was surprised to see a trail of honey. His fingers slid slyly toward the stuff. Our porcupine merchant had brought out a plate of sweet-meats, and he was automatically lifting them to his gaping mouth as he listened to the members of the mob bellow one accusation after another. Ma the Grub craftily covered the ashes in the funeral urn with honey. He slid the urn beneath the merchant's fat fingers, and the hand lifted again and again to the insatiable maw....

"Monster!" Ma shrieked in horror. "Fang, look what these fiends are doing! First they try to steal the incarnation of your beloved mother, and now they devour her very ashes!"

"Cannibals!" screamed Pawnbroker Fang. He pried the merchant's mouth open and peered into the black hole. *"Mother, speak to me!"* he howled.

Chaos ensued, and the soldiers in the courtyard converged upon the screaming pandemonium, and we dragged the flag and the basket to the rear of the roof. We climbed in, and I grasped the lanyards.

"I have decided to ask the Yama Kings to let me be reborn as a three-toed sloth, and Ox wishes to become a cloud. Do you have any preference?" Li Kao asked Miser Shen.

"A tree," Miser Shen said promptly. "In this life I have done nothing but foreclose mortgages, and when I am reborn I would like to provide free shade for the weary, free roosts for the birds, free fruit for the hungry, and free firewood for woodcutters when I am old and useless. Peasants name their favorite trees, and it is the dearest wish of Miser Shen to be known as 'Old Generosity.'"

"I shall hang by my tail from one of your branches," said Master Li.

"I shall drift overhead and bring rain for your roots," I said.

"I am overcome," Miser Shen sniffled.

"Farewell, tree."

"Farewell, cloud."

"Farewell, sloth."

I pushed off, and we plunged toward the cobblestones like three bugs clinging to a boulder. I consigned my soul to Heaven, and then the flag billowed wide, and we halted in mid-air so suddenly that my arms were nearly pulled from their sockets.

"We really must stop somewhere and collect some pearls for Lotus Cloud," said Miser Shen.

"And jade," I agreed.

"Incredible," sighed Master Li.

The wind caught the flag, and we drifted lazily away across the treetops toward a green valley where a river sparkled in the distance. The tower dwindled behind us, and we landed quite gently, and in the first village we bought a small boat and a great deal of wine.

The Duke of Ch'in, like all his predecessors, continued his tax trip past the terrible Desert of Salt, and after drifting uneventfully downstream for six days Li Kao found the landmark he was looking for. It was a tiny trail that ran from the bank toward a low hill, and the boat was light enough so that I could carry it over my head until we reached water again. It was a small, rapid stream, and as the days passed it grew narrower and shallower. The air became very hot and we began to perspire freely, and on the fourth day we floated around a bend and I realized that the stream was disappearing, vanishing into cracks in the hard-caked earth. A blinding white glare was all that I could see of the horizon. The boat scraped bottom, and we climbed out to the bank, and Li Kao pointed ahead to the glare.

"The Desert of Salt," he said. "Peasants swear that

when the Duke of Ch'in passes this way on his tax trip,
his army reaches this point and then vanishes for days."

He searched for another landmark, and pointed to a
faint line that was barely visible beneath the white expanse of salt.

"Too straight to be the work of nature," he said. "Swirling salt will cover hoofprints and wheel tracks, but the
underlying traces of a road will remain if it is used every
year."

"Do you think that it leads to another treasure trove?"
I asked.

"Well, it's an idea, and even a bad idea is better than
none," said Master Li. "Error can point the way to truth,
while empty-headedness can only lead to more empty-
headedness or to a career in politics. Miser Shen, now is
the time when a wise man would turn back. If we keep
chasing the duke we will eventually get back to Lotus
Cloud, but the Desert of Salt has swallowed whole car-
avans, and our deaths are not likely to be pleasant."

"What is life without Lotus Cloud?" Miser Shen asked,
quite reasonably from my point of view. "Besides, after
a lifetime of disgrace, the least I can do is die with dignity."

I was really astonished to see what a splendid fellow
had been lurking behind a skinflint's exterior, and that
night I learned a great deal about Miser Shen. We emptied
our wine jars and filled them with water, and I cut the sail
of the boat to make a tent. Then we followed the faint
path into the desert, and just before dawn we crawled
into the tent to protect ourselves from the direct rays of
the sun. Miser Shen was afraid that we might think badly
of Lotus Cloud for having accepted the love of someone
so old and ugly as him, and he begged to be allowed to
tell his story.

"Many years ago I was a happy man," he said in a shy,
halting voice. "I was a peasant, and I was poor, but I had
a small farm and a wife who loved me and the most ador-
able little daughter in the world. We almost always had
enough to eat, and I never dreamed of asking for more.
Then our village fell on hard times. The rain would not

fall, or if it did, it fell so hard that our dikes broke and our crops were washed away. Our animals fell sick, and bandits bullied us and stole our rice, and then one day we learned that the Duke of Ch'in, the father of the present duke, had doubled the taxes. We could not possibly pay such a tax. The men of the village drew lots, and I was the unlucky one who was sent to plead to the duke.

"There were many peasants waiting to plead for lower taxes, so I spent hours rehearsing my speech. When my time came, I fell upon my knees in front of the throne and I told the duke of all the hardships that had come to my village. I know that I told my story well. When I had finished I raised my eyes to the terrible tiger mask, and the voice of metal frightened me but the words brought joy to my heart.

"'Shen Chunlieh,' said the duke, 'today I have heard many tales from those who wish to cheat me, but your story rings true. I am convinced that you cannot pay my tax, and I will grant you a very special favor. Go home to your village, and tell your family and friends that never again shall the village of Shen Chunlieh be asked to pay taxes to the Dukes of Ch'in, not so long as the stars shine in the sky and the fish swim in the sea.'

"I kissed the floor and bowed backward from the presence of the duke, and my feet had wings as I raced over the hills. I could not run as fast as his horsemen could ride, however, and when I had climbed the last hill I stared down at smoldering ruins. The duke had sworn that never again would we pay taxes, and then he had destroyed my village as an example to others. The only villagers who had been spared were those who had been away, fishing at a nearby lake, and one of those was my wife. We wept in each other's arms, but do you remember that I had a little daughter? Her name was Ah Chen, and I loved her more than anything in the world, and she had been left behind in the village and had been killed with the others.

"I was wild with grief. I saw the face of my little girl everywhere, and at night I would hear her crying in the woods and I would run out and shout, 'Ah Chen, your father is here!' They said that I would feel better if I sent a prayer to her. I could not read or write, so I went to a priest who wrote down my prayer and burned it to send to Hell, where my little girl had gone to be judged. I did not feel better. I could not work and I could not sleep, and one day a traveler told of a great magician who lived in a cave at the end of Bear's Path, high in the Omei Mountains. 'He is called the Old Man of the Mountain,' the traveler told me. 'He is the wisest man in the world, and he can surely bring your little girl back to life, but you must bring money. You must bring a great deal of money, because the Old Man of the Mountain does not sell his secrets cheaply.'

"I had no money, so I set out to make some. Like anyone else who sets out to make money I lied and cheated and I ruined my friends, but nothing mattered except getting enough money to bring little Ah Chen back to life. 'Beloved husband, you must forget our daughter,' my wife told me. 'If you continue this way, you will surely go insane.' Then she fell ill, but I was too busy making money to care for her. She died, and I wept, but I went right on making money. The money mattered, only the money, and I could not spend a penny of it because I would need it all for the Old Man of the Mountain. I was not aware of losing my mind, but as the years passed I forgot what the money was for. Now and then I would remember, but I would tell myself that I needed twice as much money to pay the wisest man in the world to bring my daughter back to life. I buried gold in chests and ran out to grab for more. I became Miser Shen, the greediest and most miserable of men, and so I would have remained if Lotus Cloud had not bankrupted me and brought me to my senses.

"Noble Sirs, there are women who can see right into the heart of a man, and I would like you to know that Lotus Cloud never accepted the love of Miser Shen. She accepted the love of a poor peasant who loved his little girl too much, and who went insane."

18.
The Hand of Hell

We traveled at night, and spent the days huddled in the tent while we fried in the heat. When we peeped through the folds we saw multiple images of the sun reflected in the glaring white salt, surrounded by orange and violet halos that spun round and round and made us sick to our stomachs. Whirlwinds danced in mad patterns, and the wind howled horribly. Even at night the heat never released us from its blazing fingers, and often the moon and stars were obscured by flying salt. The faint trace of what we hoped was a road ran on and on, seemingly without end, and it was a relief when the mirages began, because they gave us something to look at.

I would see a castle with a silver dome, standing in the center of an emerald lake. "No, no!" Miser Shen would say. "It is a large rock in the middle of a river, and the rock is covered with nesting birds. Seagulls, I think, although I cannot imagine what seagulls are doing in a desert." Master Li would snort and say, "Nonsense. I can clearly see a large pleasure barge floating in a pond, and the banks are lined with bright green trees."

Then the mirage would dissolve into nothingness, and we would gaze at an endless expanse of white salt.

We saw cities and cemeteries and armies arrayed in battle formation, and always there was water and a green oasis of some sort. As the days passed we had to ration water, and thirst began to torment us. Then one day Miser Shen pointed ahead.

"Look at that ghastly mirage!" he exclaimed.

"Mirage?" I said. "Shen, it's the nightmare of a demented baboon."

Li Kao studied the shimmering image carefully and said, "Tell me what you see."

"Well, I see the usual green oasis, but it is standing in the middle of a mess of shattered stones," said Miser Shen. "Geysers of steam are hissing up from the bowels of the earth, and I smell a horrible stench of sulphur."

"The whole mirage is surrounded by a broad belt like a moat, and it's filled with a strange fiery liquid that makes a sickening sort of bubbling sound," I said.

"My friends, I regret to report that I see precisely the same thing," Master Li said grimly. "That is not a mirage, and the path we are following leads straight to it."

As we came closer we realized that we were looking at the ruins of a once great city, but what a terrible catastrophe had befallen it! The walls were tumbled ruins. One narrow span of what had once been a mighty stone bridge still crossed a moat that had formerly held blue water and white swans and golden fish, and now bubbled with fiery red-black lava. On the other side a pair of enormous bronze gates stood open, but bent and twisted by some unimaginable force, and when we nervously crossed the moat and passed through the gates a terrible sight met our eyes. Steam hissed like the breath of angry dragons through great gaping holes in the earth, and pools of murderous lava heaved and bubbled, and it seemed to me that the harsh wind that howled through the ruins was wailing death, death, death. A lunatic tangle of side streets branched from both sides of a central avenue—if one could call them streets, since not one building remained standing—and in the distance we saw a great mass of tumbled stones. It had probably been the palace of the king, and we decided to climb to the top of it to try to find the green oasis that we had glimpsed from a distance.

It had certainly been a palace. We climbed over smashed statues and beautiful stone friezes, and then we stopped dead in our tracks and stared. Ahead of us was a wall about thirty feet high and perhaps five times as long, and the three of us had the same thought at once.

"That wall could not possibly have survived the catastrophe!" I cried. "It must have been built afterward, from the toppled stones."

"I would not like to meet whatever it was that knocked a hole in it," Master Li said thoughtfully.

Nor would I. Some incredible force had jerked out enormous stone slabs and tossed them aside like pebbles. A great gaping hole confronted us like a screaming mouth, and when we cautiously stepped through it we stared at great piles of human bones. Miser Shen turned quite pale.

"I swear that those poor souls were chewed!" he gasped.

He was right. Nothing but monstrous grinding teeth could have shredded bones like that, and not only bones. Armor had been pulverized as well, and Miser Shen and I were greatly relieved when Li Kao examined it with critical eyes and said:

"This armor is in the style of five hundred years ago, or more. Perhaps a thousand years would be closer. Whatever the creature was, it has been dust for centuries."

He bent over and examined the mangled skeletons.

"You know, I recall a monster that could have done this to armed warriors," he said thoughtfully. "It was discovered frozen in the ice of a Mongolian glacier. Half mammal, half lizard, one hundred feet from head to tail, and equipped with teeth like steel doorposts. The sages wanted to preserve it for scientific study, but we had an exceptionally idiotic emperor at the time, and I regret to say that the imperial dolt had the beast cut up and boiled for a state banquet. The fact that it smelled like two thousand old unopened rooms and tasted like diseased whale blubber didn't bother the Son of Heaven one bit. He happily awarded himself the medal 'Heroic Slayer of Inedible Monstrosities,' which he wore on all state occasions."

I was staring at a large toppled slab.

"Master Li, I think this is covered with writing, but the script is so ancient that I can't make any sense of it," I said.

He examined the slab with interest, and brushed a layer of salt from it. Time and the wind had made much of the writing illegible, but enough remained to make my hair stand up on my head.

"It begins with a prayer to the gods," he said. "Then some words are missing, and then it says: '. . . punished for our sins, and the earth opened with a great roar and flames engulfed us. Fiery black rock sprayed up like water, and for eight days the earth heaved and shuddered, and on the ninth day the earth vomited forth the Hand That No One Sees, from the very depths of Hell.'"

"The what?" Miser Shen asked.

"The Hand That No One Sees, but don't ask me what it means," said Master Li. "More words are missing, and then it says: '. . . sixth day of our doom, and we labor on the wall but we are faint of heart. We pray and sacrifice, but the gods remain implacable. The queen and her ladies have chosen the more merciful death, and have jumped into the lake of fiery molten rock. We did not try to stop them. The Hand moves closer. Our spears are hurled at nothingness and bounce away from nothingness. The wall is beginning to shake. The Hand . . .'"

Li Kao straightened up. "That's all there is," he said quietly.

"Whoof!" Miser Shen gasped. "I don't care how many centuries ago that happened. I want to get out of here."

So did I. I scrambled up to the top of the wall and peered around.

"I see the oasis!" I cried. "There's a lake of lava covering the back of the palace, so we'll have to try to reach the oasis through the side streets."

That wasn't as simple as it sounded. Time and again we came to dead ends where scalding steam or bubbling lava blocked the way, and we were not the only ones who had reached dead ends. Skeletons, chewed to pieces in their useless armor, littered almost every side street.

"Whatever that thing was, it certainly ate well," Miser Shen said nervously.

We tried street after street with no success, and finally we were almost back where we had entered the city. Li Kao looked at the huge bronze gates and the narrow span of bridge and shrugged his shoulders.

"Perhaps we had better go back across the moat and see if there is another bridge on the side where the oasis is," he said.

We started forward, and then we stopped and gaped with eyes that nearly popped from the sockets. Those gates weighed tons. Nothing was touching them, but they were creaking shut! They came together with a terrible crash of metal, and a mark appeared in the layer of salt upon the ground. It took several moments for my brain to believe what my eyes were showing me. I was staring at the print of an enormous thumb, and four huge fingerprints followed, and then an immense sliding mark. An enormous invisible hand was crawling toward us, dragging the palm and heel behind the terrible fingers.

Miser Shen and I stood rooted to the spot in horror, but Master Li whirled around and gazed back at the tangle of the side streets. Then he yelled, "Ox, pick us up!"

I scooped up Master Li in one arm and Miser Shen in the other, and Master Li grabbed the dragon pendant that dangled from the chain around my neck. His fingers found the place where the dragon had stopped after leading us to the treasure trove.

"I should have realized at once that this place was another labyrinth," he said grimly. "Turn into the second street on the right, and I would advise you to hurry."

Even though I was carrying the two of them I doubt that my record for the course will be surpassed until a Tibetan snow leopard tries it, but the Hand That No One Sees was almost as fast. Those great invisible fingers were stretching out twenty or thirty feet, and salt was billowing up behind the sliding palm. "First left!" Master Li yelled. "Second left! . . . Fourth right! . . . Third left! . . . First right!..." I panted through the maze, leaping over lava and darting around geysers of steam, and at last I saw the tops of green trees and realized that the dragon was leading us to the oasis. Then I skidded to a halt.

"May Buddha have mercy on our souls!" howled Miser Shen.

There was the beautiful green oasis, right in front of us, but it was encircled by a moat of bubbling lava. A narrow stone bridge led safely across the fiery rock, but the Hand That No One Sees had taken a shortcut. The bridge was far too narrow for the monster to cross, but that would do us no good unless we were on the other side, and I stared in horror at the salt on the ground in front of the bridge. Great invisible fingers pawed, and salt billowed, and then the Hand from Hell began crawling toward us, blocking any path to the oasis.

At the edge of the moat was the only upright building that we had seen, a watchtower, probably, tall and narrow and teetering upon cracked stone slabs. I unceremoniously dumped Li Kao and Miser Sheen and raced up and put my shoulder to the thing. I heaved with everything that I had, and the tower began to tilt. Then I heaved with more than I had, and when I heard a snapping sound I assumed that my spine had split in half. Instead it was one of the supporting slabs that had split, and the tall tower dissolved into a shower of stones that toppled down into the moat.

The lava was nearly as dense as the stones, and they sank very slowly. I ran back and scooped up Li Kao and Miser Shen, and then I raced to the edge of the moat and jumped. My feet touched the first stone and I vaulted to the second. My sandals were smoking and my lungs were raw from bubbling sulphur as I hopped from stone to stone, and the last one had nearly sunk out of sight. I sent a prayer to the August Personage of Jade and leaped, and my toes touched the searing surface and I leaped again, and perhaps the August Personage of Jade gave me a helpful shove because I landed with my face buried in green grass.

I was dimly aware that Master Li and Miser Shen were

shouting in my ears and pounding my back, but the world was spinning before my eyes, and I felt as though I were falling down a hole that had no end. Then a cool, peaceful blackness closed around me.

19.
Bamboo Dragonfly

I awoke to see Li Kao smiling down at me, and Miser Shen tilted a gourd filled with delicious spring water to my lips. It revived me as if by magic. Soon I was able to get up and examine the little oasis, which had clearly been used as a pleasure garden.

Trees and shrubs from every corner of the empire had been planted there, and the variety was astonishing. Silver bells had once tinkled in the branches, and paper lanterns had glowed in the night like fireflies, and lovers had walked hand in hand through mazes of moonflowers. Then the horrible eruption, and the Hand That No One Sees. I wondered what terrible crime the city had committed to deserve such a fate, but then I decided that I didn't want to know. I turned around and shuddered as I saw the marks of invisible fingers angrily pawing in the salt at the other end of the narrow bridge. The Hand was waiting.

A clear path led through wildflowers toward the bronze roof of a pagoda that sparkled in the light of the setting sun. We started toward it, and as we drew closer we saw that the pagoda had escaped destruction because it was nearly solid stone. Only the wooden doors had rotted away. The sun sank below the horizon, but the moon had already lifted into the sky, and a pale path of moonbeams reached through the hole where the door had been and touched something that sparkled. Tears began to trickle down Miser Shen's cheeks as he stared at a pile of treasure that was even larger than the one at the Castle of the Labyrinth.

"Cured!" he cried joyfully. "I could not be sure before, but now when I look at this loot, my fingers itch only for the pearls and jade, and that is because I would like to give them to Lotus Cloud."

Li Kao's eyes met mine, and I nodded. Both of us had instinctively studied the top of the pile of treasure for a ghost shadow, and there it was. I was getting rather good at it, and the shadow blanket lifted easily over my head.

I was looking at the same ghost! No, not the same, but dressed in the same ancient fashion, and with the same streak of blood where a blade had pierced her heart. Again I sensed that she was making a terrible effort to appear before us, and I felt the same searing wave of agony when her lips parted.

"Take pity upon a faithless handmaiden," she whispered. "Is not a thousand years enough?" Ghost tears like transparent pearls trickled down her cheeks. "I swear that I did not know what I had done!" she sobbed. "Oh, take pity, and exchange this for the feather. The birds must fly."

Then she was gone.

Miser Shen had seen nothing, and he gazed in wonder at the stunned expressions on our faces. I snarled and scrambled up the pile, and slid back down with an identical jade casket in my hands. I jerked the lid open, and then I cried out in despair.

Inside was not the Heart of Power, which was supposed to be the ultimate, but two more tiny tendrils. They were the Arms of the Great Root, and if the Legs had failed, what more could we expect from the Arms? The ginseng aroma made my eyes water, and I turned the casket upside down. Something else fell to the floor.

Li Kao got down on his knees and carefully examined a tiny crystal ball, about the size of the miniature flute.

"Miser Shen, I would advise you to sit down and prepare for a rather unusual phenomenon," he said grimly. Then he spat on his hand and reached out and cautiously rubbed the crystal surface.

The ball began to glow with a strange inner light. Then it began to expand. It grew until it was several feet in diameter, and the inner light grew brighter and brighter, and then we all cried out in wonder as a picture appeared, and then we heard sounds.

We were looking at the interior of a pretty little cottage where an old lady snoozed on a stool. We could hear her peaceful snores, and the sounds of chickens and pigs, and the gentle murmur of a stream. Birds sang and bees droned drowsily, and the sun-dappled leaves of a tree rustled outside the window.

An ant scurried across the floor, carrying a tiny crust of bread. After a moment a roach took notice, and began to scuttle after the ant. A rat stuck its head from a hole and dashed after the roach. A cat bounded after the rat, and then a dog bounded through the door and raced after the cat. The whole procession charged beneath the old lady's stool and tipped it over, and she sat up and rubbed her eyes, unleashed a torrent of peasant profanity, grabbed a broom, and started in hot pursuit of the dog that was chasing the cat that was chasing the rat that was chasing the roach that was chasing the ant that was carrying the crust of bread.

It is difficult to describe in words, but the scene that unfolded was incredibly comic. Around and around they went, racing through the door, climbing back inside through the window, smashing through the flimsy walls, reappearing through a hole in the roof, and reducing the furniture to splinters. The variations appeared to be endless, and they were so ingenious that Miser Shen and I held our sides as we howled with laughter. At one point the old lady's slashing broom sent every piece of pottery flying into the air, and they all came together with a crash. The fragments fell to the floor, and as one piece landed upon the other, they formed a solemn statue of the Sacred and Venerable Sage of Serenity. The mad procession raced outside and splashed through a pond, and when they crashed back inside through another ruined wall there was a huge bullfrog squatting upon the old lady's head, croaking indignantly.

Miser Shen and I might have laughed ourselves to death if Li Kao hadn't reached out and touched the crystal ball. The glow faded, and the sounds and the picture vanished, and the ball shrank down to its former size.

"Shen, have you ever seen anything like this?" Master Li asked, as soon as Miser Shen had recovered enough to breathe.

Miser Shen scratched his head and said, "Well, I can't be sure. Surely I have never seen anything like that incredible scene, but I once saw a tiny crystal ball that resembled this one in an ancient painting. It was in the Cavern of Bells. An old lame peddler with his back to the viewer was facing three young ladies who were dressed in the style of many centuries ago. In one of his hands he held three feathers—"

"Feathers?" Master Li yelped. "Girls dressed in the ancient style?"

"Ah . . . yes," said Miser Shen. "In the other hand the peddler was holding a ball that resembled this one, and a tiny bell, and a miniature flute."

Li Kao grunted in satisfaction and unsnapped one of the fake shells on his belt.

"Like this?"

"Precisely like that," said Miser Shen as he examined the tiny tin flute. "I don't remember much else about the painting except that it was said to be very mysterious and that the old lame peddler was thought to be divine. The Cavern of Bells has become a shrine in his honor, and it is tended by a small order of monks."

Li Kao placed the flute back into the shell, and added the crystal ball and the Arms of the Great Root of Power to his smuggler's belt.

"Let's get some sleep. In the morning we'll find out

how to get off this island, and our first stop will be the Cavern of Bells," he said.

He spoke too soon. When we made a circuit of the oasis the following morning we discovered that it was indeed an island, completely encircled by murderous lava, and the narrow bridge was the only exit. Fingerprints pawed in the salt, and my heart sank to my toes as I realized that we would never be able to get back to the children of Ku-fu. I could not stop the tears that welled in my eyes and trickled down my cheeks, and Miser Shen looked at me and then hastily averted his eyes.

"Number Ten Ox, this is not such a bad place in which to spend the rest of our days," he said shyly. "We shall live like kings on fruits and berries and pure spring water, while the rest of the world enjoys war, famine, and pestilence."

And death, I thought. I heard weeping and mournful bells, and I saw a long row of small coffins disappearing into the ground.

"Of course, the rest of the world will also be enjoying Lotus Cloud," Miser Shen said thoughtfully.

"You have a point," I sniffled.

We were sitting upon the grass with our backs against the trunk of a huge palm tree. Li Kao trotted up and joined us, and I saw that his eyes were sparkling.

"Gentlemen, how much do you know about the great Chang Heng?" he asked.

I dimly recalled schoolroom lessons. "Didn't he invent the seismograph, about five hundred years ago?"

"And the Fire Drug," said Miser Shen.

"He did indeed, and his achievements did not stop there," said Master Li. "The great Chang Heng was a superb poet, a competent painter, an engineer and astronomer without equal, and the world's greatest student of the phenomenon of flight. He perfected the science of latitude and longitude, determined the value of pi, revolutionized the armillary sphere, and constructed kites that could carry men through the air for long distances. One day he happened to be sitting as we are, with his back against a tree, and something brushed his face."

Li Kao lifted his right hand and opened it, displaying a tiny object.

"A sycamore seed?" said Miser Shen.

"Precisely," said Master Li. "Chang Heng had seen thousands of them, but never before had he thought to examine one closely. The more he studied it, the more convinced he became that he was gazing at one of the marvels of nature."

Miser Shen and I stared fixedly at the seed. It was nothing but a tiny stem and a circle of fan-shaped blades.

"Observe," said Master Li.

He blew gently into the palm of his hand. The fan-shaped blades began to revolve, faster and faster, then the seed lifted straight up into the air. The breeze caught it and away it went, spinning into the sky, sailing over the treetops, dwindling to a tiny speck in the distance.

"Chang Heng was gazing at one of the most efficient flying machines in the world, and he immediately began to build a sycamore seed that could carry a man," said Master Li. "The emperor graciously provided pilots from the ranks of criminals who had been sentenced to death, and one after another the wailing wretches were strapped into Chang Heng's flying machines and pushed off the tops of the cliffs. One of them encountered a strong updraft and actually flew for several hundred feet, but the end result was the same. The blades could not whirl fast enough to compensate for the weight, and the pilots all crashed to their deaths. Do you know what Chang Heng did then?"

"We are as ignorant as apples," sighed Miser Shen, speaking for both of us.

"The great Chang Heng mixed sulphur, saltpeter, and charcoal, and invented the Fire Drug," Master Li said. "We use it mostly for fireworks, but he had something else in mind. By adding resin, he managed to produce a compound that would burn steadily instead of exploding, and he packed it into long tubes of bamboo. He built a wicker carriage and attached it to a revolving pole. On top of the pole he placed fan-shaped blades and at the bottom he added a wheel to which he attached his tubes of Fire Drug. The emperor and all the top officials gathered to watch what promised to be a spectacular execution, and the weeping convict was strapped to the seat in the carriage. Chang Heng lit the fuses. There was a spurt of flame, and than another and another, and a great cloud of black smoke obscured everything. When the smoke cleared, the astonished audience saw that the contraption had lifted straight up into the air, with the blades whirling furiously. A trail of smoke and flame stretched out behind as it flew through the air, and the screams of the pilot could faintly be heard as the thing streaked toward one of the palace towers. The emperor cheered and the audience applauded madly as it hit the tower and exploded with a great roar, and it was said that pieces of pilot rained down for a week, although that may be a slight exaggeration. The great Chang Heng locked himself in his workroom, and one month later he had completed the final design of the most marvelous of all his inventions: the incredible Bamboo Dragonfly."

Li Kao smiled happily. "The plans for which I have seen in the Forest of Culture Academy in Hanlin," he said.

There was a moment of silence.

"You can't possibly mean..." Miser Shen whispered.

"Right above us is a circle of palm branches that are light, strong, and fan-shaped," said Master Li.

"Surely you don't intend to..." I said weakly

"Bamboo is all around us, and so is resin. The lava is full of sulphur. There are natural deposits of saltpeter all over China, and probably on this very island, and if a former peasant like Miser Shen can't make a little charcoal, I will be very surprised indeed."

"But it would be suicide!" I exclaimed.

"Insanity!" cried Miser Shen.

"We will have no hope of survival at all," Master Li agreed. "Ox, you get the palm branches and resin and bamboo. The charcoal will be Miser Shen's department, and I will search for saltpeter and extract the sulphur from the lava. I suggest that we hurry, because with every passing moment I grow closer to expiring from old age."

For a week a series of explosions shook the little island, followed by the furious screams of Li Kao. His beard was singed and blackened and his eyebrows were nearly scorched off. So many fires had started in his clothes that he looked as though he had been attacked by a million starving moths, but finally he found the right formula and his tubes of Fire Drug began to behave. Miser Shen and I were rather proud of our handiwork. The basket was woven from reeds, and quite comfortable to sit in, and the palm-leaf blades revolved very nicely around the bamboo pole. The bamboo wheel to which the tubes were attached was balanced carefully, and although we had no steering mechanism, we hoped to be able to control our flight by shifting our weight.

"Of course this is madness," I said as I climbed into the basket.

"Moronic," said Miser Shen as he climbed in beside me.

"We are totally deranged," Li Kao agreed as he lit the fuses.

He hopped into the basket, and I covered my eyes and waited for death. The basket shuddered as the tubes of Fire Drug began to spurt flames. The wheel started to revolve, and the blades began to whirl round and round. I peeked through my fingers and peered through a cloud of black smoke and saw that the grass beneath us was bending beneath a blast of wind.

"We are rising!" I yelled.

"We are falling!" howled Miser Shen.

Both of us were right. We had suddenly lifted into the air, and now we were dropping back down. Unfortunately we had also moved fifty feet to the left, and we were dropping straight toward bubbling lava.

"Lean back!" Master Li yelled.

We shifted our weight and the Bamboo Dragonfly suddenly straightened out and began to skim just above the fiery surface toward the other side of the moat, and we stared with horrified eyes at the prints of immense fingers that were eagerly pawing the salt.

The Hand That No One Sees almost got us. A slashing

invisible finger ripped off one of the palm-leaf blades, which proved to be a blessing because we had apparently used one too many. As soon as it was gone our flying machine lifted into the air and began to perform very nicely indeed, except that it was flying around in circles. Around and around it flew, moving slowly across the ruins of the city, while great lunging marks of furious fingers kicked up clouds of salt beneath us.

"That horrible thing is crawling up on top of the ruins of the palace!" Miser Shen yelled. "If it gets on top of the wall and we keep circling like this we'll run right into it!"

He was right, but nothing could persuade the Bamboo Dragonfly to change course. Flames and black smoke spurted out behind us, and with one more circle we would be in the clutches of the Hand from Hell.

"Take off your tunics!" Master Li yelled. "Try using them as rudders!"

We ripped off our tunics and spread them behind us to catch the wind, and by some miracle it worked. Just as we reached the wall we suddenly veered to the left, and the Hand must have snatched at us because the slabs on top of the wall began to teeter precariously. Then the wall fell apart, and stones tumbled down into the lake of lava, and then there was an enormous splash that sent fiery molten rock a hundred feet into the air.

The monster slowly rose to the surface. What had been invisible was now covered with black lava, and we gazed in terror at an enormous hairy hand, perhaps sixty feet long. The palm was up, and the fingers were tightly clenched, and suddenly it jerked convulsively and the fingers opened. They weren't fingers at all, but the legs of a giant spider, and the heel and palm was a loathsome bloated sac! A cluster of evil eyes glared up at us, and a hideous round mouth opened and displayed a circle of gigantic pointed teeth, and then lava poured into the mouth and the Hand That No One Sees sank forever beneath the fiery surface of the lake.

The Bamboo Dragonfly flew steadily on, and the tragic shattered city faded behind us. We sat in shaken silence, and finally Li Kao cleared his throat.

"I suspect that it was simply an oversized relative of the common trapdoor spider," he said thoughtfully. "Invisible, because before the eruption it had lived underground, where there was no need for sight perception. Nature is astonishingly adaptable, and there are a great many sea creatures that have become transparent to the point of invisibility, and a few insects."

He turned and gazed back as the city dwindled to a tiny speck in an endless expanse of white salt.

"It really is a pity that we couldn't keep the body to study. I would have liked to learn how it managed to eat during the centuries after it devoured the inhabitants of the city, and whether its eyes were atavistic or acquired. A remarkable specimen! Nonetheless," said Master Li, "I do not think that we will mourn its passing."

20.
The Cavern of Bells

Hour after hour the palm-leaf blades whirled overhead and flames and smoke spurted out behind us as the incredible Bamboo Dragonfly flew across the searing white salt. We used our tunics to guide us around whirlwinds, and the heat from the desert was like fiery fingers that pushed us higher and higher into the sky. With the last light of the setting sun, Miser Shen pointed ahead to a long dark line on the horizon.

"Those are trees!" he exclaimed. "The Desert of Salt is coming to an end."

The best proof of that lay in the dark clouds that were building up. Lightning flickered in the distance, and I doubted that it had rained in the desert for a thousand years.

"Gentlemen, we could be in bad trouble if the basket that we're riding in fills with water," Li Kao pointed out.

We pried three bamboo pieces from the framework at the bottom of the basket, which not only made a drainage hole but also provided us with three poles for umbrellas. Thin strips from the circular rim provided the frames, and our trousers served as the covers. We finished just in time. Lightning flashed and thunder roared and rain fell in torrents, but we clutched our umbrellas and sailed through the storm quite comfortably.

"I have always wanted to fly through a thunderstorm!" Master Li shouted happily.

"Magnificent!" Miser Shen and I yelled as one.

It really was spectacular, and we were rather disappointed when the storm passed and the moon and stars came out. Wind whistled around our ears and a river gleamed like silver far below us. The Bamboo Dragonfly flew steadily on, and flames and smoke spurted out behind us as we drifted gently across the deep purple sky of China; a tiny spark that flickered beneath the glow of a million billion trillion stars.

Miser Shen dozed off, and then Master Li, and I rode through the night staring up at the stars and down at the moonlit earth far below. The sensation of flight was far different from that which I had experienced in my dreams, and to tell the truth, I far preferred dream flight. Then I was like a bird, using the wind like the current of a stream, delighting in almost total freedom, but now I was simply a passenger riding in a basket beneath whirling blades, and I silently chided myself for being too cloddish to appreciate properly an experience that was very close to being miraculous. Master Li was also chiding himself, as I learned when he began to mutter in his sleep, but for a different reason.

"Fool," he muttered. "Blind as a bat. Use your head." Then he shifted restlessly and scratched his nose. "Why not *on* the island, waiting at the end of the bridge?" he muttered angrily. "Stupid! Makes no sense."

He fell silent again, and it occurred to me that if he was dreaming about the Hand That No One Sees, he had a good reason to think that it made no sense. Assuming that the Hand guarded the duke's treasure trove, as the tide had guarded the first one, why not put the monster on the island silently and invisibly waiting at the other end of that narrow bridge? Anyone who approached the treasure would simply be serving breakfast in bed to a hungry spider.

"Children," Master Li muttered, restlessly turning and shifting. "Games. Stupid or childish? A little boy?"

He sighed and his breathing grew more regular, and then I heard nothing but deep snores. Miser Shen was dreaming too, and a tear was trickling down the sharp curve of his nose. He was making faint sounds, and I leaned close.

"Ah Chen," he whispered, "your father is here."

He said no more, and finally I too fell asleep. When I awoke I discovered that we were flying through pink and orange clouds, pale against a turquoise sky, and the morning sun was shining upon mountain peaks all around us as Li Kao and Miser Shen used their tunics to guide the Bamboo Dragonfly through a narrow pass where fantastic trees precariously perched, spreading their branches to capture wisps of clouds and to weave them into the patterns of dreams, like the landscapes of Mei Fei. I yawned and spread my tunic behind me like a rudder, and we passed so close to one high jagged peak that I let go with one hand and reached out and scooped up a handful of snow, which tasted delicious. Then we sailed through the pass and began to fly over a beautiful green valley, where tiny wisps of smoke drifted up from fields where farmers were burning weeds, and the breeze was fragrant with wet earth and trees and grass and flowers.

Around mid-morning the tubes of Fire Drug began to sputter and fizzle. The palm-leaf blades whirled slower and slower, and we began to descend toward a small village nestled beside a broad river. You may be sure that peasants gathered from miles around to watch the gradual descent of a fire-breathing bird from Heaven. We hovered above the village square, and the Fire Drug produced one final spurt of flame and puff of black smoke, and then we settled lightly to earth. The crowd gaped at three Chinese gentlemen, tastefully attired in loincloths and money belts, who stepped grandly from the basket clutching umbrellas.

"My surname is Li and my personal name is Kao, and there is a slight flaw in my character," said Master Li with a polite bow. "This is my esteemed client, Number Ten Ox, and this is Old Generosity, formerly known as Miser Shen. We hereby donate the incredible Bamboo Dragonfly to your delightful village. Build a fence around it! Charge admission! Your fortunes shall be made. And now you may direct us to the nearest wineshop, for we intend to stay drunk for a week."

Miser Shen would have liked to do just that, but by some incredible stroke of luck our flying machine had brought us very close to the Cavern of Bells. It was only a short distance downstream, so we bought a boat and shoved off into the current, and two days later Miser Shen pointed ahead.

"Stone Bell Mountain," he said. "The entrance to the Cavern of Bells is at the water's edge, and we should be able to sail right inside."

Li Kao nudged my arm.

"Ox, I have heard that the duke's tax trip takes him past Stone Bell Mountain," he whispered. "If the painting in the Cavern of Bells is as Miser Shen described it, then the Duke of Ch'in may have more than a casual interest in the place."

I remembered his earlier warning, and I peered around fearfully for two-hundred-foot armor-plated winged water moccasins as our little boat glided through the dark entrance. But then I cried out in wonder and delight. It was like sailing into one of those beautiful undersea palaces in Buddhist fairy tales. Sunlight from the entrance struck emerald water that glittered like green fire, and then the rays bounced up the stone walls that were studded with crystals that sparkled with every color of the spectrum. It was a world wrapped in rainbows. The strangest rocks that I had ever seen pointed up through the water and down from the roof. They were like spears, but turned around so that the thick handles pointed out. Li Kao had never visited the cavern before, but he had read a great deal about it.

"The bell stones," he said. "When the water rises, it strikes the stones on the bottom, which ring like bells, and the vibration causes the stones on the ceiling to respond with bell sounds of their own. The phenomenon is called sympathetic resonance. Deeper in the cavern are other stones formed from soft rock, through which tiny holes have been worn, and when the water rushes through the holes it provides more music to accompany the bells. Su Tung-po has written an interesting monograph on the subject."

We reached a wooden pier and tied our boat to one of the posts. A flight of stone stepes led up to the great hall of the cavern, where a shrine had been set up. We appeared to be the only visitors, and the shrine was tended by four monks. Three of them wore black robes, and the fourth wore crimson, and the one in crimson came trotting up. He was a tiny fellow with a high squeaking voice.

"May Buddha be with you," he said with a deep bow. "I am the custodian of the Temple of the Peddler, and my three brother monks belong to a different order nearby. In the passage to your left you will find the sacred painting of the deity of the Cavern of Bells. It is very ancient and very mysterious, and neither I nor my predecessors truly understand it. It is undeniably divine, and I live in hopes that some day a visitor will be able to explain it to me. May you be the wise visitors I seek," he said with another bow. "Will you forgive me if I do not accompany you? My brothers and I are slowly going mad as we attempt to balance our subscription books."

The little monk pattered back to join the others, and we walked down the passageway that he had indicated. At the end of it there were flickering torches that framed something upon the wall, and Miser Shen pointed to it.

"The painting that I spoke of," he said, while Li Kao and I stared at ghosts.

There could be no question about it. The painting depicted an old peddler with his back to us who was facing the murdered maiden whose ghost we had seen at the Castle of the Labyrinth. To her left stood the murdered maiden whose ghost had appeared on the island, and to her right stood a third girl who could have been their sister.

Li Kao snatched one of the torches from the brackets

and went over the painting inch by inch. The peddler's robe was covered with colored pearls and lotus blossoms, and he was supported by a crutch beneath his left armpit. His hands were extended to the maidens. In the left hand he held three tiny white feathers, and in the right hand he held a miniature flute and crystal ball that were precisely like the ones in Li Kao's belt, as well as a tiny bronze bell. The painting was very ancient, but what did it mean?

"The emblems on the lame peddler's robe usually signify Heaven, in which case this might be a painting of T'ieh-kuai Li, the Fourth Immortal," Master Li said thoughtfully. "But two things are wrong, and one of them rules out such an interpretation. He should be carrying a large calabash on his back, and he could not possibly be leaning upon a wooden crutch. After all, the name means Li with the Iron Crutch."

He went back over the painting, with his eyes no more than an inch from the surface.

"On the other hand, the emblems on the robe can signify the supernatural, and that includes the evil supernatural," he muttered. "We know that two of the girls were murdered, and I am willing to lay enormous odds against the possibility that the third girl died peacefully in bed. The maddening thing is that I can find no trace of something that should be included."

I looked at him inquiringly.

"Ginseng," he explained. "Ox, for some mysterious reason our quest for the Great Root and the ghosts of the handmaidens are linked together, and so are the games of children, the village of Ku-fu, Dragon's Pillow, nonsense rhymes, feathers, birds that must fly, the Duke of Ch'in—all of the dukes, come to think of it—and Buddha knows what else."

He straightened up and shrugged.

"If we ever figure it out, it should make a marvelous story," he sighed. "Let's go see if those monks can tell us something useful."

The three monks in black had disappeared, but the little monk in crimson was more than helpful. "No, we have never been able to grasp the meaning of the trinkets and the feathers," he said. "The feathers are particularly puzzling, because there is another painting deeper in the cavern that depicts feathers. It is so old that most of the paint has worn away, but one can clearly make out feathers and the symbol of the constellation Orion. Again I have no idea what it means."

Li Kao's eyes were sparkling. "Ox, in ancient times a roof, three beams, and the number three formed the ideograph for Orion. It was also used to signify ginseng, particularly when the symbol for heart was at the point of the beams, and that would mean the Heart of the Great Root of Power," he whispered.

I was beginning to catch some of his excitement myself, and we eagerly followed the little monk to the opening of another tunnel. He offered us torches from the wall brackets.

"You will find the painting at the end, and in the meantime you will learn why we are certain that the Peddler is divine," he said. "Fortunately you have arrived during the rainy season, and the water has begun to rise in the Peddler's cavern. Soon it will strike the bell stones, and only Heaven could produce such music. The stones are deep beneath the tunnel, but there are side passages that will enable you to hear the music clearly."

Miser Shen's previous visit had been during the wrong season for bell music, and he was rather skeptical about it. As we moved down the low dark tunnel the slap of our sandals was joined by the sound of water lapping against rocks, far below us and to the left side. Then the water rose high enough and we knew that the monk had not lied. This was the music of Heaven.

A stone bell chimed. Just as the echo was fading away it was answered by a second bell that was soft and sweet and slightly blurred, as though the sound were sifted through honey. Another bell answered, higher and clearer and perfectly in harmony, and then bell after bell chimed in: big bells, small bells, loud bells, soft bells, clear bells, cloudy bells, and we walked along in enchantment while our torches cast immense shadows upon the stone walls.

I cannot describe the beauty of the stone bell song. Then the water reached the soft rocks and began to rush through tiny holes, and the bells were joined by the sound of a thousand silver lutes being stroked by a million murmuring bees. The combination of sounds was lifting our souls right out of our bodies, and ahead of us was a side passageway that was large enough to enter. The music poured from it, and we turned as one and trotted down the passageway toward the ravishing song. Tears were streaming down Miser Shen's cheeks. He began to run, with his arms spread wide to catch and embrace the music, and we were right at his heels while our shadows leaped and jumped all around us. A rock moved beneath Miser Shen's foot, and I heard a harsh metallic *whang*.

Miser Shen lifted into the air and flew backward into my arms, and I stared stupidly at the iron shaft of a crossbow bolt that was protruding from his chest.

21.
A Prayer to Ah Chen

We dived to the floor, but no more bolts flew. I laid an ear against Miser Shen's chest. His heart was still beating, but faintly. "The painting is a trap," Master Li whispered in my ear. "The acoustics of the tunnel permit the monks to hear what's being said, and when they heard that we recognized the maidens and linked them to the Duke of Ch'in, the monks in black slipped ahead to cock a crossbow and set the trigger."

He cautiously lifted his torch and waved it around, and finally we spotted it. A single crossbow, fixed in a wall bracket and aimed at the center of the passageway.

"Why only one?" Master Li muttered. He carefully felt beneath the stone that Miser Shen's foot had pressed. There was a metal rod which ran back beneath the surface of the path. "Ox, do you see that large flat white stone?" Master Li whispered. "It has raised slightly, and I rather believe that we are supposed to step on it as we run for our lives."

I picked up Miser Shen and we carefully inched around that stone as we made our way back to the main tunnel.

Li Kao picked up rocks and hurled them, and on the third
try he hit the raised white stone. With a horrible crash a
good fifty feet of the roof collapsed, and a great cloud of
dust and whining splinters of rock shot from the mouth
of the passageway. Anyone in there would have been
crushed like an ant beneath an elephant's foot.

"We can't trust the acoustics," Li Kao whispered in
my ear. "If we go back, they'll probably be ready for us.
We have to follow the tunnel and trust to luck."

He led the way with a torch in one hand and his knife
in the other. The tunnel was sloping up, and the beautiful
bell song was growing fainter. The only other sounds were
the hiss of the torch and the slap of our sandals, and then
Miser Shen groaned. His eyes opened, but they were
feverish and puzzled and he did not seem to recognize
us. We stopped and I set him down, with his back propped
against the tunnel wall, and his lips moved.

"You are the priest?" he said hoarsely to Li Kao. "My
little girl has been murdered by the Duke of Ch'in, and
they tell me that I will feel better if I burn a prayer and
send it to her, but I do not know how to write."

For Miser Shen it was forty years ago, when the death
of his daughter had begun to drive him insane.

"I am the priest," Master Li said quietly. "I will write
down your prayer for you."

Miser Shen's lips moved silently, and I sensed that he
was rehearsing. Finally he was ready, and he made a
terrible effort to concentrate on what he wanted to say
to his daughter. This is the prayer of Miser Shen.

"Alas, great is my sorrow. Your name is Ah Chen, and
when you were born I was not truly pleased. I am a
farmer, and a farmer needs strong sons to help with his
work, but before a year had passed you had stolen my
heart. You grew more teeth, and you grew daily in wisdom, and you said 'Mommy' and 'Daddy' and your pro-
nunciation was perfect. When you were three you would
knock at the door and then you would run back and ask,
'Who is it?' When you were four your uncle came to visit
and you played the host. Lifting your cup, you said,
'Ching!' and we roared with laughter and you blushed and

covered your face with your hands, but I know that you thought yourself very clever. Now they tell me that I must try to forget you, but it is hard to forget you.

"You carried a toy basket. You sat at a low stool to eat porridge. You repeated the Great Learning and bowed to Buddha. You played at guessing games, and romped around the house. You were very brave, and when you fell and cut your knee you did not cry because you did not think it was right. When you picked up fruit or rice, you always looked at people's faces to see if it was all right before putting it in your mouth, and you were careful not to tear your clothes.

"Ah Chen, do you remember how worried we were when the flood broke our dikes and the sickness killed our pigs? Then the duke of Ch'in raised our taxes and I was sent to plead with him, and I made him believe that we could not pay our taxes. Peasants who cannot pay taxes are useless to dukes, so he sent his soldiers to destroy our village, and thus it was the foolishness of your father that led to your death. Now you have gone to Hell to be judged, and I know that you must be very frightened, but you must try not to cry or make loud noises because it is not like being at home with your own people.

"Ah Chen, do you remember Auntie Yang, the midwife? She was also killed, and she was very fond of you. She had no little girls of her own, so it is all right for you to try to find her, and to offer her your hand and ask her to take care of you. When you come before the Yama Kings, you should clasp your hands together and plead to them: 'I am young and I am innocent. I was born in a poor family, and I was content with scanty meals. I was never willfully careless of my shoes and my clothing, and I never wasted a grain of rice. If evil spirits bully me, may thou protect me.' You should put it just that way, and I am sure that the Yama Kings will protect you.

"Ah Chen, I have soup for you and I will burn paper money for you to use, and the priest is writing down this prayer that I will send to you. If you hear my prayer, will you come to see me in my dreams? If fate so wills that you must yet lead an earthly life, I pray that you will come again to your mother's womb. Meanwhile I will cry, 'Ah Chen, your father is here!' I can but weep for you, and call your name."*

Miser Shen fell silent. I thought that he had died, but then he opened his eyes again.

"Did I say it right?" he whispered. "I practiced for a long time, and I wanted to say it right, but I am confused in my mind and something seems to be wrong."

"You said it perfectly," Master Li said quietly.

Miser Shen appeared to be greatly relieved. His eyes closed and his breathing grew fainter. Then he coughed, and blood spurted from his lips and the soul of Miser Shen departed from the red dust of earth.

We knelt beside Miser Shen and clasped our hands. In my mind the image of Ah Chen was mingled with the images of the children of Ku-fu and I could not speak through my tears, but the voice of Li Kao was firm and strong.

"Miser Shen, great is your joy," he said. "Now you are released from the prison of your body, and your soul is reunited with little Ah Chen. Surely the Yama Kings will allow you to be reborn as a tree, and for miles around the poor peasants will know you as Old Generosity."

I finally found my tongue.

"Miser Shen, if fate so wills that I am reunited with Lotus Cloud, I will tell her your story, and she will weep for you and she will not forget you, and so long as I live you will live in the heart of Number Ten Ox."

We said prayers together and made the symbolic sacrifice, but we could not bury the body in solid rock, so we begged his spirit to forgive us for not observing the customary decencies. Then we stood up and bowed, and Li Kao picked up the torch.

---

*Lin Yutang has translated Miser Shen's prayer to Ah Chen slightly differently. See *The Importance of Understanding* (World Publishing Co., New York, 1960).

"Master Li, if you ride on my back we can move quickly if we have to make a run for it," I suggested.

He climbed up and I started down the tunnel. It continued to slope upward, and in an hour the song of the bells faded away. (If any of my readers happen to be in the vicinity, I urge them to visit the Cavern of Bells, because the music truly comes from Heaven and was simply put to evil use by evil men who are no longer with us.) The beautiful song had just dwindled into silence when I turned a corner in the tunnel, and the light from the torch in Li Kao's hand reached out to touch a familiar figure. The little monk in the crimson robe was standing in front of us with a smirk on his face.

"Stop, you idiot! Have you learned nothing from the death of Miser Shen?" Master Li yelled as I leaped forward.

I tried to pull up, but it was too late. My hands were outstretched to strangle the monk and my weight was forward, and I took one more step and landed upon a reed mat that had been cleverly painted to resemble rock. I fell through it as though it were water, and tumbled down head over heels and landed with a crash that knocked the breath from my body. The torch fell with us, and when I had recovered enough to look around I saw that we had fallen into a pit that was about eight feet wide and fifteen feet deep, with walls made from large stone slabs fitted tightly together. I heard a grating metallic sound and looked up, and my heart nearly stopped beating.

The little monk was pulling a heavy chain with all his might, and an iron lid was slowly sliding across the top of the pit.

Li Kao's hand was cocked behind his right ear. "A present from Miser Shen!" he yelled, and torchlight glinted upon the blade of his knife as it flashed through the air. The monk dropped the chain. He clutched at his throat and clawed at the hilt that was buried there, and his eyes rolled to the top of his head and blood spurted, and he gurgled horribly and toppled over the edge of the pit.

I lifted my hands to catch him, but he never landed. His legs became entangled in the chain and he jerked to a halt in midair, and I gasped as I saw that his weight was pulling the iron lid farther and farther across the opening of the pit, and then it slammed shut with a harsh metallic clang. In an instant I had grabbed the chain and had climbed up over the dangling monk. I shoved at the lid with all my might, but it was wasted effort. That sheet of iron had slid into grooves in solid rock, and I had no leverage at all.

"Master Li, I can't budge it!" I panted.

I dropped back to the floor, which was solid stone. Our torch was burning yellow, but soon it would burn orange, and then blue, and then it wouldn't burn at all. The last thing that we would see before we suffocated would be the blackness of the tomb.

I have a horror of small closed places. *"Saparah, tar-ata, mita, prajna, para—"* I mumbled hoarsely.

"Oh, stop that mumbo-jumbo and get to work," Master Li said testily. "I have no objection to Buddhism, but at least you can babble in a civilized language—either that or learn something about the one that you're massacring."

He picked up a couple of rocks and handed me one. Li Kao worked carefully around the circumference of the pit, tapping the slabs in the walls, while I climbed the chain and tapped the slabs higher up. On his second tour around the walls Li Kao heard a faint hollow echo as he rapped with his rock. He peered closely and saw that the slab had not been perfectly cut and joined, and that a tiny strip of mortar ran around the edges.

I jumped down, and he turned and bowed politely to the dangling corpse. "Many thanks for returning my knife to me," he said, and he jerked the knife from the monk's throat, which produced quite a mess on the floor. Half an hour later the mortar was gone and the slab was loose, but how were we supposed to work it out of the hole? My large clumsy fingers couldn't possibly fit into those narrow cracks, and even Li Kao's fingers were too large. When he tried to shift the slab with his knife, the only result was that the blade snapped in half. We were no better off than before, and that damned dangling monk was grinning at us. I growled and slapped the silly smile on his face, and as the corpse swung back and forth the creaking chain produced a sound like mocking laughter.

Li Kao watched the monk with narrowed eyes. "Ox, smack him again," he commanded.

I smacked the corpse again, and the chain laughed even louder as it creaked back and forth.

"Got it," said Master Li. "Something about our dear friend was trying to speak to me when I watched him swing around. Unless I'm greatly mistaken, he was born for the job of pulling stones from walls."

I shoved the little monk over to the slab, and his tiny fingers easily slid into the cracks. I forced the fingers in as far as possible and pressed his thumbs around the edges and held them tight. How long I squeezed the cold corpse hands I cannot say, but it seemed several eternities before the body turned rigid. It was our last chance. The flickering flame of the torch was turning blue when I gently pulled the monk backward. His fingers clutched that slab with the rigid grasp of death, and the slab slid out with no effort at all and crashed to the floor.

We did not rejoice. No fresh air had come out of the hole with the slab, and when Master Li inserted the torch, we saw a long low tunnel with many passageways branching out on both sides.

"It's another labyrinth, but my old lungs won't last much longer," Li Kao panted, and I could believe it because his face was nearly as blue as the torchlight. "Ox, tie me to your back with the cord from the monk's robe. We'll have to extinguish the torch, so you must follow the dragon by feel."

I tied him to my back, and we barely fit through the hole in the wall, and when Li Kao extinguished the torch my throat constricted so tightly that I nearly suffocated then and there. Blackness was pressing down upon me like a heavy shroud as I began to crawl, and what little air was left was foul. My fingers traced the path of the green jade dragon as it wound through the holes in the red coral pendant, while I groped for openings in the walls with the other hand. Third left . . . First left . . . Fourth right . . . Li Kao was almost unconscious, and the words that he muttered faintly in my ear made no sense.

"Ox . . . not a tiger but a little boy . . . games . . . rules of games . . ."

Then he sighed, and his body lay limply upon my back, and I could scarcely sense a heartbeat. There was nothing to do but crawl ahead, and my own consciousness was slipping away with every gasp of my aching lungs, and death was beckoning me to join my parents in the Yellow Springs Beneath the Earth. Second right . . . Second left . . .

"Master Li, the dragon can lead us no farther!" I panted.

There was no answer. The ancient sage was out cold, if not dead, and now everything depended upon the slow wits of Number Ten Ox, but what was I to do? The last direction of the dragon had led me against the stone wall of a dead end, and the dragon had wound all the way to the bottom of the pendant. It went no farther, so how could I? To turn back would be suicide, and I frantically felt around in the darkness. There was nothing but smooth unbroken stone, although my fingers found one small crack in the floor that might have been big enough for a mouse. Nothing else. No slab with mortar around the edges, no lever to pull, no keyhole. I lowered my head and wept.

It was some time before I was able to think about the strange words that Master Li had muttered in my ear, and even longer before I remembered how he had muttered in his sleep while we flew on the Bamboo Dragonfly. "Why not on the island, waiting at the end of the bridge?" he had muttered. "Games. A little boy?" Was he saying that the duke was not the Tiger of Ch'in but a child, and that the Hand That No One Sees had not been waiting for victims at the end of the narrow bridge on the oasis because the victims would have no chance, and that would ruin a game?

My head seemed to be packed with wool, and my ears were ringing. In my mind I saw the dying face of Miser Shen as he prayed to his little girl. "You played at guessing games. . . . You played at guessing games. . . . Guessing games . . . Guessing games . . ."

What was the name of the game that we were playing with the Duke of Ch'in? Follow the Dragon, that's what, and what is the rule that a child must learn when playing a follow game? Keep following. Never assume and never give up. You *can* continue to follow, if only you try hard enough. The dragon had stopped, but was it possible that it could still go somewhere, and somehow I would be able to follow?

My fingers crawled across the floor to that one tiny crack in the stone. It was a couple of inches long and irregularly oval. Lack of air had turned me into a small child, and I actually giggled as I removed the red coral pendant from the chain around my neck. It was a couple of inches long and irregularly oval, and it fit precisely into the crack.

"Follow the dragon," I giggled, and I released the pendant.

The dragon dropped down. I waited for the sound when it landed, and waited and waited, and finally, far below, I heard a click as though it had landed like a key in a lock, and then I heard a second click, as though tumblers had turned.

The stone floor tilted beneath me. I slid toward a side wall, and as the floor tilted more steeply a hole opened, and then I followed the dragon, with Master Li tied to my back, shooting out and down into moonlight and starlight and air. My lungs felt as though they were touched with fire as I gulped and gasped, and Master Li moaned softly, and I felt his lungs began to heave. We tumbled down the side of a steep hill and landed upon something that glittered.

Moonlight shone down upon a tiny glade, sunken way down in the center of Stone Bell Mountain, and upon an immense mountain of treasure. Instinctively my eyes lifted to the top of the pile to a shadow where no shadow should be. Then the third girl from that painting was gazing at me beseechingly, and blood stained her dress where a blade had pierced her heart.

"Take pity upon a faithless handmaiden," she whispered. Ghost tears trickled slowly down her cheeks. "Is not a thousand years enough?" she sobbed. "I swear that I did not know what I had done! Oh, take pity, and exchange this for the feather. The birds must fly."

Then she was gone.

I crawled up a slope of diamonds and ripped the lid from the small jade casket that the ghost had cradled in her hands. Ginseng aroma stung my nostrils, but it was not the Heart of The Great Root of Power. It was the Head, and beside it lay a tiny bronze bell.

My heart sank wearily and I closed my eyes, and sleep cradled me like a baby. I did not dream at all.

Part Three

The Princess of Birds

22.
The Dream of the White Chamber

Night rain is falling on the village of Ku-fu, glinting through moonbeams that slide through thin clouds, and the soft splashing sound outside my window blends with the drip of ink from the mouse-whiskered tip of my writing brush. I have been trying as hard as I can, but I am unable to express my emotions when the Arms and the Head of Power brought the children back from death's doorstep, and then failed to complete the cure.

Once more they awoke, but into the strange world of the Hopping Hide and Seek Game, and once more they smiled and laughed and chanted the nonsense rhyme from Dragon's Pillow. Then once more they yawned, and their eyes closed, and they sank back upon their beds. Once more they dropped into the depths of their trances.

People with nothing else to turn to must revert to the superstitions of their ancestors, and grandparents began to tie mirrors to the children's foreheads so that the demons of sickness would see the reflections of their own ugly faces and flee in terror. Fathers shouted their children's names while they waved favorite toys tied to long poles, hoping to entice the wandering souls, and mothers stood tensely at the bedsides with cords that would tie the souls to the bodies should they return. I turned and ran into the abbot's study and slammed the door.

Nothing but the Heart of the Great Root of Power could save the children of my village. I was sick with fear, and my eyes lifted to a framed quotation from The Study of the Ancients:

> *All things have a root and a top,*
> *All events an end and a beginning;*
> *Whoever understands correctly*
> *What comes first and what follows*
> *Draws nearer to Tao.*

I was a long way from drawing nearer to Tao, and children's games and nonsense rhymes and ginseng roots and birds and feathers and flutes and balls and bells and agonized ghosts and terrible monsters and the Duke of Ch'in whirled round and round in my brain without making any sense at all.

The door opened and Li Kao walked into the study. He drank three cups of wine, one after another, and then he sat down across from me and took the little bronze bell from his belt and gently rang it.

We listened to the beat of a drum, and then the beautifully trained voice of a young woman began to chant and sing the story of the great courtesan who grew old, and who was forced into the indignity of marrying a businessman. A second ring of the bell produced a lively tempo, and the hilariously pornographic tale of Golden Lotus. A third ring brought sarcasm and suppressed rage, and the story of Pi Kan, who was put to death because an idiot emperor wanted to see if it was true that the heart of a wise man is pierced by seven openings.

We had a flute that told fairy tales, a ball that showed funny pictures, and a bell that sang Flower Drum Songs. And we were supposed to exchange them for feathers.

Li Kao sighed. He replaced the bell in his belt and poured another cup of wine.

"I am going to complete this task if I have to unscrew the roots of the sacred mountains, hoist a sail on top of Taishan, and steer the world across the Great River of Stars to the Gates of the Great Void," he said grimly. "Ox, the slight flaw in my character has proved to be a godsend. When I run into something that is really foul, I can counter with the potential for foulness that resides in the depths of my soul, and that is why I can go into a place like the Cavern of Bells and come out of it with a song on my lips. You, on the other hand, suffer from an incurable case of purity of heart."

He paused to consider his words carefully, but I was ahead of him.

"Master Li, it would take twenty tons of Fire Drug to pry me loose from the quest," I said as firmly as I could, which was not very firmly. "Besides, we'll have to try to get to the Key Rabbit, and that means Lotus Cloud, and I will happily battle a tiger for the honor of hopping into her bed."

To my astonishment I discovered that what I had said was true. It was amazing what a tonic the thought of Lotus Cloud was, and I stared in wonder at hands that were no longer shaking.

"I will battle a regiment of tigers," I said with real conviction.

Li Kao looked at me curiously. We sat in silence while the sound of two fighting cats drifted into the room, and then the sound of Auntie Hua going after them with a broom. Li Kao shrugged and reached out and pressed a finger to my forehead, and quoted Lao-tzu.

"Blessed are the idiots, for they are the happiest people on earth. Very well, both of us will commit suicide, but it's Ching Ming and you must honor your dead. We'll leave in the morning," he said.

I bowed and left him to his thoughts. I took some food and wine from the bonzes' pantry and went out into the bright sunshine, and I borrowed a hoe and a rake and a broom from the tool-shed. It was the most perfect spring imaginable, glorious weather for the Festival of Tombs, and I made my way to my parents' graves. I raked and pruned and swept until their resting place was spotless, and then I made an offering of food and wine. I had saved the tassels and ornaments from the fine hat that I had worn during our visit to the Ancestress, and the silver belt with the jade trim and the gold-spattered fan. I placed the tassels and ornaments and belt in the bowl that I used for special offerings. Then I knelt to pray. I asked my mother and father to send me courage so that I would not disgrace my ancestors, and I felt much better when I had finished. Then I got to my feet and ran toward the eastern hills.

Centuries ago the great family of the Lius had ruled our valley. The estate still stood at the crest of the largest hill, although the house was seldom visited by the owners now, and gardeners still maintained the famous park that had been lovingly described by such writers as Tsao Hsueh Chin and Kao Ngoh. I knew it like the back of my hand, and I crawled through my secret tunnel in the high wall into a gardener's paradise. The ground was shimmering with yellow chrysanthemums, and the hills were thick with silver poplars and nodding aspens. A stream arched down the side of a cliff in a foaming waterfall that splashed into a bright blue lake. The banks were lined with flowering peach, and chiching trees with violet flowers growing directly from the trunks and branches, and behind them was a shady bamboo grove, and then the pear trees, and then a thousand apricot trees that were flaming with a million scarlet blossoms.

I followed the path around the moon terraces, and then turned off to a rough trail that led down through deep gorges with creepers and moss-covered great gray rocks. The trail dropped sharply down to the darkness of a cypress grove, where a quiet stream rippled past the Sandbank Harbor of Blossoming Purity, and I crawled beneath some low bushes and untied a small boat. I climbed in and pushed off, and drifted down a long winding gorge where willows bent their branches to brush the water, and spirit creepers wound over rocks, and clusters of fruit like red coral peeped beneath frost-blue foliage.

When I had tied the boat to a tree trunk and picked

up the trail again, it climbed toward bright clearings where winding brooks sparkled in green meadows, and always I reached hills or rocks that blocked the view and then opened to even more beautiful vistas on the other side. The path climbed steeply through masses of boulders toward a great glorious rock that reached to the clouds, and on the other side was another gorge that was spanned by a narrow wooden bridge. Then the path climbed again, and suddenly leveled to a small ridge where orchids grew, and orioles sang, and grasshoppers chirped in the bright sunshine. Far below I could see my village, spread out like a picture from a book.

At the end of the ridge was a willow grove. I slipped inside to a small green glade where a single grave lay among the wildflowers.

The head gardener's daughter was buried there. Her name had been Scented Hairpin, but since she had been a shy, quiet girl, who was timid with strangers, everyone had called her Mouse. She had the most beautiful eyes that I had ever seen, and she had not been timid when we played the Hopping Hide and Seek Game. Mouse almost always lasted longest and became the queen, and she had also not been timid when she decided that some day we would be man and wife. She had fallen ill when she was thirteen. Her parents had let me hold her hand on her deathbed, and she had whispered the last words of Mei Fei: "I came from the land of Fragrance; to the Land of Fragrance I now return."

I knelt at the grave. "Mouse, it is Number Ten Ox, and I have something for you," I said.

I placed the gold-spattered Szech'uen fan in her offering bowl, and I prayed, and then I sat on the grass in the golden sunlight that filtered through the leaves and told her my story. I could not explain it, but somehow I knew that Mouse wouldn't mind the fact that I was in love with Lotus Cloud. I poured out my heart and felt it grow lighter, and the sun was setting as I finished. The breeze always picked up at the approach of evening, and I stayed to watch the willows.

Mouse's heartbroken father had used his art to honor

his daughter. The wind sighed through the trees, and the willows began to bend, and then one branch after another reached out and gently swept the young girl's grave.

That night I had a very strange dream. At first it was a tangle of images: Henpecked Ho weeping with a silver comb in his hands, and Bright Star dancing down the path toward a door that always closed, and Miser Shen praying to his daughter, and the Hand of Hell and the Cavern of Bells. Again and again I fled from a great golden tiger mask, and then I ran through a door into a world of whiteness, milky and soft and glowing, and I felt comfortable and safe. Something was forming in the whiteness. I smiled happily, because Mouse had come to see me. She carried the Szech'uen fan, and her beautiful young eyes looked fondly at me.

"How happy I am," she said softly. "Ever since we held hands and recited the Orphan's Song, I knew that you would fall in love with Lotus Cloud."

"Mouse, I love you too," I said.

"You must trust your heart," she said gravely. "Ox, you have grown very strong. Now you must use all of your strength to touch the queen before the count reaches forty-nine. It must not each forty-nine, which can mean for ever and ever and ever." Mouse was fading back into the milky whiteness. "Is not a thousand years enough?" she said faintly, as though from very far away. "The birds must fly.... The birds must fly.... The birds must fly...."

Mouse was gone, and for some reason I knew that it was important for me to understand the glowing whiteness around me. Suddenly I understood that the world was white because I was inside a giant pearl, and with awareness came awakening, and I sat up and blinked in the morning sunlight.

23.
Doctor Death

"*The extraordinary effect of the tendrils of the Great Root* leads to a basic assumption, and that is that the Heart of Power is indeed the ultimate healing agent in the whole world," said Master Li. "The Duke of Ch'in would never hide such a thing in a treasure trove where he might have to cross all China to get to it. He would keep it with him, right next to his loathsome skin, and you and I are going to have to murder the bastard and take the root from his corpse."

We were passing once more through the shadow of Dragon's Pillow, where crows gathered to watch us and make rude comments.

"Master Li, how are we going to murder a man who laughs at axes?" I asked.

"We are going to *experiment*, dear boy. Our first order of business will be to find a deranged alchemist, which should not be very difficult. China," said Master Li, "is overstocked with deranged alchemists."

In the city of Pingtu, Li Kao examined the faces of

street vendors until he found an old lady with gossip written all over her.

"A thousand pardons, Adoptive Daughter, but this humble one seeks an eminent scientist who may be living nearby," he said politely. "He is a devout Taoist, somewhat seedy in appearance and rather wild of eye, and there is an excellent chance that his house is placed halfway between a cemetery and a slaughterhouse."

"You seek Doctor Death!" the old lady gasped, fearfully glancing toward a ramshackle house that teetered at the top of a hill. "None but the criminally insane dare climb that path to his House of Horrors, and few ever return!"

He thanked her for the warning and started briskly up the path.

"Almost certainly a gross slander," Master Li said calmly. "Ox, Taoists are guided by a rather peculiar blend of mysticisms. On the one hand they exalt sages like Chuang Tzu, who taught that death and life, end and start are no more disconcerting than the passage of night and day, but on the other hand they engage in frantic quests for personal immortality. When a scientific genius becomes involved in the mystical mumbojumbo, the result is likely to be a lunatic whose quest for eternal life massacres everything in sight, but such poor souls wouldn't willingly harm a fly. Besides," he added, "it's a perfect day for a visit to a House of Horrors."

There I could agree with him. Trees in the cemetery sighed in the wind like a moan of mourners, and behind the slaughterhouse a dog howled horribly. Black clouds muttered dark spells above the mountains, and sulphurous lightning streaked the sky, and the ramshackle house upon the hill creaked and groaned in a rising gale that dripped with a thin, weeping rain. We walked through the open door into a room that was littered with carcasses, and where a little old man with a bloodstained beard was attempting to install a pig's heart into a man's cadaver, while cauldrons burped and kettles bubbled and seething vials emitted green and yellow vapors.

Doctor Death sprinkled the heart with purple powder

and made mystical gestures with his hands. "Beat!" he commanded. Nothing happened, so he tried yellow powder. "Beat, beat, beat!" He tried blue powder. "Ten thousand curses, why won't you beat?" he yelled, and then he turned around "Who you?" asked Doctor Death.

"My surname is Li and my personal name is Kao, and there is a slight flaw in my character, and this is my esteemed client, Number Ten Ox," Master Li said with a polite bow.

"Well, my surname is Lo and my personal name is Chan, and I am rapidly losing patience with a corpse that absolutely refuses to be resurrected!" Doctor Death yelled, and then his face and voice softened until he looked to be as gentle as a snowflake and as innocent as a banana. "If I cannot resurrect a stubborn corpse, how can I hope to resurrect my beloved wife?" he said softly.

He turned toward a coffin that had been set up as a shrine, and tears trickled down his cheeks.

"She was not pretty, but she was the most wonderful wife in the world," he whispered. "Her name was Chiang-chao, and we were very poor, but she could make the most delicious meals from a handful of rice and the herbs that she picked in the woods. She sang beautiful songs to cheer me when I was depressed, and she sewed dresses for wealthy ladies to help pay for my studies. We were very happy together, and I know that we will be happy together again. *Don't worry, my love, I'll have you out of that coffin in no time!*" he yelled.

He turned back to us.

"It's simply a matter of finding the purest ingredients, because I already have an infallible formula," he explained. "You use ten pounds of peach fuzz—"

"Ten pounds of tortoise hairs," said Master Li.

"Ten pounds of plum skins—"

"Ten pounds of rabbit horns—"

"Ten pounds of membranes of living chickens—"

"One large spoonful of mercury—"

"One large spoonful of oleander juice—"

"Two large spoonfuls of arsenic oxide—"

"For the toxin generates the antitoxin—"

"And in death there is life, as in life there is death."

"A colleague!" Doctor Death cried happily, and he wrapped Li Kao in a bloody embrace. "Tell me, Venerable One, do you know of some better method? This one is bound to work sooner or later, but it has been such a very long time, and I fear that my dear wife is growing weary of her coffin."

"Alas, I am only aware of the classic formula," Master Li sighed. "My own specialty is the Elixir of Life, but I foolishly left home without an adequate supply, which is why I have come to you."

"But how fortunate! I have just made a fresh batch." Doctor Death rummaged in a drawer and pulled out a greasy vial that was filled with thick purple liquid. "One spoonful after each meal and two at bedtime and you will surely live forever," he said. "I need scarcely mention to a colleague that the Elixir of Life can occasionally have distressing side effects, and that it is best to try it first on a rat."

"Or a cat," said Master Li.

"Or a crow."

"Or a cow."

"And if you happen to have a useless hippopotamus—"

"Actually, I was planning to try it on an elephant," said Master Li.

"A wise decision," Doctor Death said approvingly.

"A small donation," Master Li said, piling gold coins on a table between somebody's lymph glands and lungs. "May I suggest that you employ a professional grave robber? Digging up corpses can be terribly hard work."

Doctor Death looked down at the gold with a strange expression on his face, and his voice was so soft that I barely heard him.

"Once there was a poor scholar who needed to buy books, but he had no money," he whispered. "He sold everything he had to buy a tiny piece of gold, which he concealed in the hollow handle of an alchemist's ladle, and then he went to the house of a rich man and pretended to turn lead into gold. The rich man gave him money so that he could learn how to turn large pieces of lead into gold, and the scholar happily ran to the city to buy the books that he needed. When he returned he discovered that thieves had broken into his house. They had heard that he knew how to make gold, so they had tortured his wife to make her tell where he had hidden it. She was barely alive. He held her in his arms and wept, and she looked at him but she did not know him. 'But gentlemen,' she whispered, 'surely you do not mean to kill me? My husband is a brilliant scientist and a dear sweet kindly man, but he needs someone to look after him. What will he do when I am gone?' And then she died."

Doctor Death turned to the coffin and shouted, *"Don't worry, my love! Now I can afford to buy a better grade of corpses, and ..."* He clapped a hand to his mouth. "Oh dear!" he gasped, and he turned and trotted over to the cadaver on the table.

"I did not mean to offend you," he said contritely. "I'm sure that you will do splendidly, and perhaps it would help if you realized how important it is. You see, my wife was not pretty but she was the most wonderful wife in the world. Her name was Chiang-chao, and we were very poor, but she could make the most delicious meals from a handful of rice...."

He had forgotten that we existed, and we tiptoed out and started down the hill in the rain. Li Kao had been quite serious about trying the Elixir of Life on an elephant. At the bottom of the hill was a poor old beast that was used to haul logs to the sawmill, and its master was not kind. There were cruel goad marks on the elephant's shoulders, and it was nearly starved. We climbed the fence and Li Kao put one tiny drop of the Elixir on the tip of his knife blade.

"Do you consent?" he asked softly.

The elephant's sorrowful eyes were more eloquent than words—for the love of Buddha, they said, release me from the misery and return me to the Great Wheel of Transmigrations.

"So be it," said Master Li.

He gently pressed the blade against an open wound.

The elephant looked surprised for an instant. Then it hiccupped, hopped high into the air, landed on its back with a mighty crash, turned blue, and peacefully expired.

We raised reverent eyes to the House of Horrors.

"Genius!" we cried, and the thin rain wept softly, and an old, cracked, crazy voice drifted upon the cold wind:

> *In front of our window*
> *Are the banana trees we planted,*
> *Their green shadows fill the yard.*
> *Their green shadows fill the yard,*
> *Their leaves unfold and fold as if*
> *They wish to bare their feelings.*
>
> *Sadly reclining on my pillow*
> *Deep in the night I listen to the rain,*
> *Dripping on the leaves.*
> *Dripping on the leaves—*
> *That she can't hear that sound again*
> *Is breaking my heart.*

I decided that the oceans had been formed from tears, and when I thought of the tears that had been shed and the hearts that had been broken to serve the greed of the Duke of Ch'in, I was delighted that we were going after him with mayhem on our minds.

We caught up with the duke in Tsingtao, where he was staying at the palace of an enormously wealthy woman whose oldest son served as the duke's provincial governor, and with lavish bribes Li Kao arranged for us to slip past the guards one night. My heart was in my mouth as I grabbed the vines and began to climb, but then the breeze shifted, and an unmistakable fragrance reached my nostrils. I quivered all over.

"Lotus Cloud!" I planted. "Master Li, my heart will break if I don't see her!"

Under the circumstances there was little that he could do except swear and box my ears as I swung rapidly across the vines. When I lifted my head over the windowsill I saw that Lotus Cloud was all alone, but then my joy turned to ashes.

"What's wrong with you?" Master Li whispered.

"I forgot to bring my pearls and jade," I said miserably.

Li Kao sighed and fished in his pockets. At first he found only diamonds and emeralds, which didn't interest Lotus Cloud at all, but finally he came up with a pearl that he had saved because of its rarity: jet-black, with one small white flaw in the shape of a star. I would have preferred a ton of the stuff, but it was the symbol that mattered, so I leaned over and rolled the pearl across the floor toward my beloved's feet. Soon she will see it, I thought. She will look up and grin and yell, "Boopsie!" and all my cares will vanish.

She looked up all right, but not at me.

"Fear not, my turtledove!" some lout bellowed. "Your beloved Pooh-Pooh approaches with yet another hundred pounds of pearls and jade!"

The door crashed open and the provincial governor staggered inside with an armload of loot, which he dumped upon my black pearl. I sighed and sadly climbed back down the vines.

"Pooh-Pooh?" said Master Li. "Pooh-Pooh? Ox, it may be none of my business, but I must strongly advise you against getting involved with women who call their lovers Boopsie, Woofie, and Pooh-Pooh."

"She likes to keep pets," I explained.

"So I have noticed," he said. "Thank Heaven she doesn't keep all of you in the same kennel. The noise at feeding time would be deafening. And now, if you have no objection, I suggest that we return to the matter of disposing of the duke and getting that ginseng root."

I climbed rapidly to the duke's window and cautiously raised my eyes above the sill. The Duke of Ch'in was all alone in the room, seated upon a stool in front of a desk. Candlelight glinted upon his great golden tiger mask, and the feathers in his cloak shimmered like silver, but his gold mesh gloves lay upon the desk and his surprisingly small hands were bare as he added up on an abacus the amount of treasure that his tax trip had accumulated. Li Kao's eyes glistened as he looked at the duke's bare fingers.

"He lives for money, so he can die for money," he whispered.

He reached into his pocket and pulled out the most valuable of his diamonds. The moon was very bright. Part of the vines were wild rose, which I had been careful to avoid because of the thorns, and he found a sharp cluster just below the windowsill. Li Kao placed the diamond in the center, and turned it this way and that until the moonbeams caused it to explode with blue-white brilliance, and then he doused the thorns with the vial of the Elixir of Life.

I slid back until we were concealed behind vines, and Li Kao began scratching the stone wall with his dagger— a very annoying sound. For some time we heard only the click of the beads as they slid rapidly over the strings of the abacus, but then a table scraped against the floor as it slid back, and heavy footsteps approached the window. I held my breath.

The terrible tiger mask leaned out and peered down, and the diamond was sparkling like cold fire. The bare fingers hovered like a hawk, and then they pounced. I could clearly see punctures. At a modest estimate the Duke of Ch'in had received enough Elixir of Life to assassinate all of China and half of Korea and Japan, and I waited for him to topple over and turn blue. Instead he lifted the gem to the eye-slits in the mask and turned it appreciatively, and the metal voice that oozed through the mouthpiece held a definite note of pleasure.

"Cold!" whispered the Duke of Ch'in. "Cold... cold... cold..."

I was so stunned that I forgot to hold on to the vines, and we plunged forty feet before I managed to grab them again and break our fall. Unfortunately we were then dangling about ten feet above the heads of some soldiers who were leaning against the wall swapping war lies.

"Wait for a cloud," Master Li whispered.

It seemed forever, but eventually a black cloud cov-

ered the moon, and I swung over the vines to the nearest
window and crawled into a room that was pitch-black.
The darkness vibrated with heavy snores. Li Kao slipped
off my back and tiptoed across the floor and cracked the
door open. He closed it hurriedly.

"Soldiers guarding the halls," he whispered.

We started back toward the window and froze. That
damned cloud decided to move away from the moon, and
we were pinned in bright yellow beams, and the snores
stopped suddenly, and a grotesque figure sat up in bed
and leveled a gangrened finger.

"What have you done with that ginseng root?" roared
the Ancestress.

24.
There Are No Accidents in the Great Way of Tao

Soldiers dragged me across the floor toward the throne upon which sat the Duke of Ch'in, and thrust my face forward so that it practically touched the terrible mask. A hissing sound came from the mouthpiece as the clammy mind crawled over mine, and then the golden tiger jerked back.

The great and powerful Duke of Ch'in was terrified. Saliva trickled from the mouthpiece, and the gold-meshed gloves trembled upon the arms of the throne, and an acrid stench of fear stung my nostrils.

"I see the three handmaidens!" the metal voice whispered. "I see the ball and the bell and the flute! I see the Legs and the Arms and the Head of Power!"

The duke was trembling so hard that his cloak of feathers fluttered as if for flight, but he finally forced himself to lean forward once more. The slimy brain moved fearfully over mine, and then I sensed relief and growing joy.

"But I do not see the birds, or the feathers, or anything

else of importance," he said wonderingly. "I see only those useless children, and the right quest for the wrong reason. You and your antiquated companion have followed paths that cannot be followed, defeated guardians that cannot be defeated, escaped from places where escape was impossible, and you have not had the slightest idea of what you were really doing, or where you were really going, or why!"

Now the metal voice held a cruel gloating pleasure.

"You have managed to annoy me, and you shall discover what it means to annoy the Duke of Ch'in." The mask moved to the soldiers. "Take the old man and the boy to the torture chambers. They shall die by inches in the Shirts of Iron," he commanded.

Only the duke could have ordered such an execution, and I hasten to point out that in every other part of China the Shirts of Iron had long been relegated to museums that displayed the ghastly aberrations of the Dark Ages. Actually they aren't made from iron at all, but from steel mesh that can be uniformly tightened by means of a neck loop or a screw in back. The shirts are tightened around the victim's bare torso until flesh bulges through the holes in the mesh, and then the executioner picks up something hard and rough, a rock will do, and slowly scrapes across the shirt until there are no bulges. The flow of blood is carefully stopped, and the next day the shirt is shifted slightly and the process is repeated—and the next day and the next. A competent executioner can keep a victim alive for months, and the only hope the victim has is that he will go stark staring mad fairly early in the game.

Li Kao and I had been wrapped in so many chains that we couldn't move a finger, and the soldiers groaned under the weight as they carried us down a seemingly endless flight of stone steps. I counted eleven landings, each one guarded by more soldiers. The air grew thicker and fouler, and slimy green water dripped from the black stone walls. Finally we reached the bottom-most dungeons. Brass-bound doors crashed open, and the panting soldiers carried us into a torture chamber that was decorated with blood and entrails. The executioner did not view us with friendly eyes. He was a fat fellow with a bald gray skull, a bright red nose, four yellow teeth, and a grievance.

"Work, work, work!" he snarled as he bustled around us with a tape measure. "Do you realize that each Shirt of Iron must be individually tailored for the victim? Do you realize that it takes two full days to make a decent one? Do you realize that the duke has ordered me to finish your shirts in two *hours*? And then I have to give you your first scraping, and do you realize that a decent job of scraping takes another two hours?"

He stepped back and leveled an indignant finger.

"Look at those chains!" he snarled. "Do you realize that it will take another hour just to unlock, unwrap, rewrap, and relock those things? And do you realize that the Ancestress has ordered me to draw and quarter another prisoner? And do you realize that a decent job of drawing and quartering takes another two hours? When am I to rest, I ask you? Is there no pity? Is there no concern for the welfare of the working man?"

He was not the only one with a grievance.

"How about us?" the soldiers yelled. "We have to stand guard in this slimy hole until the prisoners die, and if you're halfway decent at your job, that will take months! And that crud of a master sergeant refused to issue earplugs, and we'll be stone deaf from the screams inside of a week! Look at those cockroaches! Look at those leeches! Look at that slimy dripping water! There's fever down here as sure as you're born, and even if we live to return to our wives, what good will it do us? The duke made us wrap these poor bastards in so many chains that they can't move, and carry them down eleven flights of stairs, and quadruple hernias have made eunuchs of us all!"

It appeared to be a day of grievances.

"Woe!" somebody howled as feet pattered down the stairs. "Woe! Woe! Woe!" wailed the Key Rabbit as he trotted into the torture chamber. "The duke has ordered me to be present at the torture of my dearest friend and the most generous protector that my dear wife has ever had, and to make a full report of their sufferings! Good evening, Lord Li of Kao. Good evening, Lord Lu of Yu.

It is delightful to see you again, but how can the duke do this to me?"

The little fellow posed dramatically, one forearm across his brow and the other hand outflung.

"I become violently ill in butcher shops!" he howled. "I faint when I cut my finger! Crimson sunsets make me dive beneath my bed! Bloodhounds drive me into screaming fits! I once threw up all over a very distinguished nobleman who introduced me to his blood brother! I disgraced myself at a state banquet when I was informed that I was eating blood pudding! And now I must witness the bloodiest execution ever invented by man! Woe!" wailed the Key Rabbit. "Woe! Woe! Woe!"

"Damn it, get out of the way and let a man work," the executioner snarled.

He began to bang furiously on strips of steel mesh, and the soldiers panted and groaned as they carried us into an adjoining dungeon and dumped us upon the floor. They staggered out, clutching their hernias, and slammed the door, and we stared at the fellow who was to be drawn and quartered. He was attached to the wall with a leg chain, and he was eating a bowl of rice.

"What are you doing here?" Master Li asked.

"At the moment I am eating my last supper," said Henpecked Ho. "Good evening, Li Kao. Good evening, Number Ten Ox. It is a great pleasure to see you again, although one rather regrets the circumstances. May I offer you some rice? They have even given me a small jar of wine. Quite decent of them, don't you think?"

"Wine, by all means," said Li Kao.

Henpecked Ho's leg chain was just long enough for him to reach us and pour wine down our throats. They really were treating him with consideration because it was very expensive wine: Wu-fan, which is jet-black and so sweet that it tastes like molasses flavored with engraving acid.

"Have you really been sentenced to be drawn and quartered?" I asked.

"It's a very distressing story." He sighed. "Do you

remember that I had spent sixteen years trying to decipher fragments of clay tablets?"

"A very ancient ginseng fairy tale," said Master Li.

"Precisely, and do you remember that those grave robbers dug up a very large clay tablet? Well, it turned out to be the key to the whole thing. I could scarcely believe how quickly the pieces fell into place, and the story that emerged was so interesting that I could scarcely wait to see what came next. Then one day I entered my workshop and discovered that every clay fragment was gone, and I ran around weeping and tearing my hair until my dear wife told me to stop making a fool of myself. The Ancestress had remarked that fiddling with clay tablets was a frivolous hobby for a grown man, so my dear wife had ordered the servants to dump the tablets into the river, where, of course, they dissolved into mud."

"I would have slit her miserable throat," Master Li growled.

"Indeed you would have, and I thought about you a great deal," said Henpecked Ho. "You had advised me to use an axe, so I stole an axe and went after my dear wife."

"Did you get her?" I asked.

"I chopped her to pieces, and then I chopped her seven fat sisters to pieces. It was delightful," said Henpecked Ho. "Then I came here to try to chop the Ancestress to pieces, but her soldiers caught me first. Oh well, I suppose that one can't have everything."

"Ho, you did splendidly!" Master Li said.

"Do you really think so? Some people might consider my behavior rather gross," Henpecked Ho said dubiously. "I was maddened beyond endurance because now I will never know how the story came out, and it concerned two delightful deities that I had never heard of, even though I am familiar with the entire Heavenly Pantheon."

Li Kao thoughtfully chewed a wisp of his scraggly beard, which was about all the movement that he could manage.

"Ho, as a matter of rather academic curiosity, have you ever encountered a deity called the Peddler? He wears a robe covered with Heavenly or supernatural symbols, he leans upon a crutch, and he carries a flute and a ball and a bell."

"The Peddler is not one of the six hundred named gods, but our knowledge of the Pantheon is incomplete," Ho said thoughtfully. "It must be remembered that the first Duke of Ch'in destroyed the temples and priests and worshippers of any cult that annoyed him, and knowledge of many minor deities disappeared from the face of the earth. The Peddler might have been among them, and I am morally certain that the two delightful deities in the story on the tablet also suffered the duke's displeasure. After all, peasants treasure ginseng fairy tales, and they would never willingly abandon a story about the handsomest god in Heaven and the most beautiful girl in the world and a crown and three feathers and—"

"What!" Master Li yelped.

"Er... and a crown and three feathers."

"And three faithless handmaidens?"

"Well, I don't know about faithless, but three handmaidens were indeed briefly mentioned. Their names were—"

"Ho, let's hear it in sequence," said Master Li. "Your unmatched memory has surely retained every word, and I cannot imagine a better way to pass the time before being tortured to death than to listen to a fairy tale."

"Would you really like to hear it?" Henpecked Ho said eagerly. "I had so hoped to be able to share it with somebody, and perhaps my years of labor won't have been wasted after all. Even in half-completed form it's a very good story."

One of my clearest memories of the whole baffling affair is that of lying upon a dungeon floor, wrapped in chains from my neck to my toes, listening to the gentle voice of Henpecked Ho while the executioner banged upon our Shirts of Iron in the next room.

It was, as Henpecked Ho promised, quite a good story.

"Long ago there was a little girl who lived in a little village with her loving parents. Her name was Jade Pearl.

One day the village was raided by bandits, and Jade Pearl was picked up and carried off by a bandit who thought that he might be able to sell her, and several days later they reached a beautiful city, but the bandits were recognized and had to run away and in the confusion Jade Pearl managed to escape.

"The little girl wandered into a park where beautiful flowers were growing, and Jade Pearl sat down beside the loveliest plant of them all and began to weep. Now this was a very long time ago, before men had recognized the ginseng plant for what it was, and the lovely plant beside Jade Pearl was nothing less than the Queen of Ginseng. The queen listened to the sobs of the frightened child and her heart was moved, and when Jade Pearl uncovered her eyes and looked up she saw to her astonishment that a tall woman with a cheerful brown face and laughing eyes was smiling kindly at her.

"'Little girl, are you lost?' the queen asked.

"Jade Pearl told the kindly woman what had happened, so far as she understood it, and the Queen of Ginseng took her by the hand and told her not to worry because she was going home. Many days later they reached the little village, and the little girl's parents ran out joyfully to greet her, but when Jade Pearl turned to introduce the kindly lady who had brought her home the queen had vanished into thin air. The queen returned to the other plants that grew in the beautiful city, but after a while she realized that she had grown very fond of the little girl and would like to see her again.

"One day Jade Pearl heard somebody call her name, and she ran into a bamboo grove and there was the kindly lady with the laughing eyes. The queen became the little girl's godmother, and visited her often, and it was because of the contact with ginseng that Jade Pearl grew in health and comeliness. By the time she was eighteen she was the most beautiful girl in the whole world, although she did not know it, and it was then that she had another marvelous visitor.

"During the rainy season in Heaven, the Great River of Stars is filled with raging water. The young god who

is called the Star Shepherd must stride through the waves
day and night, guiding the stars to safety with his long
shepherd's crook, but during the dry season he is free to
travel as he pleases. One day during the dry season the
Star Shepherd decided to visit earth, so he floated down
from Heaven and landed beside a small village. He wandered around admiring the sights, and then he came to a
lovely grove of bamboo and he found a path and strolled
inside. In the center of the grove was a clearing where
wildflowers grew, and in the center of the clearing was a
pool where tiny fish of many colors swam, and in the
center of the pool was a peasant girl who was bathing.
Her skin was ivory brushed with honey, and her eyes
were black almonds flecked with gold, and her hair was
a cloud of soft swirling smoke, and her lips were ripe and
full and bursting with sweetness, like plums. There were
many other items of interest about the peasant girl, and
you may be sure that the Star Shepherd didn't miss any
of them. 'Oh!' cried Jade Pearl as she saw a face reflected
in the water, and when she looked up, the most beautiful
girl in the world was gazing at the handsomest god in
Heaven.

"One thing led to another, as it usually does, and one
day in Heaven an old retainer who had been granted
the right to fish in the Great River of Stars came panting
into the palace of the emperor and demanded an audience
with the August Personage of Jade. 'Your Heavenly Majesty, the rainy season is upon us but the Star Shepherd
has not returned from earth!' he wailed. 'The Great River
is filled with wild waves, and terrified stars are crashing
into the great black rocks, and many are badly damaged
and some have even sunk!'

"The August Personage of Jade could not believe that
his favorite nephew would so neglect his duties, but he
rushed outside to see for himself, and when he saw that
it was just as the old retainer had said, he uttered a great
roar of rage and flew down to earth and landed with a
terrible clap of thunder in the middle of the bamboo grove.
The emperor grabbed the Star Shepherd by the hair and

swung him around like a toy on the end of a string, and then he hurled him clear up to the constellation Aquila.

"'Back to your duties, you insolent puppy!' he roared. 'I swear by the name of my predecessor, the Heavenly Master of the First Origin, that never again will you be allowed to visit earth!' Then he turned to Jade Pearl. 'On your knees, strumpet!' he yelled. 'Prepare to face the wrath of Heaven!'

"Jade Pearl fell upon her knees and clasped her hands together. 'Your Heavenly Majesty, there is no need to punish poor Jade Pearl,' she sobbed. 'I have given my heart to the Star Shepherd, and if I am never to see him again, I shall die.'

"The August Personage of Jade took a close look at Jade Pearl, and remembered that he too had once been young. He took a second look, and remembered that only recently he had sworn that the Star Shepherd had more common sense in his little finger than his other nephews had in their whole bodies. He took a third look, and he began to think deep thoughts about his beloved wife, the Queen Mother Wang, who used more powder and paint with less effect than any other woman he had ever known. He took a fourth look and said, 'Ten thousand curses!'

"The emperor sighed and sat down beside the pool, and after a moment he patted the grass beside him. 'Come sit here beside me, my child,' he said.

"So the peasant girl sat down beside the Emperor of Heaven, and he took off his sandals and they dangled their feet in the water. The emperor watched tiny gold and scarlet fish glide around his toes like brightly painted snowflakes, and then he said, 'Jade Pearl, I have sworn upon the sacred name of the Heavenly Master of the First Origin that the Star Shepherd will never again be allowed to visit earth. That oath cannot be broken.'

"Jade Pearl began to weep bitterly.

"'Well, you should see what that boy did to the Great River of Stars!' the emperor yelled. 'Every hospital in Heaven will be filled with broken stars for at least six months, and you don't know what misery is until you try to bandage a broken star!'

"Jade Pearl continued to weep, and the emperor's eyes softened as he looked at her. Finally he shrugged his shoulders and muttered, 'I'm going to regret this. I feel it in my bones.' Then he reached into the left sleeve of his robe and pulled out a small golden crown. 'Peasant girl, since the Star Shepherd cannot visit you on earth, I will allow you to visit him in Heaven,' he said.

"'Your Majesty honors me far beyond my worth!' cried Jade Pearl.

"'That is precisely true, and I do not want to think of what will happen when my beloved wife, the Queen Mother Wang, finds out about it,' he muttered grimly. 'However, Heaven could use a little brightening up, and you have at least confirmed my suspicion that the Star Shepherd is the most sensible of my nephews.' The emperor cheered up at another thought. 'Besides, my wife owes me something after that disgraceful affair with her blasted Peaches of Immortality, and Chang-o, and that loathsome White Rabbit that keeps twitching his nose at me when I fly past the moon. Take my advice, young lady, and stay away from rabbits!'

"The August Personage of Jade reached into the right sleeve of his robe and pulled out three tiny white feathers, which he carefully placed upon the rim of the crown. 'What day is it?' he asked.

"'Your Majesty, it is the seventh day of the seventh moon,' said Jade Pearl.

"'Very well,' said the emperor. 'Jade Pearl, these are three feathers from the Kings of Birds. So long as you wear them on your crown, you will be Princess of Birds, and all the birds of China will be your loving subjects. I hereby decree that on the seventh day of the seventh moon you will be allowed to summon the birds, who will build a bridge for you to climb, so that you may rejoin the Star Shepherd in Heaven, but it is illegal for one who has not completed the full cycle around the Great Wheel of Transmigrations to spend a full year in Heaven. On the first day of the first moon you must summon the birds once more, and they will build the bridge that will return you to earth, and on the seventh day of the seventh moon you will be allowed to climb once more to Heaven, and so it will continue throughout eternity because if the Star Shepherd doesn't give you the Peach of Immortality, he's a greater fool than I think he is.'

"The August Personage of Jade waggled a finger in front of the peasant girl's nose to emphasize the importance of what he was saying.

"'Jade Pearl, do not forget the seventh day of the seventh moon! The conditions will be entered in the Imperial Book of Etiquette, which not even I am allowed to disobey, and if you fail to return to the Star Shepherd on the appointed day you will pass from the protection of Heaven. The Imperial Book of Etiquette does not allow for excuses,' the emperor said urgently. 'The gods will be forbidden to help you, and none but a mortal can restore you to Heaven, and at a conservative estimate the odds against somebody pulling off a trick like that are once in ten thousand billion trillion. Do you understand me?'

"'I hear and obey,' Jade Pearl whispered.

"So the peasant girl knelt before the Emperor of Heaven and he placed the little gold crown upon her head. 'Arise, Princess of Birds!' he commanded, and when Jade Pearl stood up she was astonished to see that she shone with a divine light. 'Call your subjects!' the emperor commanded, and when she called to the birds a great song of joy arose, and all the birds of China came flying toward their princess. They carried green twigs and branches, and with these they built a bridge that stretched up to the stars. Jade Pearl climbed the bridge to Heaven, and the Star Shepherd married the Princess of Birds and gave her the Peach of Immortality, and on the first day of the first moon they parted with many tears and the beautiful Bridge of Birds returned Jade Pearl to earth.

"Heaven saw to it that her little village lacked for nothing, so that the princess could spend her time singing songs and weaving daisy chains. She had three girls from her own village as handmaidens, Snowgoose, Little Ping, and Autumn Moon, and she had a goat and a cat and a little dog to help her pass the time. Still, it seemed an eternity before the seventh day of the seventh moon ar-

rived. Jade Pearl kissed her handmaidens and bowed to
her parents. Then she called to the birds, and the peasants
of China gazed up in wonder and delight as the Bridge of
Birds ascended to the stars, and the Princess of Birds ran
to the arms of the Star Shepherd, and they lived..."

Henpecked Ho sighed and shrugged.

"Happily ever after?" he said. "You see, that's as far
as I had gone when my dear wife had the fragments destroyed. If they lived happily ever after, I cannot imagine
why half of the tale remained to be deciphered, although
at some point it would most certainly have returned to
ginseng lore. What do you think, Li Kao?"

"Ho, they did not live happily ever after, and I strongly
suspect that your tablets did not preserve an ancient fairy
tale," Master Li said grimly. "When history crumbles into
dust, the events of history are sometimes preserved in
the form of myth or fable, and I am rash enough to believe
that if Ox and I can get our hands on one or two more
missing pieces, we will have the solution to a rather baffling puzzle."

Li Kao chewed thoughtfully on his beard, and then he
said,

"Ho, Ox and I are wrapped in so many chains that we
can't move, you are attached to the wall by a leg chain,
this dungeon is solid rock, the torture chamber is crammed
with soldiers, we are eleven stories beneath the earth, and
each landing is guarded by more soldiers. The palace is
swarming with the army of the Ancestress, the army of
the Duke of Ch'in is camped outside the walls, and Ox
and I must escape from here immediately. Unless you
look forward to being drawn and quartered, I suggest that
you accompany us."

"I think that's a splendid idea," said Henpecked Ho.

25.
The Triumph of Henpecked Ho

You who know so much more about the world than does Number Ten Ox will have already figured out six or seven different ways to escape from that place, and if you will bear the momentary indignity of imagining that you are soldiers in the service of the Duke of Ch'in we will see if any of your methods is similar to that of Li Kao.

Very well, you are soldiers who have been forced to stand guard in a loathsome torture chamber deep in the bowels of the earth, where slimy green water drips from black stone walls, and sickly white cockroaches crawl through puddles of blood, and fetid feverish odors mingle with the stench of discarded intestines and eyeballs. A horrible scream splits the air! The Key Rabbit topples over in a dead faint, and you follow the executioner into an adjoining dungeon where a ghastly spectacle greets your bulging eyes.

An elderly gentleman of scholarly mien lurches in lunatic circles at the end of a leg chain, frantically clawing at his throat. His face and hands are covered with loathsome black splotches, and his blotched black tongue protrudes most unpleasantly, and black saliva spurts and dribbles from his blotched lips. His eyes roll up until only the whites are visible, and he does an acrobatic somersault and lands upon his back. His hands spastically pound the floor. He bounces rigidly up and down, jerks, twitches, spurts more saliva, and finally comes to rest as stiff as a board.

Another gentleman who is even more ancient, and who is wrapped in so many chains that he can't move, views the scene with eyes that bulge in terror and screams, "The cockroaches! For the love of Buddha, look at the cockroaches!"

The black wine called Wu-fan is invisible upon a black stone floor, and you cannot possibly see that the pounding hands of the deceased scholar have uncovered a trail of it, and that the trail leads to large invisible ideographs that are traced upon a black stone wall. What you do see is that ten thousand repulsive white cockroaches are scrambling frantically across the floor, dashing up the wall, and writhing in artistic patterns upon thick sweet invisible lines that spell out the following message from the Board of Health:

> RUN FOR YOUR LIVES!
> IT IS THE PLAGUE OF
> THE TEN THOUSAND
> PESTILENTIAL PUTRESCENCES!

I sincerely doubt that you will stand there and make learned comments concerning the calligraphy of insects.

It was all up to Henpecked Ho, and his timing couldn't have been better. The executioner turned and fled. Ho jerked his leg chain taut and the executioner tripped and fell to the floor, where he was pounded into jelly by the feet of the fleeing soldiers who dashed back into the torture chamber, scooped up the Key Rabbit, who had just regained his consciousness and his feet, and carried him up the stairs like a minnow riding the quest of a tidal wave. "Run for your lives!" they screamed. "It is the plague of the ten thousand pestilential putrescences!" The

pounding feet and shrieking voices faded away and Henpecked Ho collected the keys from the flattened form of
the executioner. His eyes were worried as he unlocked
his leg chain and started to work on ours.

"Do you think that I overdid the saliva?" he asked in
a small voice.

"It was perfect," I said.

"Do you really think so? I was afraid that the final
spurt and dribble might appear to be in poor taste."

"When you do it again, don't change a single spurt or
dribble," Master Li said firmly.

The last chain fell away, and it felt marvelous to stand
up and stretch my limbs. We walked into the torture
chamber and collected weapons. Li Kao filled his belt
with daggers, and I took a sword and a spear. Henpecked
Ho had his heart set on the monstrous axe that was used
for decapitation, but since he was quite incapable of lifting
it, he was forced to settle for a small double-bladed model.
Li Kao started leisurely for the stairs.

"There is no hurry," he explained. "The soldiers from
the torture chamber will have collected the soldiers on
the landings, and by the time they burst into the palace
they will have become a large screaming mob. Anyone
who isn't trampled flat will dash into the courtyard, where
they will collect a couple of divisions from the army of
the Ancestress, and when they hit the wall I doubt that
a stone will remain standing. They will then collect the
army of the Duke of Ch'in and bolt hysterically through
the city and reduce it to rubble, and the citizens who
survive will follow in their wake. It is quite possible that
we will have to walk to Hangchow before we see another
living soul."

There was a flaw in his reasoning. We climbed the
stairs and saw nothing but a few flattened bodies, but
when we stepped through the door to the throne room,
we ran right into a creature who would not have blinked
an eye if the South China Sea had suddenly turned into
soy sauce. A bloated figure with a crown on her head
leveled a finger like a sausage.

"There is no such thing as the plague of the ten thousand pestilential putrescences," the Ancestress snarled. "Soldiers, chop these dogs to pieces!"

Her bodyguards closed in on all sides, and we would have been killed instantly if it hadn't been for Henpecked Ho. He whooped with joy and charged straight toward the throne, and his axe was whirling so swiftly above his head that if he had spurted a little flame and smoke he would have resembled the Bamboo Dragonfly.

"Chop-chop!" he howled happily. "Chop chop-chop-chop-chop!"

Of course he ran right into the spears of the soldiers. We gave him up for dead, but the distraction allowed us to clear a path. Li Kao filled the air with flying daggers and four soldiers fell. "Quick, Master Li, climb upon my back!" I yelled. He hopped up and I raced straight toward the throne, planted the butt of my spear, vaulted over the head of the Ancestress, and took to my heels.

It was a losing game. The soldiers knew the palace and we did not, and sooner or later we were going to reach a dead end. I raced up staircases while Li Kao snatched vases from pedestals and smashed them over the heads of the soldiers below, but there were simply too many soldiers. I ran down a long hallway and tugged at a pair of massive bronze doors. They were locked. I turned and started back, and skidded to a halt as the hallway filled with soldiers. Two columns of men started toward us along the walls, while the captain of the bodyguards led a double rank down the center. We stared at a solid line of glittering spears, and I consigned my humble soul to the August Personage of Jade.

Then an elephant charged into the hall and squashed the captain flat. At least I thought it was an elephant until I realized that it was the Ancestress, and I gaped at an incredible sight.

"Chop-chop!" yelled Henpecked Ho. "Chop-chop-chop-chop-chop!"

He had no right to be alive. Blood spurted from twenty wounds with every step that he took, but he kept right on taking them. "Save me!" the Ancestress howled, and then her five hundred pounds flattened three more soldiers who might have saved her. It was over in a few minutes.

The Ancestress ran around in circles and squashed everything in front of her, and Henpecked Ho swung his axe and whacked everything in sight, and Li Kao slipped through the carnage slitting throats, and I flailed away with my sword. Toward the end it became rather messy, because we were slipping and sliding upon pieces of the Ancestress, and there was a lot of Ancestress to go around. Then we staggered away from the last fallen soldier and knelt beside Henpecked Ho.

He lay on his back with his axe still clutched in his hands. His life was draining away in red rivulets, and his face was ashen, and his eyes strained to focus on us.

"Did I get her?" he whispered.

"Ho, you chopped that monster into a hundred pieces," Master Li said proudly.

"I am so happy," the gentle scholar whispered. "Now my ancestors will not be ashamed to greet me when I arrive in Hell to be judged."

"Bright Star will be waiting for you," I said.

"Oh no, that would be far too much to ask," he said seriously. "The most that I dare ask of the Yama Kings is that I may be reborn as a beautiful flower, so that sometime, somewhere, a dancing girl might choose to pluck me and wear me in her hair."

I blinked through my tears, and he patted my hand.

"Do not weep for me, Number Ten Ox. I have grown so weary of this life, and I long to return to the Great Wheel of Transmigrations." His voice was very faint, and I leaned down to hear his last words. "Immortality is only for the gods," he whispered. "I wonder how they can stand it."

His eyes closed, and the axe fell to the floor, and the soul of Henpecked Ho took leave of his body.

We carried him outside to the garden. It was cold and overcast, and a tiny silver rain pattered down as I dug the grave. We gently placed the body into the hole and I recovered it with earth, and then we knelt and clasped our hands.

"Henpecked Ho, great is your joy," said Master Li. "Now your soul has been released from the prison of your body, and you are being greeted with great honors in Hell. You have rid the world of a woman who was an abomination to men and gods alike, and surely the Yama Kings will allow you to see Bright Star again. When it is time for you to be reborn, your wish will be granted, and you will become a beautiful flower that a dancing girl will wear in her hair."

"Henpecked Ho," I sniffled through my tears, "I will miss you, but I know that we will meet again. Master Li will be a three-toed sloth, and Miser Shen will be a tree, and you will be a flower, and I will be a cloud, and some day we will come together in a beautiful garden. Probably very soon," I added.

We said the prayers and sacrificed, and Li Kao stood up and stretched wearily.

"Immortality is only for the gods; I wonder how they can stand it," he said thoughtfully. "Ox, the last words of Henpecked Ho may be significant in more ways than one."

Master Li stood lost in thought for a moment. Then he said:

"If I were to try to count the incredible coincidences of our quest on my fingers, I would wind up with ten badly sprained digits, and I am far too old to believe in coincidences. We are being led toward something, and I strongly suspect that Henpecked Ho has also supplied the question that we must ask before we continue the quest. Only the wisest man in the world could answer it, and can it be a coincidence that we happen to know where to find the wisest man in the world?"

I stared at him stupidly.

"Miser Shen," he explained. "Ox, it was no accident that Miser Shen told us that when he was trying to bring his little girl back to life, he learned that the wisest man in the world lives in a cave at the end of Bear's Path, high in the Omei Mountains."

"Are we going to the Omei Mountains?" I asked.

"We are indeed, and we will begin by looting this palace. The Old Man of the Mountain," said Master Li, "does not sell his secrets cheaply."

Rain still fell, but one corner of the sky was turning blue, and as a final tribute to Henpecked Ho I shoveled the largest pieces of the Ancestress into a wheelbarrow and trundled them to the kennels and fed them to the dogs. In the distance a rainbow formed.

26.
Three Kinds of Wisdom

Should you decide to travel to the end of Bear's Path, high in the Omei Mountains, you will eventually reach a small level clearing in front of a cliff. In front of the black gaping mouth of a cave you will see a stone pillar, upon which hangs a copper gong and an iron hammer, and carved upon the pillar is a message.

> *HERE LIVES THE OLD MAN OF THE MOUNTAIN.*
> *RING AND STATE YOUR BUSINESS.*
> *HIS SECRETS ARE NOT SOLD CHEAPLY.*
> *IT IS PERILOUS TO WASTE HIS TIME.*

I hope that you will carefully consider the last sentence. The wisest man in the world is not to be trifled with, not even by those who are so distinguished as are my readers, and I myself have no intention of ever again traveling to the end of Bear's Path. I am only Number Ten Ox, who had no business being there in the first place, but it is said that the great leaders of men have been making that journey for three thousand years and will be

225

doing so three thousand years from now, and that one only has to look at the state of the world to prove it.

The panting mules who hauled our cartload of treasure were nearly exhausted when they plodded around the last bend in the path and arrived at the clearing in front of the cave. Li Kao read the message on the pillar, and then he lifted a goatskin flask and swallowed some wine.

"Admirable conciseness," he said, nodding at the inscription. "Not one wasted word." Then he picked up the iron hammer and rang the gong, and when the echoes died away he took a deep breath and yelled, *"Old Man of the Mountain, come forth! I have come to purchase the Secret of Immortality!"*

The echoes shouted immortality, immortality, immortality, and then they faded away into silence. For many minutes we listened to the tiny sounds of small animals, and the sighing wind, and the distant scream of an eagle, and finally we heard the faint slap of shuffling sandals. A voice that sounded like gravel scraping across iron drifted from the blackness of the cave.

"Why does everyone ask for immortality? I have so many other secrets to sell. Beautiful secrets, beastly secrets, happy secrets, horrible secrets, lovely secrets, lunatic secrets, laughing secrets, loathsome secrets..."

The man who shuffled from the cave and blinked in the bright sunlight looked like the oldest and ugliest monkey in the world. Pieces of filthy straw were tangled in his matted hair, and his beard and robe were stained with spilled food. His seamed and pitted face was even older than Li Kao's, but his eyes were jet-black and so piercing that I caught my breath and instinctively stepped backward. He dismissed me as unimportant, and looked with interest at Li Kao.

"A sage, I perceive, with a slight flaw in his character," he said with a little snicker. "Surely a sage can think of a more interesting secret to buy from the Old Man of the Mountain? I can teach you how to turn your friends into flowers and your enemies into cockroaches. I can teach you how to transform yourself or anything else into whatever you like, or how to steal the spirits of the dead and make them your slaves, or how to control the creatures that lurk in the black bowels of the earth. I can teach you how to remove varicose veins or cure pimples, yet you come to me for the Secret of Immortality, which is so simple that it is scarcely a secret at all."

"I will give all I have for that one secret," said Master Li, and he brushed away the straw that covered the pile of loot in the cart. The Old Man of the Mountain plunged his hands into the treasure.

"Cold!" he said delighted. "It has been years since I touched treasure as cold as this! In fact, this treasure is so cold that I will tell you the secret at once, instead of toying with you as is my usual custom."

Li Kao bowed and offered the wine flask, and the Old Man of the Mountain drank and wiped his lips with his beard.

"You know the seamless robes of the gods? The jade girdles and golden crowns? Any of those items will do," he said. "Simply wait until the New Year, when the gods descend to earth to make their tour of inspection, and steal a robe or a crown. So long as you possess it, you will never age, but I would advise you to hurry. I myself was well past two hundred when I stole a jade girdle, and not even the Old Man of the Mountain has learned the secret of restoring youth."

Master Li threw back his head and laughed.

"Do you take me for an idiot? What use is it never to age when you can be extinguished in an instant by the bite of a mosquito or a slip upon the stairs? Immortality is a meaningless word unless invulnerability goes with it. Old Man of the Mountain, I am beginning to suspect that you are a fraud."

The Old Man of the Mountain winked at him, and passed the wine flask.

"You would goad me into indiscretion, my friend with the flaw in his character? Do you think that I cannot sense that in your pocket you carry a business card with the sign of a half-closed eye? Or that I would not wonder what an old fox is doing traveling with a young chicken?"

He turned and crooked a finger at me. "Boy, come here,"
he commanded.

The jet-black eyes burned a hole in my heart and I had
no will of my own. I found myself walking toward him
like a mechanical toy, and his eyes looked into my mind.
What the Duke of Ch'in had done was but a feeble imitation of the Old Man of the Mountain.

"Well, I'll be the Stone Monkey!" he exclaimed. "There
are those three handmaidens, and the flute and the ball
and the bell, and the feathers and the crown too, although
dimly perceived. So you hope to steal the Great Root of
Power, do you? Boy, you are nothing but a walking
corpse."

He sniggered and released my mind, and I staggered
backward and nearly fell.

"Let the chicken go ahead and get killed," he said softly
to Li Kao. "He couldn't tell a turd from a turnip, but
you appear to have some common sense. Go steal something that belongs to a god, and then return with ten times
this much treasure, and if it is as cold as this stuff I will
sell you the Secret of Invulnerability, which, as you have
correctly pointed out, gives meaning to the word immortality."

Li Kao tilted the wine flask, and passed it back to the
Old Man of the Mountain.

"But is there such a secret?" he wondered. "Anything
with a heart can be killed, and though there are hundreds
of peasant stories about men without hearts, I have always
considered them to be allegorical fables. Quite sophisti-
cated fables, at times, but depicting character rather than
actual physiology."

"Not one in a hundred of such stories is true, but when
you hear one that is you may be sure that the wisest man
in the world is involved, for I alone have found the secret," said the Old Man of the Mountain. "You doubt it,
my slightly flawed friend? Marvel at the man who rivals
the gods!"

When he opened his robe I nearly fainted, because
there was a hole where his heart had been. I could look
right through it and see the stone pillar behind, shining

in the sunlight, and the gong and the hammer, and the black gaping mouth of the cave."

"Fantastic," Master Li said admiringly. "You are truly the wisest man in the world, and a dolt like myself must bow before your genius."

The Old Man of the Mountain simpered with pleasure and passed the wine flask, and Li Kao bowed and drank thirstily.

"It would seem to me that your heart must still be beating somewhere," Master Li said thoughtfully. "Would it be safe to transform it into a pebble or a snowflake? A heart that is transformed is no longer a heart. A simplistic statement, but perhaps intuitively true."

"Almost entirely true," the Old Man of the Mountain said approvingly. "A heart cannot be transformed into a snowflake without killing it unless the entire person is also transformed into a snowflake. But a heart can be hidden. Of course the value of that depends upon how well it has been hidden, and you cannot believe the stupidity of some of the pupils that I've had. Why, one of those dolts was so mindless that he hid his heart inside the body of a lizard that was inside a cage that was on top of the head of a serpent that was on top of a tree that was guarded by lions, tigers, and scorpions! Another cretin, and may Buddha strike me if I lie, concealed his heart inside an egg that was inside a duck that was inside a basket that was inside a chest that was on an island that was in the middle of an uncharted ocean. Needless to say, both of those numbskulls were destroyed by the first half-witted heroes who came along."

He took the flask and drank deeply, and passed it back again.

"Now you would not be so stupid," he said. "Try to find treasure that is as cold as this stuff—a man who has no heart likes things cold, and there is nothing colder than treasure—and when you return, I will remove your heart and you will hide it well. So long as it beats, you cannot be killed, and nothing is worse than death."

I suddenly realized that Li Kao was controlling himself with an immense effort. He was clenching and unclenching his hands, and he could no longer keep a trace of revulsion from creeping into his voice.

"Some things are far worse than death," said Master Li.

The Old Man of the Mountain stiffened. I drew back in fear as I saw his eyes burn with cold fire.

"My secrets are not sold cheaply," he said softly.

The Old Man of the Mountain stamped his foot, and a great crack appeared in the earth, and our poor mules brayed in terror as they plunged down into blackness with the cartload of treasure; he waved his hand, and the crack closed as though it had never been.

"It is perilous to waste my time," he whispered.

The wisest man in the world lifted a finger to his lips and blew. The light was blacked out by a dense cloud, and wind howled, and we were scooped up and sent flying into the air, whirling around and around inside a black funnel that was thick with dirt and broken branches and small screaming animals. The cyclone whirled down the mountainside, and I tried to shield Li Kao's frail body with my own as branches buffeted me and shrieking wind deafened me. Down and down and around and around, and then the earth leaped up at us and we landed with a crash that separated me from my senses.

When I regained consciousness I saw that we had landed in soft shrubbery, but if we had been blown another ten feet we would have sailed over the side of a steep cliff. Far below I could see a river shining in the sunset, and a boy standing motionless upon the bank, and a village half-hidden by trees. Birds swooped high and low in the chilly wind that sighed down from snow-capped peaks, and somewhere a woodcutter was singing a slow sad song.

Li Kao had bandaged the bump on my head. He was sitting cross-legged at the edge of the cliff, cradling his wine flask. When I gazed up at the distant mountain peaks, I seemed to hear faint laughter that was like pebbles rattling in an iron pan.

"Master Li, forgive my impertinence, but if the pursuit of wisdom leads to the Old Man of the Mountain I cannot help but think that men would be better off if they stayed stupid," I said.

"Ah, but there is more than one kind of wisdom," said Master Li. "There is wisdom to take, and there is wisdom to give, and there is the wisdom of Heaven that is inscrutable to man." He tilted his flask to his lips. "In this case, Heaven is becoming scrutable," he said when he came up for air.

To my astonishment I saw that Master Li was as happy as a small boy with a large puppy.

"Henpecked Ho gave us a third of the solution to this weird quest, and now the Old Man of the Mountain has made it two-thirds," he said with satisfaction. He pointed down to the riverbank, where the boy had been joined by his friends. "What are those children doing?"

I gazed down and shrugged. "Playing games," I said.

"Children's games!" Master Li chortled happily. "Rituals, riddles, and nonsense rhymes!" Then, to my astonishment, he jumped to his feet, waved his wine flask toward Heaven, and bellowed, *"August Personage of Jade, you have the guts of a first-class burglar!"*

I nervously awaited a bolt of lightning, but none came.

"Come along, Ox, we must hurry back toward your village to collect the third piece of the puzzle," said Master Li, and he started down the mountainside at a trot.

The Old Man of the Mountain had blown us to the very edge of civilization, and we found ourselves trudging through a very strange landscape. Flat cracked earth stretched toward distant mountains with fantastic shapes, like deformed mushrooms, and a cold wind sighed across twelve hundred miles of empty steppes. Once in a while we would reach a desolate plain where endless mounds of dirt were laid out with almost geometric precision, and on top of each mound a gopher stood on its hind legs and watched us pass with bright wondering eyes. Once an enormous army of rats raced toward us, but when they swept around and past us, I saw that they were not rats but roots, the famous rolling roots of the peng plant, which were being blown by the wind toward some unimaginable destiny at the outer edge of the world.

Gradually the bare mountains acquired scattered trees, and we reached valleys that had touches of green, and finally the landscape turned into the one I knew so well. Then we climbed a hill and I saw the outline of Dragon's Pillow, hazy in the distance, and I was greatly relieved when Master Li said that it was our destination. I could not have borne the eyes of the parents if we went on to Ku-fu with no ginseng for the children.

We reached the wall as soft purple shadows were creeping like cats across the green valley, and the birds began to sing the last songs of the day while we climbed the ancient stones to the Eye of the Dragon. Li Kao sat down upon the floor of the watchtower and uncovered a bowl of rice that he had bought in the last village. For a few moments he ate in silence, and then he said:

"Ox, mysteries cease to be mysteries when they are viewed from the proper angle. In this case we must find the proper angle by recalling a comment that was made by the Duke of Ch'in not once but twice. 'You seek the right root, but for the wrong reason.' Doesn't that suggest that we might have unwittingly wandered into a completely different quest when we started after the Great Root of Power? We can assume that the duke thought that we might be trying to do something else, and the idea scared him half to death. What sort of a quest could terrify a tyrant as mighty as the Duke of Ch'in?"

He ate some more rice and watched the shadows climb the wall, and he pointed a chopstick at the songbirds.

"Let's begin by assuming that Henpecked Ho's story was factual, in the sense of history that over the centuries has been cloaked in the conventional trappings of myth," said Master Li. "There really was a minor deity called the Princess of Birds, although not necessarily as described in the story, and she really did wear a crown that was decorated with three feathers from the Kings of Birds. We would have to be as blind as neo-Confucians not to guess what happened," he said. "The Duke of Ch'in went to the Old Man of the Mountain for the Secret of Immortality, and he learned that he must begin by stealing something that belonged to a deity. He tricked and murdered Jade Pearl's handmaidens, captured her, and stole her crown. Then the Old Man of the Mountain removed his heart, which is why the jovial fellow laughs at axes and fatal dosages of poison. It's been the same duke all along, of course. The tyrant who burned the books of China has been squatting in the Castle of the Labyrinth ever since, concealed behind the mask of a snarling tiger."

My heart was sick as I thought of the duke and his playmates, such as the Hand That No One Sees. He had paid the wisest man in the world for more than heart surgery. The Duke of Ch'in had also bought the secrets of reading minds and of controlling the creatures who lurk in the dark bowels of the earth. What chance would we have against a pupil of the Old Man of the Mountain?

"Jade Pearl had something that was almost as valuable as her crown," Master Li continued. "She had a godmother. Surely a fellow as greedy as the duke would not miss the fact that the Queen of Ginseng had to be the most valuable plant on the face of the earth, and with Jade Pearl as his captive, he would probably have been able to capture her godmother as well. Now I will make one more assumption: The Great Root of Power *is* the Queen of Ginseng, and that is why two quests are intertwined."

Li Kao gazed thoughtfully up at Heaven.

"Ox, the Heaven of the Chinese is superior to all others because nothing is absolute except the rule of law. The supreme deity is bound by the rules of the Imperial Book of Etiquette, and if he breaks those rules, he will be abruptly replaced. Thus the Heavenly Master of the First Origin gave way to the August Personage of Jade, and the Heavenly Master of the Dawn of Jade of the Golden Door stands ready in the wings to ascend to the throne the moment the August Personage of Jade gets too big for his sandals. When the emperor's pet goddess lost her crown and failed to return to the Star Shepherd she passed from the protection of Heaven, and the Imperial Book of Etiquette does not allow for excuses. What could the emperor do? Direct intervention would cost him his throne, so if he did anything it would have to be very sneaky indeed."

Master Li bent over and laughed until the tears flowed.

"I can just see his Heavenly Majesty sitting there with that damned nursemaid of a book on his lap!" he chortled. "I can see his eyes scanning the earth, and I can see him sit bolt upright when two splendid fellows named Li Kao and Number Ten Ox set forth to find the Great Root of Power. 'What's wrong with trying to help the poor children of the humble village of Ku-fu?' he says reasonably. 'After all, things like that are the reason for my existence!' So Pawnbroker Fang and Ma the Grub pop up to tell us that the duke has the root—and if they uncover a tablet that tells the story of Jade Pearl? 'Accidents will happen,' sighs the August Personage of Jade. Fang and Ma pop up again to help us escape from a tower, along with Miser Shen—and if Shen tells us about the Old Man of the Mountain? 'Accidents will happen,' sighs the August Personage of Jade. The Bamboo Dragonfly heads straight toward the Cavern of Bells, and after we get a good look at the painting of the Peddler we are reunited with Henpecked Ho, who has deciphered the story of the Princess of Birds. 'Accidents,' the emperor sighs, 'will happen, and after all, I'm only trying to help them find the root that might save the children of Ku-fu.' So far, so good, but now let's take a look at something truly sneaky, which should not be difficult to do because we're sitting on it."

I nervously looked around the wall for something truly sneaky, but the only sneaky thing I saw was a lizard stalking a bug.

"Centuries ago, a general just happened to dream that he had been summoned to Heaven, and when he returned he discovered that his plans had been altered to place Dragon's Pillow in this ludicrous position," said Master Li. "Then a reading of the Trigrams just happened to provide a ghostly watchman named Wan, and a couple of centuries after that some of the local children began playing a game."

Master Li finished his rice and pointed a chopstick at me.

"The Duke of Ch'in very nearly eliminated all trace of the Princess of Birds when he burned the books, destroyed priests and temples and worshippers, and decapitated professional storytellers, but he forgot about a children's game," said Master Li. "Ox, there is such a thing as racial memory, which preserves events long after conventional histories have turned to dust. One of the ways in which this memory is expressed is through the games and songs of children, and when the children came to the wall that day, they began to play the Hopping Hide and Seek Game, which happens to be the history of the Duke of Ch'in and the Princess of Birds."

I stared at him stupidly.

"Jade Pearl was a ginseng child, in the sense that her godmother was the Queen of Ginseng," said Master Li. "How do you capture a ginseng child?"

"With a red ribbon," I said.

"How did the duke disguise himself when he approached her handmaidens?"

I thought of the painting in the Cavern of Bells. "As a lame peddler who leaned upon a crutch," I said.

Li Kao began to imitate the sick boys in the infirmary at the monastery, shaking his shoulders and snatching at the air. Then he imitated the girls, making swooping pulling gestures.

"The boys are pretending to be lame peddlers who must hop on one leg, although they are not consciously aware of it," he said. "They are trying to get the girls' red ribbons, and while the girls are not aware of it, they are ginseng handmaidens who are being killed. The last girl becomes Jade Pearl, but the Princess of Birds cannot be killed because she has eaten the Peach of Immortality. So the boy who takes her red ribbon hides her. He is now the duke, and the other children become the birds of China, blindfolded because the birds cannot see their princess after she has lost her crown. They try to find and rescue her by touch, but there is a time limit. All right, why does the duke count to forty-nine?"

I am not usually so intelligent, but the answer popped unbidden into my mind.

"Seven times seven," I said. "Jade Pearl could escape if she reached the Star Shepherd before the seventh day of the seventh moon. But, Master Li, why couldn't there be ten or twenty other interpretations of the Hopping Hide and Seek Game?"

"Ginseng," he said promptly. "The moment that the children of your village took the tiniest of the Great Root their racial memory was stirred, and instinctively they began to play their ginseng game. A slightly stronger taste dredged up a deeper racial memory, and an understanding that had eluded the conscious minds of the children who had first experienced it. The moment that they began to chant a nonsense rhyme, they were able to find the Princess of Birds. Ox, that was no accident when Monkey reached out and touched Fang's Fawn."

Li Kao began a slow rhythmic beat upon the rim of his rice bowl with his chopsticks.

"The ghost of poor Wan must have been very lonely," he said. "Ghosts also share racial memories, and when he saw the children play the Hopping Hide and Seek Game he realized that the question that the game asks is, 'Where is the Princess of Birds? Where has the lame peddler taken her?' Wan knew the answer. He wanted to join the game, but he was determined to play fair—how many times had he listened to the riddle games of children?—and his impromptu effort was so good that I strongly suspect that he had been far more than a simple soldier.

> "Jade plate,
> Six, eight.
> Fire that burns hot,
> Night that is not.
> Fire that burns cold,
> First silver, then gold."

Master Li tossed the chopsticks into the bowl and winked at me.

"Ever since the standard was set by Yang Wan-li, what has been the common metaphor for the moon?"

"A plate of jade," I said. "Sailing across ten thousand miles of blueblack sky."

"In relation to the moon, what can you make of 'six, eight'?"

"The sixth day of the eighth month?" I guessed.

"Try it the other way around."

"The eighth day, the sixth moon—why, that is today!" I exclaimed.

"It is indeed. We've begun with the moon, so what about the fire that burns hot?"

"The sun?" I said.

"And the night that is not?"

I scratched my head. "An eclipse?"

"It could be, but I don't recall any eclipse of the sun on the eighth day of the sixth month. Try something simpler."

"Sunset," I said. "The sun has gone, but the light remains."

"Excellent," said Master Li. "So in their game the children were asking, 'Where is the Princess of Birds?' and Wan told them that if they looked from his watchtower when the sun sank below the horizon on the eighth day of the sixth moon, they would see where the lame peddler had taken Jade Pearl. Specifically, they would see something that looked like cold fire, and that first burned silver and then burned gold. In a few minutes," said Master Li, "that is precisely what we are going to look for."

I felt myself flush, and I said, almost angrily.

"Master Li, we are trying to find the Great Root of Power for the children of Ku-fu! We are not trying to find a little goddess for the Emperor of Heaven!"

"Dear boy, don't you think the emperor realizes that? Be patient for a few minutes more," Master Li said soothingly.

The sun slowly sank behind distant mountain peaks, and the clouds began to glow with the colors of sunset. I saw nothing like cold fire. The light began to fade, and

I could see faint stars, and still I saw nothing. It was almost dark, and to tell the truth, I had no faith at all in Master Li's analysis of the nonsense rhyme.

Suddenly the concealed sun sank to an invisible gap in the western mountain range. A brilliant shaft of light shot like an arrow across the valley to the eastern mountains. At no other time in no other day of the year would the angle have been perfect, but now a small circular spot that was concealed among peaks began to glow like cold fire. It shimmered like silver, and then it faded to dull gold, and then it vanished.

Master Li motioned for me to get down on my knees and clasp my hands together.

"Well done, Wan!" he cried. "You have fulfilled the mission for which you were chosen by the Emperor of Heaven, and surely your spirit will be allowed to ascend to the stars. There you will find many children who will ask you to join their games, and the goddess of Nu Kua will be delighted to have such a sentinel to help her guard the Celestial Walls."

We performed the three obeisances and the nine kowtows and then we got to our feet. Li Kao grinned at me.

"Ox, what do you think that we're being sent to find?"

I stared at him. "Isn't that the place where the peddler took the Princess of Birds?" I asked.

"He undoubtedly took her there, perhaps to find the city where her godmother lived, but it would be quite useless for us to search for Jade Pearl," Master Li said patiently. "If the Duke of Ch'in had a brain in his head, he would also take her to the Old Man of the Mountain. She couldn't be killed, but she could be transformed, and the Princess of Birds might now be a raindrop hidden in a thunderstorm, or a petal in a field of flowers, or one special grain of sand among a billion on a beach. No, you and I and the August Personage of Jade are engaged in mutual back-scratching because there is one thing upon the face of the earth that we can use to force the duke to hand over the Great Root of Power, and it can also force him to hand over Jade Pearl: I will bet anything you like that the Emperor of Heaven will see to it that we can't get one without the other."

He stretched and yawned and scratched his scraggly beard.

"Let's get some sleep. In the morning we'll go after the sick slimy heart of the Duke of Ch'in," said Master Li.

27.
The Lake of the Dead

We left at dawn, and by the fourth day we reached the foothills. When we began to climb the mountains we left summer behind, and the green trees and fragrant flowers and rippling streams were replaced by the most depressing landscape that I had ever seen.

A strange chill gripped that mountainside. It was dead and stale, as though a monstrous iceberg had been scooped up and deposited upon a peak, where it had lain lifeless and unmelting for a thousand years. Sometimes we went for an hour without seeing a squirrel or hearing the song of a bird, and on the third day of the climb all signs of life vanished. We looked in vain for so much as an ant on the ground or an eagle in the sky.

We had been hearing the faint sound of falling water, and finally we reached the source. A meager waterfall was trickling down the side of a chaotic cliff, and when we climbed to the top we saw that the cliff was part of a gigantic rock-slide that had blocked the narrow mouth of a valley many centuries ago. In the distance we could see another waterfall trickling down a higher cliff, and the entire valley in between had become a vast lake. It was the coldest, grayest, most unappetizing body of water that I had ever seen, and I knew in my bones that it was evil. Li Kao sat down and made some rapid calculations.

"Ox, this lake is the right size, the right shape, and at the correct angle," he said. "This is what we saw that first burned silver and then burned gold, and it very much looks as though we'll have to find out what's on the bottom of it."

It turned out to be more difficult than he expected. We made a raft and paddled to the center of the lake, but when we tried to reach bottom with a stone tied to a rope of vines we went down two hundred feet without touching anything. For practical purposes the lake had no bottom at all, and Master Li turned bright red while he scorched the air with the Sixty Sequential Sacrileges with which he had won the all-China Freestyle Blasphemy Competition in Hangchow three years in a row. Finally he decided to climb the cliff at the other end of the lake and look at the problem from a different perspective.

It was a hard climb and very dangerous. The cliff was mostly shale that was held together by clay, and when we reached the top we found that the ground was soft and porous except for the path where the stream ran along a bed of solid rock. Master Li teetered at the cliff's edge and gazed down nearly five hundred feet to the gold-gray lake glinting dully in the sunlight.

"Why, it's a matter of elementary hydraulic engineering!" he exclaimed. "We can't reach bottom, so we'll bring the bottom up to us. The first order of business is to get hold of a lot of strong backs."

We had to go a long way down the other side of the mountain before we reached a village, and the villagers wanted no part of a job that required getting close to that lake. They called it the Lake of the Dead, and swore that not even fish could live in the water.

"Once a year, at midnight on the fifth day of the fifth moon, a ghostly caravan approaches the Lake of the Dead," an old woman said in a quavering whisper. "Once in my grandmother's time some foolish men crept out to

spy upon that evil process, and they were found with their
bellies slit open and their guts ripped out! Since then we
lock the doors in our village and hide beneath the beds
on the fifth day of the fifth moon."

Master Li glanced at me, and I knew what he was
thinking. That should be the time when the Duke of Ch'in
completed the final leg of his tax trip and started home
again, and his route should pass the cold mountain and
the Lake of the Dead.

It wasn't easy to persuade them, but we could offer
more money than they could hope to earn in twenty life-
times, and at last the men gathered picks and shovels and
fearfully followed us back to the cliff. They worked like
demons in order to get out of there as fast as possible.
We began by digging a trench from the bank of the stream
to a deep ravine, and then we ran connecting trenches to
other ravines until we had a ditch that ran from one end
of the cliff to the other. We felled trees and made a dam.
It wasn't easy to persuade the stream to move to a new
home, but eventually the water roared angrily from its
bed of rock and began snarling through the porous earth
at the bottoms of the ravines. We gave the men bonuses,
but they barely paused to thank us before taking to their
heels.

Master Li and I moved to the other side of the lake
and pitched a tent. We had no idea how long it would
take, and we passed the time by making divers' equipment: air tanks from the bladders of wild pigs, and breathing tubes from the intestines. We fashioned bamboo spears,
and made loops in our belts for the rocks that would give
us extra weight. It happened far faster than either of us
thought possible.

I was looking out across the smooth cold surface of
the lake toward the cliff that was shimmering in the moonlight, and Li Kao was at a table writing down songs in
the light of a lantern. Suddenly the lantern began to move.
We stared in astonishment as it slid all the way down the
table and crashed to the earthen floor, and then the floor
started to buck beneath us like a wild horse. We ran from
the tent and gazed at the cliff, and there was a rumbling,

grinding sort of sound, and the cliff moved in the moonlight. Not even Master Li had expected something so spectacular, but the stream had tunneled so deeply into the spongy earth that almost half of the mountain leaned out, hovered in the air, and then plunged five hundred feet straight down into the Lake of the Dead.

We grabbed a tree and hung on for dear life. I saw a huge mass of water, silver in the moonlight, rise into the air like a cloud. The monstrous wave appeared to move very slowly toward the dam, and we felt a blast of icy wind, and then the wave plunged over the dam and smashed into the valley below. We saw a forest turned instantly to pulp, and we saw enormous boulders picked up and hurled through the air like grains of sand. The mountain beneath us shuddered, and huge rocks ground together and screamed deep in the bowels of the earth, and an icy mist closed around us. The tree that we were clinging to jerked and pitched and strained at its roots, and it seemed forever until the earth stopped bucking and the roar of water faded away.

The mist gradually dissolved, and we stared at an incredible sight. A forest of domes and spires and towers had lifted through the shallow water that remained, and my brain finally accepted the fact that the Lake of the Dead had been covering an entire city! Li Kao whooped with delight and grabbed my waist and began dancing around in a circle.

"What a lovely place to hide a heart!" he yelled. "Absolutely lovely!"

I danced with Master Li, but I could not agree that the place was lovely. The ghostly spires were reaching up to claw at the moon like the fingers of drowning men, and the water dripped from the turrets like tears.

The night passed, and the bright sun of morning that shone upon our little raft could warm us, but nothing could warm the water of the Lake of the Dead. I checked my pig bladders and breathing tubes, and the rocks in my belt and my spear.

"Ready?" asked Master Li.

"Ready," I said. I put the breathing tube from the first bladder in my mouth, held my nose, and jumped.

The water was very cold, but my body was covered with pig grease and it was bearable until I encountered a strange icy current that nearly sent me back to the surface—I could see the tips of my fingers turn blue—but it was a very narrow current and I soon left it behind. I was sinking faster than seemed safe, so I jettisoned rocks until I was drifting down easily. A rope of vines led up from my belt, and Li Kao counted the knots as they slid through his fingers, and when my feet touched bottom, I had gone down thirty feet.

I expected total darkness, but phosphorescent rocks produced an eerie greenish glow that enabled me to see quite easily, and I walked down one of the streets of the drowned city, waving my arms like a swimmer to battle the weight of the water. The air from the pig bladder tasted terrible, but the breathing tube worked and I had two more bladders tied to my belt. I came to a house and cautiously peered through the door, and it took quite some time for me to realize that what I was seeing was impossible.

I switched to my second bladder of air and began moving as fast as I could through the city, and everywhere I saw the same impossible sight. When that bladder ran out I switched to the third one, and retraced my steps until the rope tied to my belt was leading almost straight up. Then I jettisoned rocks until I drifted up and broke water a few feet from the raft.

"Master Li!" I gasped. "Master Li!"

He told me to shut up, and hauled me aboard and rubbed me down. Then he made me drink some wine before I told my tale. I began with the strange icy current, and the phosphorescence, and then I said:

"Master Li in the first house I saw the skeletons of a woman and a baby. That lake must have taken years to build up behind the rockslide, but the woman had drowned so quickly that she hadn't had time to grab her baby from the crib!"

Everywhere it had been the same. I had seen gamblers

drowned with dice in their hands, and blacksmiths tumbled over forges, and women whose bones were mingled with the pots that they had been using to cook dinner.

"Master Li, that city was destroyed in an instant!" I gasped. "If the Duke of Ch'in was responsible for such a massacre, he must have the coldest heart in the world!"

Li Kao grabbed my arm. "Repeat that," he ordered.

"Er...if the Duke of Ch'in is responsible, he must have the coldest heart in the world," I mumbled.

The expression on Li Kao's face was rather odd, and I decided that he reminded me of a cat that was creeping up behind a large complacent bird. He waved at the thicket of towers and spires.

"Ox, this is another labyrinth, and we no longer have the dragon pendant," he said. "But do we need it? It occurs to me that when the Old Man of the Mountain told us about the stupidity of some of his pupils, he may have been slyly saying something about the Duke of Ch'in."

Li Kao hurriedly greased his body and grabbed his diving equipment.

"After all, the wisest man in the world could scarcely be pleased with a pupil who chose a vast city as the hiding place for his heart, buried it beneath hundreds of feet of water, and then left a path that would lead straight to the rather peculiar nature of the extracted organ. Ox, lead me to that strange icy current," purred Master Li.

28.
The Coldest Heart in the World

We drifted down into the eerie greenish glow, and in a minute I found the current. It nearly froze us to death before we learned that we could follow it from a safe distance by watching a tiny trail of bubbles. We followed it for hours, through a tangled maze of streets. I would swim back up to the surface and paddle the raft ahead, and then Master Li would break water and climb on board, and we would rest and replenish our air bladders. We were slowly working our way toward the center of the city, and in late afternoon we paddled the raft toward a copper dome that lifted through the water in the center of four stone towers. A boulder from the fallen cliff had crashed through the dome, and that trail of tiny bubbles was oozing up through the hole.

We squeezed through the hole and drifted down toward a pile of treasure that was so huge that it was ten times larger than the other hoards added together!

Above the loot was a large copy of the duke's tiger mask, hanging upon a stone wall. The tiger's mouth was wide open, and behind the teeth was a niche where the choicest gems were piled. I swam closer and saw that the gems were heaped around a golden casket, and my heart leaped joyfully when I saw that the bubbles were trickling out from the keyhole. My hand reached out, but Li Kao grabbed it. He nodded urgently at the mask. I noticed that the tiger's teeth were pointed steel, and I swam to one of the towers and managed to pry a stone slab from the wall. I swam back and shoved it between the terrible jaws.

The teeth snapped together and began grinding through the stone with a screech that seemed to be magnified by the water, but the stone held long enough for me to reach through the gap and grab the casket. I dropped it into a sack that was tied to my waist, just as the stone dissolved into powder and the teeth snapped shut with a terrible crash. We turned to swim back to the surface, and my heart nearly stopped beating. Three pearly figures were drifting toward us in the greenish glow, and if I had not had the breathing tube in my mouth I would have cried out in pity. They were the three murdered hand-maidens of the Princess of Birds, and their bodies were uncorrupted after all the centuries, and the horror in their eyes was blended with a strange helpless pleading. They moved through the water like fish, with small wriggles of their hips and legs, and their long black hair drifted behind them like clouds.

The hair defied the pressure of the water. It reached out in front of the girls and floated toward us like masses of snakes. The cold wet coils curled around our breathing tubes and jerked them from our mouths, and then the tendrils closed around our faces and clogged our mouths and noses. We turned turtle and dived, and jerked out the second pig bladders and inserted the breathing tubes in our mouths, and then we flipped over and swam back up, thrusting at the girls with our bamboo spears. We were wasting our time. The limp bodies had been lifeless for centuries, and the clouds of hair passed through the spears and reached out again. The second tubes were ripped from our mouths and air bubbled away from the bladders. Again we dived, and we inserted the tubes of

our last bladders, but even as I fixed my tube in my mouth
I felt heavy coils of writhing wet hair crawl over my shoulders. Then the last tubes were ripped away. I thrust desperately at the handmaidens, and I saw that their pleading
eyes appeared to be weeping, but their hair lifted to form
an impenetrable cloud. We could not pass.

I grabbed Master Li and swam to the tower and used
my spear to pry out another stone slab. The hole was just
big enough, and I shoved Master Li through it and squeezed
in after him and wedged the spear in the gap to delay the
handmaidens. I jerked rocks from our belts and we began
to rise. My lungs were bursting, and my eardrums were
exploding, and my eyeballs seared with pain. I was nearly
unconscious when our heads broke through the surface
of the water into a small air pocket just below the copper
roof. I held Li Kao's head above water while I gulped
air, and I screamed when it touched my tortured lungs.
Finally I could breathe well enough to start thinking again,
and I saw that the wall to my left had nearly crumbled
into nothingness. A few kicks knocked a hole in it, and
I carried Li Kao through the hole and climbed up upon
the flat roof.

Master Li was an inert weight in my arms. I laid him
on his face and began to apply artificial respiration. I wept
when I thought that it was too late, but I soon heard him
cough. I cried out for joy and kept at it while water spurted
from his mouth, and finally he began breathing on his
own. Then I fell back on the roof and we lay side by side,
gasping like beached fish. Finally we were able to sit up
and look around, and we saw that we were still in bad
trouble. It was more than a mile to the shore, and those
handmaidens were swimming around the tower like sharks.
Master Li pounded some water from his ears and pointed
a quivering finger.

"Number Ten Ox, we are witnessing a crime so terrible
as to transcend belief," he said hoarsely. "The Duke of
Ch'in murdered those poor girls, and then bound them
with a spell that would force them to defend the heart of
their murderer. Since he fully intends to live forever, he
has sentenced three innocent girls to eternal damnation."

He was so angry that he was turning purple.

"Not even the Emperor of Heaven has the right to sentence anyone to eternal damnation!" he said furiously. "There must be a trial, and the accused must be defended, and the Yama Kings must concur in the verdict before such a terrible sentence can be imposed!"

I growled and pulled the casket from the sack at my waist. When I held the icy thing to my ear I heard a faint thump . . . thump . . . thump . . .

"Shall I slice it or squeeze it?" I snarled.

The question was academic. Li Kao went to work with his lockpicks, but he had never encountered a lock like that one. It was the most complicated pressure lock that he had ever seen, and nothing but the proper key could open it. A dagger could not scratch the casket. I smashed it to the stone with all the strength that I had, and I couldn't even dent it. Friction could not produce the slightest trace of warmth upon the icy surface. I hurled the casket down and we sat there and stared at it. Apparently when I had grabbed the casket from the niche I had taken a few jewels as well, and Li Kao slowly reached out and picked them up: a diamond, a ruby, a pearl, and an emerald. He stared at them wonderingly.

"Checkmate," he said softly. "I told you that the August Personage of Jade was going to tie the two quests into a nice neat knot. There is only one way that we can escape from this tower, and we are going to have to make a sacred vow."

I had no idea what he was talking about.

"To find a raindrop in a thunderstorm, or a petal in a field of flowers, or a grain of sand concealed among a billion on a beach," Master Li whispered. "I am a dolt. My poor brains have turned to butter. Ox, since I can no longer trust what I used to call a mind, do you happen to remember the names of the handmaidens of the Princess of Birds?"

"Snowgoose," I said slowly, "Little Ping . . . and Autumn Moon."

Li Kao put the jewels into a seashell on his smuggler's belt and had me replace the casket in the sack and tie it securely to my waist. Then he painfully got to his feet and faced the poor girls who slowly circled the tower.

"Snowgoose," he said quietly, "Little Ping, Autumn Moon, listen to me. The quest is almost at an end. We have the flute and the ball and the bell. I know where to find the three feathers of the Kings of Birds. I know where to find the golden crown. Now I know where to find the Princess of Birds. You must let us pass. You must fight as no one has ever fought before, and let us safely reach the shore."

I stared at him stupidly. He took a deep breath.

"Handmaidens, if you can defeat the spell and let us pass, I swear by all that is holy, and in the sacred name of the August Personage of Jade, that the birds will fly!" Master Li yelled. *"On the seventh day of the seventh moon the birds of China will fly!"*

I doubt that I can ever again be decently impressed by courage, because I have been privileged to witness courage that passes mortal comprehension. Li Kao's voice echoed back from the spires of the tragic city and faded into silence. Then the bodies of the murdered girls began to spin in the water. At first I thought that they were out of control, but then I realized that they were spinning in order to wrap their hair tightly around their bodies.

I felt a searing wave of pain that nearly knocked me into the water, and while I could not hear the screams of the handmaidens in my ears, I could hear them in my heart. Master Li hopped upon my back and I dived into the water and swam toward the distant shore. A soul-shaking agony surrounded the spinning girls, and scream after scream ripped through my heart, and the water turned choppy from the jerks of their bodies. I passed so close to one of them that I could see her tears and see that she was jerking in agony hard enough to snap her spine. And then I plowed ahead and they faded behind me. The hand-maidens did not give up their terrible fight until I crawled up to safety upon the sandy bank.

We faced the maidens and banged our heads against the ground, but Li Kao did not have time to honor them properly.

"Ox, we are bound by a sacred vow, and it's time to find out how much strain those muscles of yours can bear," he said grimly. "The Castle of the Labyrinth is halfway across China, but we must reach it by the seventh day of the seventh moon. Can you do it?"

"Master Li, get on my back," I said.

He climbed up and I turned and faced south, and then I set off at a gallop.

In the late aftertnoon of the seventh day of the seventh moon we stood upon a sandy beach and gazed across the water toward a sheer cliff upon which loomed the great hulking mass of the Castle of the Labyrinth. Sunlight was shining through dark clouds and turning the Yellow Sea into molten gold, but a high wind was whipping the bay into hard choppy waves, and seagulls were sailing like snowflakes across a sky that promised rain. I could not possibly carry Master Li across those waves without killing one or both of us, and I stared at him with stricken eyes.

"I rather think that help is on the way," hc said calmly, pointing toward a small flotilla of boats that was rapidly skimming toward us.

The lead boat was a tiny fishing vessel with a bright red sail, and it was being bombarded by spears and arrows. The wind whipped screams of rage toward our cars. "My purse!... My jade belt buckle!... Grandmother's life savings!   Powdered bat manure does not cure arthritis!... My gold earrings!... There wasn't a pea under any of those shells!... Bring back my false teeth!"

The little boat ran aground practically at our feet, and two gentlemen of low appearance climbed out and shook their fists at the pursuing fleet.

"How dare you accuse us of fraud!" screamed Pawnbroker Fang.

"We shall sue!" howled Ma the Grub.

The howling mob scrambled ashore, and Ma and Fang took to their heels. We climbed into the little fishing boat and shoved off, and thc wind obligingly shifted around and caught the sail. We raced across the waves while the sunlight was extinguished, and lightning flickered across the sky, and rain began to fall. The cliff loomed in front of us, and I steered between jagged rocks and found a place where we could land.

The wind was shrieking around us, and the rain was so heavy that I could barely see as I swung a rope around my head and sent a grappling hook flying up the side of the cliff. On the third try I caught a rock that held the hook securely, and Master Li hopped up on my back and I began to climb. The sheer stone was slippery in the rain, but we had to take chances if we were to reach the labyrinth before the tide did.

We just made it. I climbed over the ledge into the little cave where we had found the first of the duke's treasure troves, and I secured a hook and a rope and climbed down the stone chimney into the labyrinth. Li Kao lit a torch and looked around thoughtfully.

"It's a pity that we no longer have the dragon pendant," he observed mildly. "If ever I could use the ironclad memory of Henpecked Ho, it would be now."

Master Li's mental processes were as alien to me as the inner thoughts of Buddha. He never wavered, even though he had to retrace every twist and turn and do it backward, and I trotted behind him listening nervously for the first metallic snarl of the tiger. The duke had not been idle since his return from the tax trip. The air reeked with blood and rotting flesh, and fresh corpses stared blindly down at us from crevices in the ceiling. I stared in terror at dark streaks that were sliding across the floor, and back in the blackness a tiger began to growl.

Li Kao grunted with satisfaction, and trotted through an archway to the cavern where a pool of water lay beneath a trapdoor high overhead. I tied a rope to a jutting rock on one side of the pool, and another rope to another rock on the other side. Then I secured both ends around my waist with a slip knot that I could release with a jerk, and I glanced up fearfully at the darkness where the trapdoor should be. If it didn't work from this side, we were going to join those happy fellows wedged in crevices.

The water was rushing in faster and faster, climbing

around my thighs. I began to float upward, treading water, with Master Li riding on my back. I heard the tiger screaming, and then the full force of the tide struck us. We were buffeted from all sides, but the ropes held firmly and we continued to lift straight up. Master Li got as high as he could on my shoulders and reached up. I could hear him strain and grunt, and then there was a screech of metal as a bolt slid through grooves. He ducked and the falling trapdoor missed his head by an inch, and I jerked the slip knot and released the ropes and climbed through the hole into the throne room of the Duke of Ch'in.

From a chance comment by the Key Rabbit some time ago, we knew that the throne room was locked at sunset, and nobody but the duke was allowed to enter. Li Kao's torch flickered palely in the darkness, and I heard the clash of weapons and the heavy tread of the soldiers who patrolled outside the golden doors. Then the storm passed as swiftly as it had come, and the wind drew the clouds as though opening curtains in front of the rising moon, and light poured through the windows. I gasped in horror and stopped dead in my tracks.

The Duke of Ch'in was seated upon his throne, and the terrible mask was glaring straight at us.

Li Kao continued to trot ahead without a care in the world. "Don't worry, Ox, it's just an empty shell," he said reassuringly, and when I forced my feet to move again I saw that he was right. Moonbeams stretched out like pale gold fingers and reached through the eye-holes in the tiger mask and touched the back of the throne. It was just a mask and a long cloak of feathers, propped upon a light metal framework.

"Well, Ox, we have a promise to keep before we can worry about ginseng roots," Master Li said. "That means that we have only a few hours to find the feathers of the Kings of Birds, the golden crown, and the Princess of Birds. We'll also need the key to a casket, so let's get started. The first time you hit the duke with that axe, it bounced right off him. Do you remember where the blade struck?"

I reached out toward three tiny white feathers that were woven into a cloak of feathers.

"Feathers that stop axes?" I whispered. "Master Li, are these the feathers of the King of Birds?"

"We'll soon find out," he said. "Try to pull them out."

The feathers could not be pulled, and they could not be cut, and Li Kao's torch couldn't even scorch them. He opened shells in his smuggler's belt and handed me three trinkets. I placed the tiny tin flute upon an arm of the throne with trembling fingers, and I reached out to the cloak.

"Snowgoose returns the flute in exchange for the feather," I whispered, and the first feather slid from the cloak as smoothly as straw sliding from warm butter. I placed the crystal ball upon the arm of the throne.

"Little Ping returns the ball in exchange for the feather," I whispered.

The second feather slid out as easily as the first. I placed the little bronze bell upon the arm of the throne.

"Autumn Moon returns the bell in exchange for the feather," I whispered, and the third feather practically jumped into my hand.

Li Kao put the feathers in his smuggler's belt.

"The rest of it isn't going to be so easy," he said grimly. "We're going to need help, so let's go find it."

We waited for the tide to go out. Then we jumped back down into the pool and Li Kao retraced our steps through the labyrinth. The rope and hook had held, and I hauled us up the stone chimney to the cave. Then we used the ropes and hooks to swing back down the side of the cliff to a sea that had calmed enough to allow me to swim across the bay to the city.

The greatest pleasure city in the world was coming to life. Laughter and oaths and the cheerful sound of smashing wine jars followed us through the streets, and lurching merrymakers swarmed around us, but we shoved them aside and hurried on. We climbed a wall to a small garden. The guard dogs knew us well, and after a few pats they made no objection when we climbed through a window. Sometimes one can find help in the strangest places, such as a modest little house where a meek little man and his gloriously greedy wife were enjoying a rare evening of domestic tranquillity.

"*Boopsie!*" Lotus Cloud yelled happily, and the Key Rabbit screamed "*Ghosts!*" and dived beneath the bed.

29.
The View Through a Half-Closed Eye

It took some time to persuade the Key Rabbit that we had really survived the terrible plague of ten thousand pestilential putrescences, but when we coaxed him out from under the bed, we made quite a happy little family group. He was even inspired to bring jars of wine from his meager cellar, and we sat around the table sipping wine and nibbling grapes. When the little fellow's long nose had stopped twitching in terror, Li Kao said as gently as possible:

"Lotus Cloud, will you catch your husband before he hurts himself? You see, Ox and I have decided to assassinate the Duke of Ch'in."

Lotus Cloud grabbed the Key Rabbit just before his head hit the floor. After several applications of smelling salts he was able to sip some wine, and color began to return to his face.

"You are going to help us," said Master Li.

Lotus Cloud grabbed her husband in the nick of time, and I ran for more smelling salts.

"Feel better?" Master Li said sympathetically when

the Key Rabbit had regained some color. "Perhaps I should begin by explaining why the duke deserves to be assassinated. It all begins with a charming story that Lotus Cloud is sure to enjoy, because it involves the handsomest god in Heaven and the most beautiful girl in the world."

"And her wicked stepmother!" Lotus Cloud said, with shining eyes.

"Oddly enough, the wicked stepmother doesn't appear. I can't imagine why," Master Li said thoughtfully.

"Thank goodness!" the Key Rabbit exclaimed. "Wicked stepmothers terrify me. Come to think of it, most things do," he added sadly.

Li Kao played the host and refilled our wine cups, and then he followed Henpecked Ho's account almost word for word as he told the tale of the Star Shepherd and the Princess of Birds. No one could ask for a better audience than Lotus Cloud, who hopped up and down in excitement when the August Personage of Jade placed the crown upon the head of Jade Pearl, and who wept for joy when the princess stepped from the beautiful Bridge of Birds and ran to the arms of the Star Shepherd. It didn't take a genius to see that my darling Lotus Cloud was daydreaming that she could be the most beautiful girl in the world, and become a goddess who could climb to the stars.

"And they lived..." Master Li refilled his cup. "No, I am sorry to say that they did not live happily ever after. You see, there was a slimy fellow who wanted to live forever. He learned that if he stole something that belonged to a god he would never age so long as he possessed it, and that he would be invulnerable if the wisest man in the world, the Old Man of the Mountain, removed his heart. So he set a trap for the most innocent and gullible deity that he could find, meaning Jade Pearl, the Princess of Birds."

"Oh no!" Lotus Cloud cried.

"Oh yes," said Master Li. "She had three handmaidens who were as innocent as she was. The slimy fellow bought three marvelous trinkets from the Old Man of the Mountain, as well as three feathers that precisely resembled the feathers of the Kings of Birds. Then he disguised himself as a lame peddler and he approached the hand-maidens with some sort of tale—he worshipped the princess from afar, for example, and would give anything to own something that she had touched—and he offered to give one small favor. Simply substitute the feathers in his hand for the feathers on Jade Pearl's crown, and bring the real ones back to him."

"They would never do such a thing!" Lotus Cloud said indignantly.

"Did the girls know that the feathers on the crown were important?" the Key Rabbit wondered.

"The Key Rabbit has put his finger on it," Master Li said approvingly. "The handmaidens didn't know that the feathers were those of the King of Birds, and one should remember that this was a thousand years ago, when feathers were used to decorate headgear of all sorts, including crowns. Why should it be a terrible crime to substitute new decorations for old ones? Besides, those trinkets were truly irresistible. But the handmaidens were firm on one point. The peddler must swear a binding oath that if for any reason the princess wanted her old feathers back, he must return them in exchange for the trinkets. Of course he took no chance of that happening. One by one they returned with the feathers, and one by one he handed them the trinkets, and one by one he stabbed them to the heart."

Lotus Cloud began to cry. "Poor girls," she sniffled. "Poor faithless handmaidens."

"And poor Princess of Birds," said Master Li. "I would imagine that the slimy fellow committed his crimes on the seventh day of the seventh moon, so that Heaven would have no warning. Jade Pearl had been commanded to return to her husband, so she called to the birds of China, but the birds could no longer hear her because she no longer wore the feathers. Poor little princess. Calling birds that did not come, turning around helplessly, gazing up at the Great River where her husband waited—and waited in vain, because the seventh day of the seventh moon had come and gone. A vow had been made, a vow that had been broken, and the Princess of Birds passed from the protection of Heaven. Then it was a very easy matter for a sly fellow in a peddler's robe to steal a crown from a simple peasant girl."

"Tragedies terrify me!" the Key Rabbit wailed.

"I'm afraid that it gets worse," Master Li sighed. "The slimy fellow returned to the Old Man of the Mountain, who removed his heart. Now he was invulnerable, and so long as he held the crown, he would never age. As the centuries passed he bought many secrets from the Old Man of the Mountain, and his power grew. And you, my dear Key Rabbit, know him better than any of us, because he became the Duke of Ch'in, and he has been sitting upon the throne ever since, concealed behind a golden mask."

I grabbed the Key Rabbit in mid-fall, and Lotus Cloud waved smelling salts.

"The same duke throughout the centuries!" he gasped when he had recovered. "One thing I beg of you. Do not force me to see the face behind the mask, for it must be the most terrible face in the world!"

"Well, maybe not, because we are talking about a very unusual man," Master Li said thoughtfully. "He burned the books of China and massacred millions to erase all records of the Princess of Birds, but why did he bother? She had already passed from the protection of Heaven, so millions died for no good reason whatsoever. He built a castle with thirty-six imperial bedrooms to confuse assassins, but the assassins couldn't harm him because he was invulnerable. He lives only for money, but does he guard his hoards with iron vaults and armies? He does not. He guards them with labyrinths and monsters that might have come from children's books, and while the monsters are frightening, they are not very effective. Great Buddha, any half-witted staff sergeant could plan better defenses!"

"Do you think that he is crazy?" Lotus Cloud whispered.

"Oh, not at all," said Master Li. "This is a fellow who arranged things so that anyone who went after him would have to wander through the landscape of a homicidal fairy tale, which makes no sense if you think of him as a great and powerful ruler, but which makes perfect sense if you think of him as he once was: a cowardly little boy lying in bed at night, staring in terror at every noise and seeing monsters in every shadow. He grew older, but it can scarcely be said that he grew up, because he was so frightened at the thought of death that he was willing to commit any crime, and even to lose his heart if it would keep him from the Great Wheel of Transmigrations. There is one more thing about the Duke of Ch'in that is perhaps the strangest of all."

Li Kao reached into his belt and pulled out the gems that I had picked up along with the casket: a diamond, a ruby, a pearl, and an emerald. He placed them upon the table.

"Key Rabbit, look at this stuff," he said. "We have been talking about a little boy who lives only for money, yet he employs you as Assessor of Ch'in. You are forced to impose his fines, and collect his share of every transaction, and accompany him on tax trips and determine what every village owes. Night after night he forces you to stay in his treasure chambers and count every penny of his loot. The mysterious Duke of Ch'in, who lives only for money, has arranged matters so that his Assessor must spend far more time with it than he does. Peculiar, isn't it?"

"Lotus Cloud was right. He's crazy," I said firmly.

"As a matter of fact, he isn't," Master Li replied. "You see, everything would fit neatly into place—the money, the monsters, the labyrinths and other trappings of fairy tales, the lack of sensible precautions and the ridiculous precautions where none are needed—if the right kind of face were concealed behind a mask. Suppose that hiding behind a terrible snarl of a tiger..."

Master Li leaned forward. His voice was hypnotic, and his eyes were as cold as a cobra's.

"Was the face of a frightened rabbit," he whispered.

Li Kao's eyes had warned me to leap, and all I needed to know was where. I smashed the Key Rabbit to the floor, and Li Kao's hands darted out and snatched a chain and jerked a key up over the Key Rabbit's head. We had once become entangled in that chain, and at the end of it was a key that was shaped like a flower, with sixteen tiny points. Li Kao pulled a golden casket from beneath his tunic. A casket that contained the heart of the Duke of Ch'in, and that was secured by a pressure lock shaped like a flower, with sixteen tiny slits. Each point had to fit into each slit with precisely the right amount of pressure, and Li Kao's forehead wrinkled with concentration as he applied the key to the lock.

Lotus Cloud, who was not the screaming type, was screaming her head off, and outside in the garden the dogs were going insane. When I lifted from the floor I was not riding upon the back of a man, but on the back of a snarling, clawing tiger.

I was in the best position that I could manage, with my arms wrapped around the tiger's throat and my teeth buried in the fur on its neck, and we went bounding around the room while Master Li struggled with the lock, and I am alive today because the Duke of Ch'in was unquestionably the stupidest of all the pupils of the Old Man of the Mountain. When he discovered that he was not dislodging me as a tiger he transformed himself into a serpent, and then into a wild boar, and then into an enormous spider, and all the while I was praying: "August Personage of Jade, cleanse this idiot's mind of all memory of scorpions!" I could almost feel the lethal tail whipping around to impale me like a bug. "Wipe his brain of all images of porcupines, cacti, quicksand, and carnivorous plants!" I don't know whether or not the August Personage of Jade had anything to do with it, but certainly the duke wasn't reading my mind at the moment because he obligingly transformed himself into a crocodile. Unfortunately, the lashing tail knocked Li Kao beneath a heavy table that collapsed on top of him, and the casket and the key went spinning across the floor. I spat out a mouthful of tiger fur, boar's bristles, spider hair, and crocodile scales.

"Lotus Cloud, open the casket!" I yelled.

The Duke of Ch'in transformed himself into a giant

ape. We went bounding around the room again while
Lotus Cloud, her eyes glazed with shock, slowly reached
down toward the casket at her feet. Then the duke transformed himself into a boulder. We crashed to the floor,
and the huge heavy thing slowly rolled over on top of me.
I gasped for breath while a pair of pink-rimmed Key Rabbit eyes appeared in the boulder. A pair of Key Rabbit
lips opened, and a piece of the rock quivered like a long
twitching nose.

"I can grow heavier," the duke giggled. "Heavier and
heavier and heavier."

The breath was being squeezed out of me, and my ribs
were cracking. I could see Li Kao wrestling with the
heavy table, and Lotus Cloud dazedly trying to fit the
key into the lock. The top of her tongue protruded from
between her lips, and she looked for all the world like a
little girl who was trying to thread a needle for the first
time. Above me the pink-rimmed eyes were glittering,
and I realized that sheer terror was driving the Duke of
Ch'in to the edge of insanity, as it had done so often in
the past.

"I shall hang you and the old man in a cage beside my
bed," he whispered. "My dear friends *shan hsiao* shall
rip your flesh with their claws and beaks, and your flesh
will grow back, and the claws and beaks shall rip it again,
and your screams will soothe me to sleep at night, and
thus you will spend eternity."

I had no breath left. The room was swimming before
my eyes, and my ears were throbbing with hurtful heartbeat sounds. The boulder grew heavier and heavier, and
I could stand it no more.

Lotus Cloud screamed. She screamed so piercingly
that a thin porcelain bowl broke in half. The open casket
fell to the floor, and a wet throbbing heart lay sickeningly
at her feet.

In an instant the boulder had become the Key Rabbit,
and he frantically tried to reach his heart. I clung to his
ankles with the last bit of strength that I had, and he wailed
in fear as he slowly dragged me across the floor. The Key
Rabbit's hand reached out, and Lotus Cloud watched him

with eyes that were wide with horror. Then that marvelous girl reached down and scooped up the slimy thing at
her feet, and she wound up in the manner of a peasant
girl who had been the terror of crows, and she hurled the
heart on a dead line across the room and through the
window to the garden. The hysterical guard dogs descended upon the heart of their master.

The Key Rabbit stood quite still. Then he slowly turned
to his wife, and he reached out with a strangely tender
gesture, and his lips parted. I will never know what he
wanted to say. The flesh withered upon the face of the
tyrant who had given his name to China, and I stared at
the clean white bones of a skull, and then the bones themselves dissolved into the dust of centuries, and an empty
robe slowly floated down and settled limply upon the
floor.

I managed to crawl over and lift the table from Li Kao,
and he staggered to his feet and dived for the wine jar.

"The Yama Kings have been waiting a long time, and
I would imagine that the Duke of Ch'in is receiving a
rather warm welcome in Hell," he said when he came up
for air.

Master Li handed me the wine jar. I drank deeply and
passed it to Lotus Cloud, who swigged like a soldier. The
wonder had overcome the horror, and her eyes were wide
and bright and filled with marvels. Master Li walked over
to the robe on the floor. He bent down and reached inside
it, and his right hand lifted with a small golden crown.

"What better place to keep the greatest of all treasures
than the hole where a heart had been?" he said.

His left hand lifted, and I cried out in joy as an unbelievable powerful aroma of ginseng reached my nostrils.
It was so strong that it revived me in an instant.

"Master Li, has our quest come to an end?" I cried.

"Not quite yet," he cautioned. "This is indeed the Heart
of the Great Root of Power, but we must remember that
it is also the Queen of Ginseng. Her Majesty must never
be forced. If she is to help the children of Ku-fu, it must

be of her own free will, and we must ask her goddaughter
to transmit her wishes."

Master Li clasped his hands together and bowed deeply
to Lotus Cloud.

"Meaning your Highness, the Princess of Birds," he
said.

Lotus Cloud stared, but her eyes were not as wide as
mine.

"Master Li, you can't be serious!" I gasped.

"I have never been so serious in my life," he said
calmly.

"Me? With my thick legs and flat face?" Lotus Cloud
exclaimed. Her sense of the fitness of things was out-
raged, and she flushed with indignation. "The Star Shepherd fell in love with the most beautiful girl in the world!"

"Mere literary convention," Li Kao said, with an airy
wave of a hand. "Beauty is ridiculously overrated, and if
that was all that the Star Shepherd wanted, he had the
young goddesses of Heaven to choose from. The Star
Shepherd had enough sense to want a peasant girl whose
eyes held all the hope and joy and wonder in the world,
and whose grin could fell an ox at fifty paces. Ask this
ox here," he said with a wink in my direction. "Ox, remind
me to change my business sign so that the eye is nine
tenths closed. I should have known that Lotus Cloud was
immortal the moment that Miser Shen reacted to her exactly as you did."

Lotus Cloud stamped her foot. "I refuse to believe one
word of this nonsense," she said angrily.

"Why should you? The Duke of Ch'in took you to the
Old Man of the Mountain, who removed your memory,"
Master Li said reasonably.

He strolled over to the table and sat down, and placed
the little crown and the Great Root of Power beside the
wine jar. Then he opened his smuggler's belt, and the
three feathers of the Kings of Birds jumped eagerly into
place when he touched them to the rim of the crown.

"It is truly said that men die like trees, from the top
down." Master Li sighed. "If my poor brains had not been
riddled by wood rot and little green worms I might have

considered the fact that Miser Shen was not jealous of Number Ten Ox, and Number Ten Ox was not jealous of Miser Shen. None of Lotus Cloud's lovers was ever jealous. Now that simply isn't human if we're talking about love, but it is very human indeed if we're talking about worship. One is not jealous of a fellow worshipper, and the pure in heart will always recognize a goddess. I have had occasion to mention the purity of Ox's heart, and beneath his repulsive exterior Miser Shen was solid gold. I have no doubt that her other lovers were equally admirable, which is why I was unable to recognize the young lady myself."

He stood up and bowed to Lotus Cloud again.

"There is," said Master Li, "a slight flaw in my character."

He sat down and filled two cups from the wine jar and slid them across the table toward Lotus Cloud and me. Then he picked up one of the jewels that he had shown to the Key Rabbit.

"My stupidity was such that I remained unaware of the obvious until I found this," he said sadly. "It is a very rare pearl, jet-black, with one small white flaw in the shape of a star. Lotus Cloud, I once gave this pearl to Ox, who rolled it toward your feet. The next time I saw it was in a drowned city, where it was lying beside the casket that contained the duke's heart. Dear girl, I knew very well that you forgot about a gift of pearls and jade ten minutes after you received it, but it never occurred to me to wonder what happened to the stuff."

He turned and thoughtfully examined the crumpled robe upon the floor.

"The Duke of Ch'in was abysmally stupid, but on one occasion he showed real intelligence," Master Li said. "After removing the memory of the Princess of Birds, the Old Man of the Mountain almost certainly offered to transform her into a raindrop or a rose petal, for a stiff price, but the duke knew better. He lived only for money, and if he left Jade Pearl precisely as she was he would have something that was worth a thousand gold mines. You see, it is in the nature of men to worship a goddess and to bring her valuable offerings, and it is in the nature of a goddess to accept their worship and their offerings. The men are not being lecherous. The goddess is neither greedy nor promiscuous. They are merely acting out roles that were ordained at the beginning of time, and to my own certain knowledge Lotus Cloud has collected more pearls and jade than the entire army of the Duke of Ch'in. Every bit of it has wound up in treasure troves guarded by monsters."

Cold fingers were crawling over my spine, and I lifted my cup and drained it at a gulp. Lotus Cloud stood frozen, with her cup halfway to her lips.

"I don't believe it," she whispered.

"I'll bet that the duke also struggled with disbelief," Master Li said. Then he began to laugh—a real belly laugh, with a happy whoop at the end. "There is something indescribably comic about the greediest man in the whole world who gets his hands on the least acquisitive goddess in history," he panted, wiping tears from his eyes. "Ox, the duke must have suffered terribly from ulcers until he discovered Lotus Cloud's one weak spot. Think about it. Think very carefully about pearls and jade, because it may help you to do something unpleasant."

He refilled my cup while I tried to think about pearls and jade. My mind refused to function at all, but something from deep down was trying to work its way up, so I stopped trying to think and let whatever it was take over. I closed my eyes tightly, and then I was inside a strange world of glowing milky whiteness, and a thirteen-year-old girl was looking at me gravely.

"Ever since we held hands and recited the Orphan's Song, I knew that you would fall in love with Lotus Cloud," Mouse said softly. "Ox, you must use all of your strength to touch the queen before the count reaches forty-nine. Forty-nine can mean for ever and ever and ever." Mouse was fading into the whiteness. "Is not a thousand years enough?" she said faintly. "The birds must fly.... The birds must fly.... The birds must fly...."

The image was gone, and I remembered that the world had been white because in my dream I had been inside a pearl, and with a sudden shock I understood the meaning of the pearl.

I opened my eyes to find Li Kao looking at me with a stern expression, but kindly eyes.

"Number Ten Ox, in a little while the watchman will rap three times, and the seventh day of the seventh moon will have come and gone," he said quietly. "For the thousandth time the Star Shepherd will gaze down from the Great River at an empty sky, and for the thousandth time he will weep bitter tears. Thus he will weep throughout eternity, considering that the Emperor of Heaven quoted the odds against bringing the princess back to the stars at one in ten thousand billion trillion. Of course there is a slight chance that somebody might want to give the Celestial Bookmaker a heart attack."

Master Li slid the crown toward me. I blinked through my tears and picked it up. This was the only life that Lotus Cloud could remember, and she backed away fearfully.

"No," she whispered. "I love you, and you love me, and we can find a desert island and live happily ever after!"

"That's the point," I sniffled. "Ever after is such a very long time."

"I am afraid," Lotus Cloud said desperately. "I don't want to be changed into something strange."

"Oh yes, you do," I said sadly. "Lotus Cloud, you yawned in the presence of diamonds. Emeralds bored you to tears. I gave you a casket of gold, which you handed to the first person who asked for it. You have never asked for a new dress, and you wouldn't know what to do with a servant, but everything changed when I brought you pearls and jade. You could never quite remember, but you could never quite forget, and your eyes grew wide with hope and wonder, and your face was transfigured by longing, and a soul-shaking desire wracked your whole body, and with trembling hands you reached not toward pearls and jade, but toward yourself."

My heart was breaking as I maneuvered her into a

corner. "Pearls and jade, and the name of the Princess of Birds," I said gently, "was Jade Pearl."

Then I reached out and placed the little golden crown upon the head of the woman I loved.

30.
China!

I suppose that there is only a slight chance that a person will be called upon to rescue a goddess, but the odds will increase dramatically if the person is as illustrious as are my readers, so I will offer two pieces of advice.

Beware of her divine light, and take cover.

No sooner had the crown touched Lotus Cloud's head than I was nearly blinded, and I sank to my knees and gazed at dancing black spots and bright orange pinwheels. Even then I could see in my heart that she had moved away from me, and when my eyes adjusted to the unearthly glow I saw that my beloved Lotus Cloud had picked up the Great Root of Power from the table and had walked outside to the garden. She was surrounded by a shimmering nimbus, and the crown upon her head flickered like fire. The Princess of Birds paid no attention to me, and I felt a hand on my shoulder.

"Dear boy, she has a great many things to think about," Master Li said kindly. "Sit down with me at the table and have a drink. Have six or seven."

In the garden the dogs crouched over the tiny pile of

dust that had been the heart of their master. They were as still as statues. Lotus Cloud lifted her face to the night sky and uttered a low cry that was neither a song nor a whistle, but something in between, and the dogs jerked their heads up and appeared to be listening to a distant echo. Then Lotus Cloud dropped to her knees and bowed her head and clasped her hands together. She prayed for many minutes, and then she humbly banged her head against the ground. Lotus Cloud got to her feet and bowed her head over the Great Root, and for another minute she silently communed with her godmother. Then the Princess of Birds turned and lifted the Queen of Ginseng toward the huge looming shape of the Castle of the Labyrinth.

Master Li grabbed the wine jar. He told me to follow his example, and then he crawled beneath the sturdy table and arranged some heavy pillows for further protection. "Ever since I was a wee lad, I have been addicted to spectacular endings," he said nostalgically. "Pass your cup."

"Master Li, I don't think that I can handle any more wine," I said shakily, as I stared with terrified eyes at the vast fortress upon the cliff.

"Nonsense! Try saying 'forty-four dead stone lions.'"

"Forty-four dead stone lions."

"Sober as a Confucian," Master Li declared.

I could not dispute it. We were speaking the Peking dialect called Mandarin, in which "forty-four dead stone lions" comes out as *ssu shih ssu ssu shih shih*, if it comes out at all, so I passed my cup.

I was not the only one who gazed in terror at the Castle of the Labyrinth. It was slowly twisting upon its foundations, as though it were being squeezed by a giant hand, and screams and shrieks rang through the streets of the greatest pleasure city in the world, and merchants and merrymakers and priests and prostitutes fell upon their knees and began babbling prayers and promises to repent.

That monstrous monument to temporal power was dissolving. Invincible walls were bending like soft wax, and great stone slabs were spraying down like scattered grains of sand, and enormous steel gates were ripping apart like flimsy parchment. The iron towers melted into mud, and the drawbridges toppled into the moats, and the face of the solid cliff cracked and splintered, and the water from the moats shot over the edge of the cliff and glittered in the moonlight like silver as it plunged in a foaming cascade to the sea. Tunnels and torture chambers collapsed and buried forever the terrible secrets of the Duke of Ch'in, and in the depths of the labyrinth the tiger screamed for the last time.

A great cloud of dust and debris billowed up and blotted out the moon, and stones and steel rained down upon the duke's city. Small pieces of wreckage crashed through the roof and pounded like drumsticks upon the table and covered us. Then a great gust of wind blew down from Heaven and the dust cloud vanished as though it had never been, and I stared in wonder at the Castle of the Labyrinth as you will see it today: a great twisted mass of wreckage scattered across the face of a cliff overlooking the Yellow Sea.

Li Kao's eyes were shining, and he happily punched my shoulder. "One should not be so miserly when it comes to a spectacular ending, and unless I am greatly mistaken, we are in for a whopper," he said. "Listen."

The sound was faint at first. Then it grew stronger and stronger, deepening in pitch as the chorus swelled, and resolved itself into a great song of joy as a million birds, a billion, a trillion, every bird in China, including those that had to break out of cages, came flashing across the face of the moon toward their princess. The mobs in the streets jumped to their feet and took to their heels, howling in terror while the trees and shrubs bowed beneath a great wind of wings, and billions of blossoms whirled through the air and turned bawling bonzes into bouquets, and fleeing felons into flower arrangements.

The great Phoenix, mightiest of all, led the way, and his flaming crown of feathers streaked across the sky like a meteor. Behind him flew the Eagle and the Albatross, the kings of the birds of land and sea. Then came the Owl, prince of the birds of night, and the Lark, prince of the birds of day, and the Swan, prince of the birds of rivers, and the Crane, prince of the birds of marshes, and the Parrot, prince of the birds of jungles, and the Petrel, prince of the birds of storms, and the Raven, prince of the birds of prophecy—I shall not give the entire list. Henpecked Ho might have drawn it up, since it covers twenty pages. Behind the officers flew the legions, and the world was fragrant with the sharp scent of the green twigs and branches that they carried in their claws.

The crown upon the head of Lotus Cloud was shining even brighter than the crown on the Phoenix. She uttered another low cry, and the mighty Falcon, prince of the birds of war, slid silently down from the sky and landed in the garden. It was as big as a horse, and its talons glittered like swords, and its wise old yellow eyes glowed like smoky torches. Lotus Cloud ran up and wrapped her arms around the Falcon's neck and rested her cheek against its head. She stood like that for some time, and then she turned, unconsciously imperial, and looked straight at two gentlemen who were still crouched beneath a table. We found ourselves crawling out, and walking obediently into the garden. The Princess of Birds reached out and placed the Great Root of Power in my hands.

"My godmother wishes to go with you," she said softly. "She has suffered much, and she prays that in the village of Ku-fu she may be able to perform the task for which she was born. I have spoken to the Falcon, who alone of all living creatures may be able to get you there in time."

She turned to Li Kao.

"I have a message that I do not understand," she said simply. "The August Personage of Jade says that he will reserve a place for you in the constellation Scorpio, where you will rule as the red star Antares, whose sign is that of the fox, on the condition that you do not try to sell him any shares in a mustard mine."

"Conditions, conditions," Master Li grumbled, but I could see that he was immensely pleased.

Lotus Cloud gestured, and the Falcon bent down and Li Kao and I obediently climbed upon its back. Lotus Cloud leaned forward; her lips softly brushed my cheek.

"I will never forget you," she whispered. "Not through all eternity."

The princess stepped back. For the last time I saw her incredible grin, and she waved, and the great wings pumped once, twice, and then the prince of the birds of war shot up into the air. The Falcon wheeled around, and the wings flashed so swiftly that they were nearly transparent in the moonlight, and Master Li and Number Ten Ox set sail across the night sky of China.

I turned and looked back, blinking through tears. A billion birds were beginning to build a bridge with their twigs and branches, and their princess was placing her foot upon the first step. Never again would I see her. Never again would I hold her in my arms. The Falcon turned its head, and its voice was surprisingly soft and gentle.

"Number Ten Ox, why do you weep?" the Falcon asked. "The Princess of Birds has vowed to remember you throughout eternity, and by now you should know that men cannot come any closer to immortality without going insane."

The beautiful Bridge of Birds was climbing slowly toward the stars, and a great song was spreading across China. Faster and faster we sped through the sky, and on the ground below the peasants were running from the cottages and lifting little children in their arms to gaze at glory.

"You see?" said the peasants. "That is why you must never give up, no matter how bad things may seem. Anything is possible in China!"

We shot over a ridge to a small valley where men stood frozen in awe and wonder, and I began to feel a certain respect for Pawnbroker Fang and Ma the Grub, who were taking the opportunity to pick the pockets of their own lynch mob. The Falcon's burning eyes were lighting up the night like lighthouse beacons as we flashed past, and then we swooped over another ridge and down into another valley toward an old well and a bricked-up hole in a wall.

The Falcon was right. Why should I weep? Bright Star

had shed enough bitter tears for both of us, but now her tears came from joy as she gazed at the Bridge of Birds, sparkling in the distance. The dancing girl and her captain were giving a great scholar the respectful attention he deserved, and Henpecked Ho gestured grandly at the glorious sky.

"So the peasant girl knelt before the Emperor of Heaven, and he placed the little gold crown upon her head. 'Arise, Princess of Birds!' he commanded, and when Jade Pearl stood up she was astonished to see that she shone with a divine light. . . ."

The Falcon flashed past, and mountains and valleys disappeared as though China were being folded up like a map beneath us, and we shot down the side of a low mountain where three more ghosts were seated upon a rock, gazing up at the Bridge of Birds.

"You know, I feel in my heart that I had something to do with this, although it scarcely seems possible," Miser Shen said wonderingly. "I cannot imagine how anything so beautiful could be associated with someone as ugly as myself."

His wife kissed his cheek, and the lovely little girl in his arms looked up in surprise. "But, Daddy, you are very beautiful," said Ah Chen.

They vanished behind us. Another mountain and another valley vanished in a blur, and then the Falcon slowed and feathered its wings above a cemetery, where a tired and lonely old man was trudging between gravestones with a cadaver on his back. He tilted the head of the corpse toward the Bridge of Birds.

"Now look here, if the birds can pull off a trick like that, surely you can manage something so simple as resurrection," Doctor Death said reasonably. "Perhaps it would help if you understood how important it is. My wife was not pretty, but she was the most wonderful wife in the world. Her name was Chiang-chao, and we were very poor, but she could make the most delicious meals from a handful of rice and the herbs that she picked in the woods. She sang beautiful songs to cheer me when I was depressed, and she sewed dresses for wealthy ladies to help pay for my studies. We were very happy together, and I know that we will be happy together again."

The Falcon dropped like a rock, and the great talons shot out, and there was a dull thud. We lifted back up into the air while the old man toppled to the ground, and his ghost lifted from his body, and another ghost came running with open arms, and Doctor Death and the most wonderful wife in the world embraced beneath the Bridge of Birds.

The stars above us were blending into a continuous blur and the landscape below was unrolling like a painted panorama: the hills and valleys that we had trudged across on our quest, and the Desert of Salt, and Stone Bell Mountain. We shot up the side of another mountain toward a stone pillar and a hammer and a gong and the black mouth of a cave. The wisest man in the world was standing there, gazing at the Bridge of Birds, and for a moment I thought that it might not be such a bad thing to lose one's heart. There was real pleasure in his eyes. Then I saw that his hands were caressing a small pile of jewels, and I remembered that a man with no heart likes things cold, and there is nothing colder than treasure.

"Cold," crooned the Old Man of the Mountain. "Cold... cold... cold..."

Then the wisest man in the world turned his back upon the beautiful Bridge of Birds, and shuffled down into the darkness of his cave.

Another valley disappeared beneath us, and another river, and more hills, and we swooped up the side of another peak, and Master Li and I cried out as one: "But surely they have paid for their folly!"

We stared down at the bodies of the three handmaidens, who still floated upon the cold water of the Lake of Death. The Falcon turned its head.

"In life they were faithless, but in death they were faithful beyond belief," said the prince of the birds of war. "Their courage has been brought to the attention of the judges of Hell, and even now the Yama Kings are making their decision."

We watched the bodies peacefully dissolve into dust,

and we felt an indescribable wave of joy as the soul of Snowgoose and Little Ping and Autumn Moon shot past us to rejoin their mistress in Heaven.

The mighty heart pounded beneath us, and the wings beat with all the Falcon's strength, and we left the Bridge of Birds far behind, and China vanished. My eyes swam with tears from the wind, and I could see nothing, and I held on for dear life. For an hour I had no idea where we were, but then the racing wind began to bring a hundred familiar odors to my nostrils. The pace slackened, and I pried my eyelids open, and the Falcon slid down from the sky and dipped its wings in salute above the watchtower on Dragon's Pillow. As the monastery grew closer we could see the watching bonzes point in wonder from the roof, and then the bells began to ring. Lower we drifted, and then the Falcon landed lightly in the courtyard.

Li Kao and I climbed off and bowed deeply, and the prince of the birds of war looked at us with its yellow smokey eyes.

"I shall not say good-bye. The Raven has told me that we are destined to meet again, at the great confrontation with the White Serpent in the Mysterious Mountain Cavern of Winds. The Raven is never wrong," said the Falcon, and its wings beat once, twice, and then it shot into the air and sailed away to rejoin its bridge and its princess.

Li Kao and I raced into the infirmary, where the abbot ran to meet us. He was wasted with weariness, and one glance told us that the endurance of the children was almost at an end.

"We have the Great Root!" I yelled. "Master Li found the Queen of Ginseng, and she has agreed to help us!"

Master Li and the abbot began preparing the vials, and I ran from bed to bed. I held the root toward the children's faces and recited their names and gave brief ancestries. I suppose that it was a foolish thing to do, but I remembered that the story of Jade Pearl had begun when the Queen of Ginseng had taken pity upon a child and had asked if she was lost, and the children of my village were lost indeed. Then I ran up to Master Li, and reverently placed the root in the first vial.

I cannot possibly describe the aroma when Li Kao finally removed the vial from the pan of boiling water and removed the stopper, but old Mother Ho, who caught some of the steam full in the face, tossed her cane away and hasn't used it since. The abbot and Master Li began making the rounds: three drops upon each tongue.

The children's faces flushed, and the covers lifted with deep breathing, and they sat up and opened their eyes to the private world of the Hopping Hide and Seek Game.

The second treatment of three drops, and the happy smiling faces turned as one toward Dragon's Pillow. *"Jade plate, six, eight, fire that burns hot, night that is not, fire that burns cold, first silver, then gold!"* chanted the children of Ku-fu.

The third and final treatment, and there was just enough essence to go around. The children suddenly stopped chanting, and they sat motionless, with wide unseeing eyes. Nobody dared to breathe. The monastery was completely silent until Big Hong could stand it no more. He ran to his son and waved his hand in front of the boy's bright eyes. Nothing happened.

Big Hong fell on his knees, and his head sank to the little boy's lap, and he began to weep.

Master Li is convinced that the true story of the Bridge of Birds is far too crude to please priests and palace eunuchs, and that suitably polite and pious legends will be invented to account for the extraordinary event that stunned the empire on the seventh day of the seventh moon in the Year of the Dragon 3,338 (A.D. 640), and that there will probably be a lover's festival that celebrates a meek little goddess who waves seamless robes and a meek little god who milks cows, with a few magpies tossed in for comic effect. Perhaps, but in the village of Ku-fu in the valley of Cho we will continue to celebrate the moment when the Queen of Ginseng probed and tested, and then tentatively reached out and took *ku* poison into her heart. Little Hong blinked. His eyes lowered.

"What's the matter, Daddy?" he asked.

Her majesty was gaining confidence, unleashing all of her power, and child after child blinked and shook his head, as though clearing cobwebs, and wanted to know why his parents were weeping. They were very weak.

"Outside!" Master Li yelled. "Carry the children out to the courtyard!"

A long row of beds moved out to the courtyard, and the children stared in wonder at a strange glow upon the horizon, like the rising of a second moon, and then the Bridge of Birds lifted above Dragon's Pillow. Surely the Queen of Ginseng smiled to see her beloved goddaughter provide the final step to the cure. The world was wrapped in the fragrance of green twigs and branches, and a divine light climbed higher and higher toward the stars, to the great song of billions of birds. A trillion wings splintered moonbeams into rainbows, and a roar of thanksgiving came from the Great River, and the Star Shepherd hurled his crook away and bounded across waves and rocks, and the untended stars began to spill over the banks. The August Personage of Jade ordered all Heaven to erupt with bells and gongs and trumpets, and the children of Ku-fu jumped from their sickbeds and began to dance with their parents, and the abbot and his bonzes swung lustily through the air as they hauled on the bell ropes, and Master Li did the Dragon Dance with Number Ten Ox, and showers of stars, torrents of stars, great glorious explosions of stars streaked across the sky of China while the Bridge of Birds reached the boundary of paradise, and the Star Shepherd opened his arms to receive my darling Lotus Cloud, the Princess of Birds.

I shall clasp my hands together and bow to the corners of the world.

May your villages remain ignorant of tax collectors, and may your sons be many and ugly and strong and willing workers, and may your daughters be few and beautiful and excellent providers of love gifts from eminent families that live very far away, and may your lives be blessed by the beauty that has touched mine.

Farewell.

About the Author

Barry Hughart was born in the Midwest and raised on a ranch in Arizona. He has been kicked out of Andover and Columbia, with, he says, "briefer stops at other asylums." Since then, he has worked at too many occupations to list, all of them boring, he claims. His interest in the Far East began during military service in Japan and focused upon China when he discovered that vast numbers of Chinese deities had really originated as characters in novels.

Bridge of Birds is his first novel, but he promises that Master Li and Number Ten Ox, with the panorama of the magnificent culture they represent, will probably surface again. Mr. Hughart lives in Arizona.